Megan's arms slipped around his waist.

"I don't expect you to take on my problems. You're my boss, not my fairy godmother."

Daniel chuckled. "Yeah, I'd look pretty silly in a dress carrying a fairy wand, and I'm not such a great boss at that."

"Why do you say that?" She looked up at him through watery green eyes. "You're great."

"Because a good boss doesn't go around kissing his employees." He stared down at her damp cheeks, his belly flipping. "Right now, I want to be a very bad boss."

Her eyes flared with desire. "How so?"

"I want to kiss you. Again."

She sucked in a breath and bit down on that lip before saying, "I told you, I quit. That means you're not my boss."

He leaned his forehead against hers and sighed. God, he wanted to kiss her. "I'm not accepting your resignation."

"You don't have a choice," she said, her lips so close.

* * *

**Be sure to check out the next books
in this miniseries.**
The Coltons of Oklahoma: **Family secrets
always find a way to resurface...**

**If you're on Twitter, tell us what you
think of Harlequin Romantic Suspense!
#harlequinromsuspense**

Dear Reader,

I grew up the daughter of a career US Air Force father, moving with our family of six from Washington to Montana, California and Texas. My father's home and heart was in the state he was born and raised, Arkansas. The twenty years he was in the air force he dreamed and worked toward returning to his home. Vacations were spent traveling from those other states back to Arkansas to visit family.

People say home is where the heart is, and that is true, mostly. To the kids in my family, home was wherever we lived. To my father, his roots were Arkansas. Most of the nineteen kids he grew up with still lived in Arkansas.

Dad bought forty acres forty miles north of where he grew up. When he retired, he moved us to Arkansas, where he built a house and made it his home. It proved you could take the boy away from home, but you couldn't take the home out of the man.

My hero in *Protecting the Colton Bride* might be the bastard child of the owner of the Lucky C Ranch, but he dug his roots into the ranch, the only place he considered a real home. He'll do anything to protect it and the people he loves from danger, just like my father.

I love my father for making each place we lived home and protecting us even when he deployed to the far reaches of the world.

Happy reading!

Elle James

PROTECTING THE COLTON BRIDE

Elle James

HARLEQUIN® ROMANTIC SUSPENSE

Special thanks and acknowledgment are given to Elle James for her contribution to the Coltons of Oklahoma miniseries.

ISBN-13: 978-0-373-27933-3

Protecting the Colton Bride

Copyright © 2015 by Harlequin Books S.A.

Recycling programs
for this product may
not exist in your area.

Printed in U.S.A.

New York Times and *USA TODAY* bestselling author **Elle James** is a former IT professional and retired army and air force reservist. She writes romantic suspense, mysteries and paranormal romances that keep her readers on the edge of their seats to the very end of every book. When she's not at her computer, she's traveling to exotic and wonderful places, snow-skiing, boating or riding her four-wheeler, dreaming up new stories. Learn more about Elle James at ellejames.com.

Books by Elle James

Harlequin Romantic Suspense

Deadly Allure
Secret Service Rescue
Deadly Liaisons
Deadly Engagement
Deadly Reckoning

The Adair Affairs

Heir to Murder

The Coltons of Oklahoma

Protecting the Colton Bride

Harlequin Intrigue

Thunder Horse Redemption
Triggered
Taking Aim
Bodyguard Under Fire
Cowboy Resurrected
Christmas at Thunder Horse Ranch

Visit Elle's Author Profile page at Harlequin.com, or ellejames.com, for more titles.

This book is dedicated to my father, who left his home in Arkansas to join the US Air Force and gave twenty years of his life to his country. He ultimately followed his heart all the way back home, where he lives today and is happy to stay there. Home was where his heart was, and his heart was in Arkansas. I love you, Dad!

Chapter 1

Daniel Colton swept the brush over Rider's black coat, comforted by the scent of animal hide, manure and fresh-cut Bermuda. With every swish of the horse's full black tail, hay dust sparkled in the air, reflecting the afternoon sunlight streaming through the open door of the Lucky C breeding barn.

This was home and there was nowhere else Daniel would rather be.

"Are you about done brushing Rider? Halo's practically champing at the bit to get outside for her afternoon run."

Daniel lifted his head and stared over the black quarter horse stud's back at the woman on the other side. She was brushing the beautiful palomino mare, one of Daniel's many successes in his quarter-horse-breeding program at the Lucky C Ranch.

His chest tightened and his breath caught. It wasn't the horse he couldn't take his gaze off. It was the halo effect the sun gave Megan Talbot's strawberry blond hair. The palomino's registered name was Angel's Golden Halo, but the woman deserved the moniker more than the animal. For the first time in the four months since Megan had come to work for him, she'd worn her hair loose. Normally those long, curly locks were twisted into a braid, pulled back from a face sprinkled lightly with freckles. Some would call them flaws in her pale complexion, but Daniel found each freckle adorable and hard to resist.

A light breeze blew through the door, lifting Megan's hair, making it dance in the sunshine. The horse shifted nervously and Megan patted her backside. "Shh. We'll leave soon." She turned and smiled at Daniel with her bright green eyes. "Ready to saddle up? I don't know if Halo can wait any longer. She's more hyper than usual."

Daniel jerked his attention back to his horse, reminding himself that he was the boss, Megan worked for him and he had no business staring at her hair or any other part of her perfectly shaped face or lithe, athletic body.

"Let's saddle these two." He was ready to get out of the barn and gallop across the pastures of his father's ranch. Working around the animals, training, feeding and riding, he was more at home than at the big house with the rest of the Coltons.

Big J Colton was the patriarch of the Oklahoma Coltons and the owner of the Lucky C Ranch. As his bastard child, Daniel had grown up with his half brothers and half sister, accepted by everyone except his stepmother, Abra Colton. Because of her antagonism toward him and the fact that Big J had taken in a child who wasn't hers, Daniel had never felt he quite fit in with the others.

Megan was first to the tack room. When she emerged, she carried a blanket. "Is Greta back from Oklahoma City?" she asked.

"Not that I've heard. Why do you ask?"

With a shrug, Megan threw the blanket over the mare's back and followed Colton into the tack room. "I thought I saw her earlier. I might have been seeing things. With a wedding to plan, I doubt she has time to go back and forth between Tulsa and Oklahoma City often."

Daniel snorted. He grabbed his saddle and a blanket and squeezed by Megan in the confines of the barn. The scent of strawberries wafted in his direction from Megan's hair hanging down around her shoulders. Why did she have to be so darned beautiful? If she wasn't also so efficient and helpful, he might reconsider her employment at the ranch. She was a distraction and growing more distracting every day. "Don't know what takes so long in planning a wedding. All you need is a bride, a groom, a preacher and a ring."

Megan laughed as she lifted her own saddle. "I'm with you. If you know you love someone, why all the fuss, anyway? Married is married whether you have a big wedding or stand in front of a justice of the peace, say I do, sign the papers and call it done."

Daniel chuckled. "And I thought all women were romantics."

Megan's pretty coral lips twisted. "I think it's just me. My parents tried to convince me to earn an M-R-S degree, but I was too busy studying genetics and cell biology to be interested in the boys on the UCLA campus."

"M-R-S?"

Her brows rose. "You know. Mrs. someone." She shook her head. "They wanted me to marry well, be a social butterfly on the arm of my husband and stop playing in yucky stuff like parasites, tissues, and horse and cattle semen." Megan tossed her saddle up onto the mare's back with little effort.

Strong and beautiful, and she knew what she wanted out of life. In Daniel's mind, that was a killer combination. Why waste brains and talent by making her some man's arm candy?

He threw the blanket on Rider's back, followed by the saddle. "Didn't you grow up on a ranch? You know your way around horses like you've been doing this all your life."

Megan reached beneath the horse to grab Halo's girth, threaded the strap through the ring and tightened it. "My parents own a nice spread in California," she answered, pulling hard. "But they didn't let me work with the animals. I was barely allowed to ride. They were afraid those big ol' horses would hurt little ol' me." She laughed, the sound brightening Daniel's day.

Daniel frowned at how he'd grown used to the sound and looked forward to it. As he cinched Rider's girth and looped the leather strap, he concentrated on sticking to facts, not emotions. "You're an excellent rider."

"I didn't get that way *because* of my parents, but more *in spite* of them. What they didn't know was that I'd go to my room, saying I wanted to read for a while. Once there, I'd slip out the window, climb down a tree and race off to the pasture. Because I didn't want to get caught, I rode bareback and without a bridle."

An image of a gangly young woman with long strawberry blond hair riding bareback across the hills of California flashed in Daniel's mind. "No bridle? How did you get the horses to go the way you wanted?"

Megan lowered the stirrup and patted Halo's neck. "They could feel the pressure of my legs and responded accordingly. I also bribed them with apples and sugar cubes."

"I'm impressed." Daniel adjusted his stirrup and slipped the bridle over Rider's head. "Your parents didn't know what they were missing. You're very good with the horses."

"They didn't need the help with their horse-breeding program. We had a staff that managed the animals on the ranch." Megan sighed. "I'd love dearly to bring my horses out here someday."

"Why don't you?"

"My parents haven't forgiven me for moving to Oklahoma. Every time I speak with them on the phone, they ask me when I'm moving back. Remember last month, when I went home because my father was sick?"

Daniel nodded. She'd been gone an entire week, and he'd missed her more than he cared to admit. "You could have brought your horses back with you then. We have room here on the Lucky C for them."

Megan gave an unladylike snort. "Don't you think I would have if I could have?" She shook her head. "My father is using them as leverage, threatening to sell them if I don't move back to California."

Daniel shot a glance her way. "And are you?"

Megan blinked. "Am I what?"

"Moving back to California?"

She laughed. "Oh, heavens, no. I love it out here. I love my parents, but they stifle me. I've been calling my father's bluff about selling the horses. I hope he has a change of heart and lets me have them. Besides, I have no desire to live their lifestyle. It's not me."

Grabbing his stallion's reins, Daniel asked, "And what lifestyle is that?"

Megan's mouth twisted. "Servants to do everything for you, smiling at people you don't know at social events you don't really care about. Wearing skirts, heels and makeup all the time. Never getting your hands dirty or breaking a nail."

Daniel studied her fresh, makeup-free, freckled face. With her light red eyebrows and blond-tipped eyelashes, she was beautiful just the way she was. He wouldn't change a thing.

Tearing his gaze away from her, he led Rider out of the barn. He walked away from the woman who was far too often in his thoughts both at work and at night when he lay in bed, trying to sleep through a growing hunger that had nothing to do with food.

Behind him, he heard the sound of hooves pawing the ground and then thumping against the hard-packed dirt.

"Whoa, Halo," Megan said, her voice tight.

Daniel glanced over his shoulder.

Halo, normally calm and gentle, reared, her front hooves pawing at the air.

Daniel took a step back into the barn, his hand still holding Rider's reins.

Megan held on to Halo's bridle, talking softly, soothingly. When the horse came back down on all four hooves, Megan chuckled shakily. "You really are raring to go, aren't you?"

"Need a hand?" Daniel asked.

Her mouth firming, Megan frowned. "I don't need your help. I'm perfectly capable of handling Halo."

A smile tugging his lips, Daniel led Rider out of the barn. "Touchy, are we?"

"I'm not fragile like my father and mother seem to think. Haven't I proven that?" she demanded.

"Absolutely," he said, unable to fight the grin spreading across his face. "If you didn't look so good in your jeans, I'd mistake you for one of the guys."

Megan's frown deepened for a moment, then cleared. Her lips quirked upward along with her brows. "You like the way I look in jeans?"

Daniel was saved from responding by Halo rearing again, jerking Megan up off her feet for a second.

"We'd better get going before Halo takes off without you." Daniel jammed his boot in the stirrup and mounted Rider. He had to remind himself Megan was his employee. He couldn't flirt with the staff. It wasn't right. He leaned down and opened the gate to the pasture, rode through and waited for Megan.

She stuck her boot in the stirrup, but before she could sling her leg over the top of the saddle, Halo spun.

Megan held on, managing to get her leg over the top. "I don't know what's got her riled, but she's not acting right."

"You want to take another horse?"

"No," Megan grunted, fighting to control the horse and aim her toward the open gate. "She needs to get out and run."

Daniel waited for Megan and Halo to pass through before he closed the gate.

Megan released one hand from the reins to pull her

hair behind her and tuck it into the back of her shirt. "I should have braided this—"

Before she finished her sentence, Halo reared, tossed her head and yanked the reins from Megan's hands. Before Megan could reach out to retrieve them, Halo leaped forward and bolted across the pasture.

Daniel dug his heels into Rider's flanks and raced after her, his pulse pounding as fast as the horse's hooves. At the speed Halo was going, all it would take was a quick change of direction or halt and Megan would be thrown.

Rider's hooves thundered across the ground. Daniel leaned forward to decrease wind resistance, slapping the reins behind him against the horse's hindquarters, urging him faster.

The stallion's eagerness to be first in the race would have made him move faster even without Daniel's bidding.

Halo had a good head start, but Rider slowly closed the gap.

Megan held on, bending over the horse's neck in an attempt to grab her bridle, without success.

As Daniel rode up beside her, pressing Rider against Halo's side, he yelled, "Grab on!" Reaching out, he looped his arm around Megan's waist.

She grabbed around his neck and held on as he lifted her out of the saddle and slammed her hard against his chest.

His legs clamping tight around the horse, Daniel adjusted his balance for Megan's weight and pulled on the reins. "Whoa, Rider."

The horse strained against the command, determined to catch up and overtake Halo.

His grip loosening around Megan's waist, Daniel's breath caught and held. If he didn't get Rider under control soon, he'd drop her and she could be crushed beneath the horse's powerful hooves.

Megan clung to Daniel.

Rider had been just as spooked by Halo's behavior as she had been. In his mad dash to catch up to the other horse, he was ignoring Daniel's one-handed attempt to bring him under control.

She was deadweight on Daniel. If she could get her leg around to the back... Swinging her leg behind her, she couldn't quite reach the back without Daniel losing his grip on her. The front was closer and had a better angle.

"Whoa!" Daniel yelled at the crazed horse.

Megan made the decision to go for the front. She looped her leg over the saddle horn and straddled Daniel's lap, facing him.

Daniel immediately released her and reached around her to take the reins in both hands.

Trying to make herself as small as possible, Megan pressed her face into his chest so that he could see over her. Daniel's thighs tensed beneath her as he dug his heels into the stirrups and pulled back hard on the reins. Rider slowed, whinnying his protest, as he settled into an agitated trot.

Daniel let off on the reins just a little.

Rider took that as an invitation to leap forward. He was instantly brought back by a sharp tug on the reins.

The horse reared.

Daniel leaned forward, his chest pressing into Megan's, his breath stirring the loose hair at her temples.

Her pulse hammered in her veins, but she kept her cool and held on until Rider stamped to a complete stop, pawing at the dirt.

When she was certain Daniel had the horse settled, she lifted her head, her face inches from Daniel's. Adrenaline spiking through her system, her breaths coming in ragged gasps, she was hyperaware of every point of contact between her body and his, from her legs resting on his muscular thighs to her chest pressed against the hardened planes of his. She could barely breathe.

His arms still around her, holding on to the reins, Daniel breathed out a long sigh. "You had me scared."

Megan let go of a nervous laugh. "You? I could do nothing to stop her. That was stupid of me to let go of the reins." The wind lifted her hair and blew it across her face. Before she could shove it behind her ear, Daniel reached out and did it for her.

"You couldn't have known Halo was going to take off like she did." Daniel's fingers curled the hair behind her ear, and he dragged the backs of his knuckles across her face, tracing a line from her ear to her jaw. "Watching her fly off like that with you on her back the reins dangling…"

Mesmerized by his gentle touch, Megan couldn't move away, nor did she want to. Daniel had never made a pass at her, nor had he indicated any attraction toward her in the four months she'd worked for him. Oh, but she'd been attracted to him from the day they met, when she'd interviewed for the job of his assistant.

Now, with her heart racing for an entirely different reason, her breath lodged in her throat and held as she waited for him to make the next move.

Daniel's gaze shifted to her mouth. He cupped her

cheek, and his thumb brushed across her lips. "You don't need makeup."

"My mother would disagree. She hates my freckles," Megan whispered, her breath mingling with his.

"I think they are one of your best features." He leaned forward and touched her freckled nose with his lips.

Megan's eyes widened. Had he just kissed her? Was she dreaming? Her lips tingled in hopeful anticipation of a kiss that met her mouth, not her nose. She swept her tongue across her suddenly dry lips, and she stared up into his eyes.

Daniel's thumb brushed her lips again. "Don't do that."

"Do what?"

"This." He leaned forward and touched his mouth to hers, his tongue sweeping across the seam of her lips.

She opened to him as naturally as a morning glory opened to the sun. Her hands curled into his shirt, dragging him closer.

Daniel crushed her to him, his arms tightening around her. His tongue slipped past her teeth, claiming her in a long, sensual kiss that made her blood burn a path all the way to her core.

When at last he raised his head, he stared down at her as if seeing her for the first time.

Suddenly she felt shy. Her cheeks heated and she stammered, "Thanks for coming to my rescue."

Her words seemed to shake him out of his trance, his body stiffening. "Right. You're welcome." He glanced away, looking anywhere but at her. "I'd have done it for anyone."

He could have stuck a pin in her ego, as deflated as she felt after that incredible kiss and then his complete brush-off. A rush of adrenaline-induced anger made her back straighten. She was sitting in his lap, for heaven's sake, and there was no mistaking his obvious attraction to her pressing against her.

"Here, let me help you down." He gripped her arms and started to lift her off him.

Megan's arms slipped around his neck, refusing to let him dislodge her from his lap. Damn it. She didn't want down. Where she sat was exactly where she'd ached to be for so long. She wanted to scream with frustration that he now seemed determined to put her back in her place.

Megan tilted her chin in challenge. "I know you would have rescued anyone. That's the kind of person you are. But would you have *kissed* anyone like you just kissed me?"

Chapter 2

Daniel helped Megan slide around him to ride double behind him. Then he turned back for the barn.

"Aren't we going after Halo?" she asked.

"We're closer to the barn. I'll come back to get her when she's had time to calm down."

All he got from Megan was a soft snort. He could feel her anger and was torn between regret and relief. She was his employee. He had no right to kiss her like he had. Instead of holding around his waist, she gripped the rim of the saddle's seat and didn't say a word.

Her silence made Daniel's gut knot. This was the reason he didn't mix business with pleasure. And holy hell, it had been all pleasure, the feel of Megan's lips on his, her body pressed tightly to his. But when you crossed the line, you couldn't go back. The easy camaraderie they'd had before the kiss might be gone for good.

Jack, the oldest of Daniel's half siblings, and his younger brother Brett stood by the barn, sunlight glinting off their dark brown hair. They draped their arms over the wooden fence rail, their brows rising when Rider turned, revealing Megan behind Daniel.

Jack frowned. "Run into trouble?"

A grin split Brett's face. "Or creating some of your own?"

Daniel glared at Brett.

As soon as they reached the barn, Megan slid off the horse's rump, her cheeks bright pink. "I'll go look for Halo," she said, turning toward the barn to find another horse.

"Don't worry about her. Jack and Brett can saddle up and help me go after her."

"Fine." Megan, her face averted, ran for the barn.

Brett's smile disappeared. "What happened?"

"Something spooked Halo."

His younger brother's gaze followed Megan. "Not the horse. Megan. What happened with Megan?" He faced Daniel.

Heat suffused Daniel's cheeks and spread all the way out to his ears. "When the horse bolted with Megan, I pulled her off. She rode back with me. That's all." He narrowed his eyes, willing his brothers to stop with the inquisition about Megan. "What did you think happened?"

Brett's mouth twisted. "I don't know, but Megan just ran off like a scalded cat."

Daniel blew out a breath. "The point is, Halo spooked and nearly hurt Megan."

Jack's brows drew together. "That's not like her. Halo's one of our gentlest mares."

"I know. All the more reason to bring her back and find out what's wrong with her." Daniel looked from Jack to Brett. "Are you coming or not?"

Brett spun and trotted toward the barn. "It'll just take us a minute to saddle up."

Daniel dismounted and led Rider to the watering trough, watching through his peripheral vision for Megan to emerge from the barn.

By the time his brothers had captured and saddled their horses, Megan still hadn't come out of the barn. Daniel knew it had been a mistake to kiss her. Now she was too embarrassed to come out while he was still around. She was the best assistant he'd had. Okay, so she was the only assistant he'd had. Now that his breeding program was doing well, he needed all the help he could get.

Megan was smart, computer savvy and great with the horses. He hoped she didn't quit because of one little kiss. One completely soul-defining, world-shattering kiss.

Daniel groaned.

"Got a bellyache?" Brett asked, leading his bay gelding out of the barn, followed by Jack.

"No, just thinking."

Jack swung up on his horse, carrying a lasso in his right hand and reining with the left. "Thinking these designer horses aren't the way to go after all?"

"No, not at all." Daniel had put a lot of thought, planning, research and sweat into the horse-breeding program, and it was just beginning to pay off. He wasn't giving up now.

"I told you, Jack," Brett said. "With Daniel's eye for excellent breeding stock and Megan's record-keeping capabilities, we're finally starting to take off. It won't be long before the Lucky C becomes a household name in progressive horse-breeding programs."

Daniel's chest swelled. "I'm determined to continue that progressive trend. Has Big J considered my proposal to purchase semen from the Kennedy Farms?"

"He's thinking about it. You already know how I feel," Jack said. "The Lucky C is a cattle ranch. We've always run cattle. The horses should be secondary, for running the cattle, not breeding."

Daniel respected his older brother's ability to manage a ranch the size of the Lucky C and his love and determination to protect his family. But the man was pragmatic and often slow to change. In order to let loose of the funding to purchase the semen needed to move their program forward, Daniel would have to convince both his father and his older brother it would be worth the investment.

"Come on, Jack," Brett said, nudging his horse to catch up with Jack's. "Daniel's already got other breeders looking at the Lucky C lines. He knows what he's doing, and it doesn't hurt to diversify our holdings."

"Yeah, well, we don't even know if the Kennedys will sell to us." Jack shot a glance at Daniel. "What's the latest?"

"They are all about the pedigree," Daniel said. "They hand-select the programs they want to contribute to."

"You have some of the best horses in the country," Brett noted. "Why wouldn't they want to add to your lines?"

Daniel snorted. "Their pedigree requirement extends to family and heritage."

"So? The Coltons are full of family and heritage.

You think they might not sell to us because of family?" Jack's brows dipped. "I'll bet the Lucky C Ranch has been in the Colton family as long if not longer than the Kennedys have owned their ranch."

"Yeah, but I'm the one running the horse-breeding program here. I'm the main contact," Daniel reminded him.

"And?"

"Well, I'm not exactly a blue blood or a purebred."

Jack reined his horse to a stop. "What the hell are you talking about?"

"Yeah, what are you saying?" Brett reiterated. "You're just as much a Colton as the rest of us."

"I'm the bastard," Daniel said, his tone flat.

"That's not how we see it," Brett said.

Jack, Brett, Ryan and Greta had always treated him as one of the family, even though Daniel's stepmother had resented the fact that Big J brought him to live with them when his own mother had died.

Abra hated Daniel. She hated that Big J had an affair with the nanny when Abra had been halfway around the world on another one of her trips. The woman couldn't stand to be around her own kids. They made her nervous.

Daniel's mother, full-blood Cherokee, had left the Lucky C when she discovered she was pregnant with Big J's child. She'd returned to the reservation, where she'd instilled in Daniel pride in his Cherokee heritage and the love of horses.

"You're as much a Colton as the rest of us," Jack said.

Brett snarled. "If anyone says differently, they can take it up with all of us."

"Not everyone sees things the way you, Ryan and

Greta do," Daniel assured them. But his heart warmed at the conviction in his brothers' tones.

When he'd come to live with them at only ten years old, he'd thought he'd be miserable, losing the mother he loved and moving in with a father he barely knew. He figured on staying until he was old enough to leave home.

And here he was twenty years later. He no longer lived at the big house, having moved out when he finished college. Now he lived in the cozy two-bedroom cabin close to the breeding barn. It was small but enough for a bachelor and away from his stepmother.

"There she is," Jack called out, pulling Daniel back to the task at hand.

Halo stood in the middle of the pasture, pawing at the ground.

As they neared, she reared and whinnied.

Rider answered, sidestepping nervously.

"She's all wound up," Brett muttered. "Did she get hold of some bad feed?"

"No telling. But whatever is bothering her isn't normal." Daniel nudged Rider forward.

"Let's go get her." Jack lifted his lasso and urged his mount forward.

Daniel rode up to the mare. With only twenty yards between them, the mare bolted and ran. Rider quickly caught up to her on one side. Jack's horse swung to the opposite side as he tossed the lasso, his aim true. The rope circled the mare's neck.

Jack tied off on the saddle horn and slowed his horse by pulling on the reins.

Halo pulled against the rope around her neck, tossing

her head, dancing sideways to avoid Jack. Daniel was on the other side. He reached over and grabbed her reins.

Between Jack and Daniel, they slowed the mare to a halt. Her chest heaved, her sleek cream-colored coat was slick with sweat and her eyes rolled, showing the crazed whites.

"Need a hand there?" Brett called out, riding nearby in case the horse broke free.

"We have her."

The two Coltons led the horse back toward the barn, Daniel speaking to her softly, trying to soothe her.

Brett was first off his horse. He took over for the other two and held the horse's reins.

When Jack loosened his hold on the lasso, Halo tried to rear, but Brett held tight, pulling her head down.

"You're right," Brett said, straining to hold on to the horse. "Something isn't right with her."

"Let's get her into the squeeze chute. I want to take a blood sample." Daniel dismounted and led Rider into the barn, tying him off to a post before helping Brett get Halo into the chute.

Jack backed away. "If you two can handle this, I'll take care of the other horses."

"We have it," Daniel assured him. "All I need is a syringe—"

Megan appeared, carrying a syringe and a couple of cotton balls soaked in rubbing alcohol.

Daniel breathed a sigh, happy that she hadn't decided to quit because of his indiscretion.

"Daniel keeps telling us how efficient you are," Brett teased. "Now you're a mind reader?"

Megan shook her head. "It's logic. Halo wasn't acting herself. There has to be a reason."

Brett and Daniel held Halo's head while Megan swabbed the horse's neck, felt for the jugular and slid in the needle.

Halo jerked, but the men held her steady while Megan pulled the plunger, filling the syringe. She removed the needle, swabbed the injection site and massaged it for a moment. "I'll put this in a tube and drop it off at the vet pathology lab in Tulsa on my way home."

"Better leave now if you want to catch them before they close for the day."

"Will do." Megan hurried back into the barn with the syringe without making eye contact with Daniel. She'd always been open and smiling around him.

Daniel could have kicked himself for ruining everything. He wouldn't have been surprised in the least if she came in the next day with her resignation. "Can you take over with Halo?"

"Sure." Brett gripped the mare's bridle and backed her out of the chute.

Daniel ran into the barn, where Jack had tied off his and Brett's mounts beside Rider. He was in the process of removing the last saddle.

Megan was nowhere in sight.

Jack shook his head. "She's in the office."

Without a word, Daniel entered the office.

Megan was at the desk they shared in the cramped space, transferring the blood from the syringe into a tube. "Is there anything else you need dropped at the lab?" Megan reached for a padded envelope and dropped the tube inside.

"No. Just that." Daniel rubbed his sweaty palms down the front of his jeans. "Megan, I want to apologize."

Megan's cheeks reddened. "Don't."

"I'm afraid my actions might have given you the wrong idea."

Her head jerked up and she stared straight into his eyes. "Are you going to tell me that you kissed me by accident? Or that it was a huge mistake?"

"No. I mean, yes." He bit down on his tongue to keep from saying something stupid.

"Save your breath, Daniel." She crossed the room with the package in her hand. Her jaw was set, lips pressed into a thin line. "I agree. The kiss was a big mistake."

He let go of the breath he'd been holding, but the tightness in his chest didn't loosen. Though he thought the kiss was a mistake, he hadn't known how he'd feel to hear her echo his thoughts. Had the kiss meant nothing to her?

"Good, then." Daniel straightened, determined not to let any of his chaotic thoughts show in his expression. "I just didn't want things to change between us. You're the best assistant I've ever had."

Megan rolled her eyes. "Daniel, I'm the only assistant you've ever had. But if you want to pretend nothing happened and everything between is just like it was this morning, I can play that game, too." She stopped in front of him and poked a finger into his chest. "But it would be a lie. You might wish you could, but you can't take back that kiss or the way it made you feel. Because I sure can't. It wasn't entirely one-sided, in case you hadn't noticed."

Megan left the office and ran out of the barn. She hopped into her Jeep Wrangler and sped down the road leading to the gate to the Lucky C Ranch. Soon she was on the highway into Tulsa, where she had a depressingly small apartment in an inexpensive but not too sketchy neighborhood.

Determined to make it on her own without her parents' vast wealth, she'd managed to put down a deposit on the apartment and pay rent and her utilities with the money she made working for the Lucky C Ranch.

The drive into Tulsa didn't take long, and soon she was on the bypass circling the city to get to the veterinary laboratory before it closed. She hadn't factored in the evening rush-hour congestion. Swerving in and out of traffic, she finally pulled into the parking lot with two minutes to spare.

She ran the blood sample inside, wrote out her request and left the package with the receptionist.

Then she drove to her apartment complex and parked, her hands shaking as she sat behind the steering wheel, letting the events of the afternoon wash over her in a tidal wave of emotions. One thought stood out over all others.

Daniel Colton had kissed her.

The incessant buzzing of her cell phone pierced her hazy cloud of schoolgirl giddiness, and she dug in her purse.

Perhaps it was Daniel calling to tell her that the kiss hadn't been a mistake and he was deeply, madly, completely in love with her. Megan found the phone, stared at the caller ID and groaned before punching the talk button.

"Hi, Mother. What do you want?" she asked, the irritation in her voice more pronounced than usual.

"Ferrence Small is back home from New York City."

"That's nice."

"I understand he's a lawyer now, working with a large

pipeline company out in Wyoming. If you can tell me the next time you'll be home, I'm sure I can set up a chance for you two to meet."

"Mother, I'm not interested."

"Sweetheart, your father's health isn't what it used to be. He's a very sick man."

"I know. I was out there last month. We had a lovely visit."

"Honey, you can't keep slaving away in the tornado-infested center of the country. I can't stop worrying. And you can imagine all the stress your father is under."

"I'm sorry, Mother. But you and Daddy can manage your ranch in California. You don't really need me there. However, the Lucky C needs me here. I have important work to do, and I don't need care packages, cards and letters begging me to come home. I'll be home for visits. That will have to be enough."

Her mother clucked. "Oh, darling, I didn't want to have to tell you…"

A sense of dread slipped over her. Her mother only used that I-hate-to-stick-it-to-you-but-I-will-if-I-have-to voice when she was about to drop a bomb on some poor unsuspecting sales clerk who displeased her while shopping. Only this time, the bomb would fall on Megan.

"Your father is on the line, and he has something to say to you."

Her hand tightening on the cell phone until her knuckles turned white, Megan sucked in a deep breath and said, "Hi, Dad. What is it you wanted to say?"

"I have an auctioneer coming out tomorrow to look at your horses."

Megan's heart plummeted to her knees. "Daddy," she said. "I've only just started putting money away for the horses. It will take me years to have what I need to pay you for them."

"I'm sorry, sweetheart, but if I can't go out to Oklahoma to talk some sense into my daughter's head, I can damn sure get her to come to me. The Triple Diamond Ranch is your legacy."

"Daddy, it's *your* legacy. You and Mother never wanted me to help with it. Now I want to make it on my own." She'd left the rich debutante lifestyle behind after she'd lost her fiancé and nearly lost her life. Megan had no intention of going back.

Her father snorted. "You do not have to work for others when you have servants who can do all that for you."

"But, Daddy, you don't understand. I love working with the horses. And I'm good at it."

"You're a woman. You shouldn't be working around animals big enough to crush you."

"Those horses are big enough to crush the men I work with as well as me. The thing is, Daddy, I know when to get out of the way."

"Damn it, Megan, you are our only child. I want to know when I die…" He coughed. "I want to know you will be here to take over the reins. You need to come home, settle down, get married and have children to shoulder your obligation to your heritage."

"I'm sorry, Daddy, but I have to live my life the way I want to, not the way you dictate."

Her mother's gasp echoed over the line.

"Very well," her father said in a steely voice. "If you're not home in one week and actively looking for a suitable spouse, I will sell all of your beloved horses to a glue factory."

Blood drained from Megan's head, and her stomach

flipped. "You can't do that. Those horses are beautiful animals, and they should be with us. The horse-breeding program at Triple Diamond Ranch is one of the best. You can't condemn them to a glue factory or even sell them just because you want me to come home."

"I can and I will. If you care about the horses, show you care about your legacy and the future of Triple Diamond Ranch. One week, Megan."

Chapter 3

Daniel tossed all night. When he actually fell asleep he dreamed of Megan, her hair flying out behind her on a runaway horse. He chased her. For a long time she was just out of reach. When he finally caught up with her, he snatched her off her horse and into his arms. Then they kissed. The kiss turned into more and suddenly they were in his bed, making love.

Daniel jerked awake, hot, sweaty and more aroused than he'd ever been in his life. All stemming from a kiss that shouldn't have happened.

Before dawn, he rose from his solitary bed in the cabin close to the breeding barn and pulled on a pair of jeans, a shirt and his boots. He couldn't go back to sleep knowing Megan would be in his dreams, lying naked in his sheets. Everything about that image was wrong.

He'd be lucky if she even showed up for work today.

And if she did, she'd probably come only to turn in her resignation.

By the time the sun came up over the horizon, Daniel had fed the horses, checked on his studs and prize mares and stacked twenty bags of feed in a corner of the barn. With his pulse still pounding and blood burning through his veins, he snapped a lunging rope on Rider's halter and walked him out to the arena.

Daniel twirled the end of the rope and clucked his tongue. Rider started at a walk, more interested in an easy pace than actual exercise.

"Come on, boy. You need this as much as I do." Daniel continued twirling the loose end of the rope. He clucked his tongue again and tapped the horse's hindquarters with the rope.

Rider stepped up the pace and trotted around the circle, tossing his black mane in protest.

The monotonous circling calmed Daniel and the horse, and they settled into a rhythm of walking and trotting. Fifteen minutes passed before a voice called out.

"Daniel!"

Daniel's hand tightened on the rope. Rider immediately came to a halt.

Heat rose up his neck and into his face as Daniel turned toward the voice.

Megan leaned over the arena's metal fence, her arms folded over the top rail, lines etched across her smooth forehead.

Though he was happy Megan had returned, Daniel couldn't erase his concern over the content of his dreams, and he worried his thoughts would be easily discernible in his eyes. Without meeting her gaze, Daniel nodded. "Good morning, Megan," he acknowledged, gathering the rope until he held the horse on a short lead.

The normally reserved and always confident young woman chewed on her lower lip, and her brows puckered. "We need to talk," she blurted.

His stomach knotting, Daniel braced himself. "Yes, we do. Let me take care of Rider first. Then we can talk uninterrupted."

"Okay," she said, biting on her lower lip again, driving Daniel nuts with the nervous movement that only drew his attention to the mouth he'd kissed so hard the day before.

He opened the gate to the arena and led Rider through.

Megan closed the gate and trailed behind Daniel and Rider, following them into the barn.

Not certain what he was going to say, Daniel chose to concentrate on the horse, putting off the talk as long as he could, hoping he could say something that would make sense and put things back on an even keel. He liked Megan. A lot. And he didn't want to lose her over something as stupid, and inconsiderate, and completely unforgettable as a kiss.

Holy hell, he couldn't even come up with an apology when he wasn't at all sorry he'd kissed her. He'd be sorry only if she left because of it.

After grabbing a brush, Daniel stalled by running the brush over Rider's back.

Megan fetched another brush and took the other side, working quickly, her strong hands smoothing over the horse's sides, meeting Daniel over the horse's hindquarters. She stared across the animal's rump and said, "Daniel, I have to quit." Then she spun and paced away from him.

"Won't you at least give me the chance to apologize properly?"

Her head down, her boot heels pounding the dirt, she marched to the end of the barn and back. "Normally I'd give two weeks' notice. But that's impossible."

His chest tightening with each of her words, Daniel stood with a brush in his hands. How could he salvage this situation and keep her on the Lucky C? "Under the circumstances, I don't blame you, but I wish you'd reconsider."

She paced, shaking her head, her long French braid whipping side to side. "If there was any other way, I wouldn't go, but I don't see another option."

"Again, I don't blame you. I blame myself." He set the brush on a workbench and gathered Megan's hands in his. "I wish there was something I could say or do to make it better. Please don't go. I need you here."

She stared up into his eyes. "I don't have a choice. If I don't leave, he'll sell them all." Her eyes swam with tears.

Daniel stared down at her. "What are you talking about?"

"My horses." She frowned. "What did you think I was talking about?"

A wave of relief nearly made Daniel weak. "I thought you were mad about yesterday."

Her frown deepening, she stared into his eyes. "Yesterday?" Then her eyes widened and her mouth formed a kissable O. "Yesterday." Twin flags of color flew high on her cheekbones. "The kiss."

"The kiss." His hands slid up her arms and stopped before he pulled her close and kissed her again. "I thought you were going to leave because I crossed the line."

"You think I'd leave because of a kiss? I thought you knew me better than that."

"You had every right to quit. As your boss, I shouldn't have kissed you."

"For your information, there were two people involved in that kiss. It was not one-sided. And that's not the reason I'm leaving."

"Then what is?"

"My father." She pulled in a long breath and let it out. "He gave me an ultimatum. He's going to sell my horses if I don't come home to live."

Daniel's fingers tightened on her arms. "I thought the horses at the Triple Diamond were quality stock. They are ranked right up there in standing with the Kennedys' breeding program."

"Yeah, well my father doesn't really give a damn about the horses. It was just a project he took on at my suggestion until I left."

"Can't you buy them from him?" Daniel couldn't wrap his mind around throwing away some of the best horseflesh in the nation.

"If I had the money my grandmother left to me." She shook her head. "But I won't get that until I'm married. It's a stipulation of her will. Even then, I'd have to purchase them through a third party. My father would never sell them to me. He wants me home, and this is his leverage."

"Didn't you say he was sick?"

"Yes, but I can never tell how sick he is. He always tries to manipulate me and make me live according to his standards. I don't want to go back, but I don't have another choice. I have to go home. I can't let him sell those horses. They're top breeders...and...my friends."

Daniel gathered her in his arms and stroked her head. "It's okay. We'll think of something."

She rested her cheek against his chest, her fingers curling into his shirt. "There's nothing to think about. I have to go. The sooner the better."

He tipped her face up. "When is he selling?"

"He gave me one week to get home or the horses go on the auction block." Her eyes filled with tears.

"Well, that gives us a week."

"One week isn't enough." She shook her head. "I don't see any other way. If he sells them as breeding stock, they'll go high. I won't be able to buy them. I barely have enough money to pay next month's rent. So you see, I have to go home." She took a step back and stood in front of him, her shoulders slumped, the first tears sliding from the corners of her eyes. "I thought he was bluffing. But I can't bet those horses on a bluff."

The anger he could handle. But as the tears slid down Megan's cheeks, it felt like a large fist had clenched around his heart and squeezed. He pulled her against him again and held her close, resting his cheek against the top of her head. "I have a little money saved."

She laid her face against his chest. "I can't take your money. This isn't your problem. It's mine."

"Well, don't do anything today. Give us some time to come up with some solutions."

"I'm out of solutions," she said, pressing her face into his shirt.

"Just promise me you won't leave right away. Can you do that?"

"It'll take time for me to organize my apartment, shut

off my utilities and inform my landlord. But once I have all that done, I have to drive to California."

"Just hold on for a day or two. We'll think of something."

Her arms slipped around his waist. "I don't expect you to take on my problems. You're my boss, not my fairy godmother."

He chuckled. "Yeah, I'd look pretty silly in a dress, carrying a fairy wand, and I'm not such a great boss at that."

"Why do you say that?" She looked up at him through watery green eyes. "You're great."

"Because a good boss doesn't go around kissing his employees." He stared down at her damp cheeks, his belly flipping. "Right now, I want to be a very bad boss."

Her eyes flared with desire. "How so?"

"I want to kiss you. Again."

She sucked in a breath and bit down on that lip before saying, "I told you, I quit. That means you're not my boss."

He leaned his forehead against hers and sighed. How he wanted to kiss her. "I'm not accepting your resignation."

"You don't have a choice," she said, her lips so close. Daniel could almost feel how soft they were. He wanted to kiss her so badly his lips tingled. The warmth of her breath feathered across his mouth. His hands shook with the effort it took to resist.

Then he pushed her to arm's length. "I can't screw this up. If we find a way to save your horses without you moving back to California, you'll still be my employee. I don't want to risk losing you as an assistant."

Megan sighed and dropped her arms. "Okay, boss,

I'll be here for another day, but I'll only be able to work half a day tomorrow. I have a lot to do to get my stuff packed for the move."

"Don't start packing yet. We'll come up with a solution. In the meantime, I need you to call the vet lab and see if they came up with anything from the sample you took in yesterday."

"They won't have had time to process it," Megan argued.

"Then research other breeding programs. The Kennedy deal might not happen."

"Why? You have a fine program here. You're a rising star in quarter horse breeding."

Daniel snorted. "As far as the Kennedys are concerned, that isn't enough."

"Why?"

"I don't want to go into it. Just do that research for me, will you?"

She popped a salute and gave him a crooked smile. "Yes, boss." Then she turned and marched into the barn office.

Daniel let go of the breath he'd been holding since the urge to kiss Megan again had nearly pushed him past reason. He had to come up with a plan to help Megan get those horses or he'd lose her. After working with her for only four months, he knew she'd be impossible to replace. In more ways than he'd ever imagined.

Megan entered the office, closed the door behind her and leaned against it. Her face burned and her heart hurt so much she could barely think straight. She'd wanted to kiss Daniel. She'd almost thrown herself at him. After yesterday's kiss, she'd thought there might be something between them. But today he'd pushed her away. Apparently he wasn't as infatuated with her as she was with him.

Since the first day she'd come to work with Daniel, she'd known he was special. The man was quiet and dedicated. He loved horses as much as she did. His Cherokee ancestry didn't hurt, either. He was tall and handsome. That dark, dark hair and even darker brown eyes made her crazy with longing. Maybe she should leave. Staying at the Lucky C and falling in love with Daniel would only set her up for a whole lot of pain.

The irony of it all was that all problems would have been solved if he'd professed a secret love for her and asked her to marry him. She'd have the man of her most sensual dreams and meet the stipulation of her grandmother's will. She'd inherit her grandmother's sizable financial holdings upon her marriage. That money would be enough to purchase the horses from her father and she'd never be subject to his threats again. Her life would be her own to live the way she saw fit.

Megan drew in a long, steadying breath and let it out on a sigh. If wishes were horses, beggars would ride. She held out no hope for another solution to her situation. But two more days with Daniel were better than nothing.

She sat behind the desk and thumbed through her contacts to find the number for the vet lab in Tulsa and called. When she reached one of the lab techs, she explained she was calling for the Lucky C Ranch.

"Oh, we're so glad you called. We had a lull in samples, so we were able to get right on the one you left last night. I'm surprised that horse is still standing. The sample you left us indicated she was poisoned." The tech gave her the scientific name of the poison, which Megan wrote on a pad.

"It affects the animal's nervous system, making her jumpy and overstimulated."

"How would a horse get hold of something like that?"

"It's not like it grows around here. Either it was present in the food she was fed, something brought it into her environment or someone gave it to her."

Megan's gut clenched at the final option. They fed all the breeding horses the same feed, and Halo was the only one to show any symptoms.

"Okay, I'll let the boss know. Thank you for the information." Megan hung up and stared at the phone for exactly two seconds. Then she pushed to her feet and ran out to the stalls.

"What's wrong?" Daniel had just finished mucking Rider's stall and stood the rake against the wall.

"The vet lab said Halo was poisoned."

"What?" He hurried to Halo's stall with Megan.

The mare stood with her head sagging, her breathing labored.

"She seemed fine early this morning when I checked on her." Daniel entered the stall and ran his hands over her neck, checked her eyes and looked down her throat. "Call the vet."

Megan ran back to the office and dialed the veterinarian who serviced the animals on the Lucky C. He was there within twenty minutes, and they spent the rest of the afternoon working to save Halo.

Megan and Daniel cleaned her stall thoroughly, took samples from her trough and searched the barn for anything contaminated that she could have come in contact with. Nothing stood out.

After the vet left with strict instructions on how to take care of the very sick horse, Megan stood by Daniel. "What now?"

"We wait and see how she does by morning. We've done all we can do."

Megan stared at Daniel's worried face. Neither one of them had eaten lunch, and the work they'd done all afternoon had depleted Megan's personal store of energy. It had to have taken a toll on Daniel's. "It's nearly supper time. Why don't we grab a bite to eat?"

Daniel shook his head. "I have deli meat and bread at the cabin. Help yourself. I'm staying with Halo."

Knowing Daniel needed to fuel his system for what appeared to be an all-nighter, Megan left him in the barn and hiked over to his cabin. It wasn't the first time she'd gone to the cabin to make sandwiches. The man didn't take care of himself. As his assistant, she'd helped him set up a robust database to track horses, feed, lineage, exercise and all the other nuances of running a breeding facility. She'd also learned what kind of sandwiches he preferred and made sure he ate.

She entered the cabin through the front door and headed for the small kitchen. Having little in the way of decorations, the cabin reflected the male occupant through the dark leather furniture and large television screen for the occasional football game he liked to watch. The furnishings were spare and serviceable.

In the kitchen, his refrigerator held five bottles of beer, a couple bottles of water, one moldy orange, a few bottles of condiments, a jug of soured milk and a package of deli meat. Megan gave the meat a smell test. Thankfully it passed.

After throwing together two sandwiches, she grabbed

the bottled water and hurried back to the barn, not wanting to be away from Daniel and Halo any longer than necessary.

Daniel was where she'd left him and Halo lay on the ground beside him.

Her heart went out to the horse. "She doesn't look good."

"The vet said tonight would be the big test."

Megan held out the sandwich she'd wrapped in a paper towel. "Eat. You're no good to anyone if you pass out from hunger."

"I don't pass out," he mumbled, refusing to take the sandwich. "I'm going to wash my hands first."

"I'll be here." Megan sank to the ground beside Halo, unfolded the napkin around her sandwich and took a bite. She had no real interest in eating when such a beautiful creature was lying sick because of some toxin with a source they had yet to locate.

Over her shoulder, she heard the jingle of the phone ringing in the office. She struggled to stand but settled back on her bottom when Daniel's deep tone said, "Hello. Yes, this is Daniel Colton. Mr. Kennedy, I'm glad you called."

Megan stiffened. From the sound of it, Daniel was talking to the owner of Kennedy Farms. Excitement had her leaning toward the office, straining to hear the conversation. This was the call Daniel had been hoping for. Marshall Kennedy didn't bother to talk to breeders unless he already had a good opinion of their programs.

Rider whinnied from his stall. Angel, Halo's mother, answered, the noise drowning out whatever Daniel was saying.

The office door swung closed, shutting out the sound

of the horses and cutting off any eavesdropping Megan hoped to accomplish.

Not that it mattered. She'd soon be on her way back to California to live the life her father and mother deemed appropriate for a debutante. All interest in the sandwich she'd prepared disappeared and she laid it on the napkin beside her.

Sleek, the black barn cat, trotted over to her side and sniffed at the discarded food.

"Go ahead. You can have it. You'll need your strength here more than I will." It appeared the cat would outlast Megan's stay at the Lucky C.

Chapter 4

"I've heard a lot about the Lucky C Ranch lately," Marshall Kennedy's voice boomed in his ear.

Daniel held the phone in a tight grip. This call might mean the difference between a good program and an excellent breeding program that could gain international attention. "Thank you, sir," Daniel said. "I've selected from only the best lineage."

"I assume that's why you're looking at purchasing semen from Striker's Royal Advantage."

"Yes, sir. I've done my research, and I believe a foal from Striker and Big J's Lucky Coin will be the most sought-after registered quarter horse in the country."

"I'm impressed with Big J's Lucky line, but I don't sell to just any farm that comes along with enough money to pay for stud service."

"I understand, Mr. Kennedy."

"I want to know my horses are being bred and cared for by a fine, upstanding family. Good family is just as important, if not more so, than money. From what I've learned about the Coltons, there are a few skeletons in the closets. You being one of them."

Daniel bit down on his tongue to keep from telling Kennedy that people couldn't always choose their lineage like people could choose a horse's bloodline. "I'm as much a part of the Colton family as any of my siblings, and I'm just as proud of my Cherokee blood." Realizing he was coming across too strong, Daniel drew in a calming breath and continued. "If my heritage will be a sticking point in this deal, perhaps this conversation is over."

"Whoa, young man. I didn't say your bloodline was at fault."

"Then what is it you need from me to convince you the horses produced from your lines will be well cared for?"

"I want you to convince me the Coltons are the right family to invest in. I'm speaking at the annual Symposium on Equine Reproduction a week from now in Reno, Nevada. I want you to attend that symposium. I'll be there with members of my family. If at that time I feel that the Coltons are worth the risk, we can discuss the details of the sale. Are you still interested?"

"Yes, sir," Daniel said, not really understanding how meeting Kennedy at a symposium would change the man's mind if he'd already made his decision. "I'll be there."

"Good." Marshall Kennedy ended the call, leaving Daniel no closer to knowing whether he'd get the semen he wanted to take his breeding program to the next level.

With one of his mares down and no guarantee she'd pull through, and his assistant likely quitting, he wondered if it was too soon to take this step. He'd be gambling a great deal of Colton money on a dream. Not all of the Colton brothers were in agreement on taking this project forward. Big J liked a family consensus before funding was released.

The bright spot in the mess of the past few days was that Kennedy hadn't said no. He hadn't said yes. But there still was hope.

He stepped out of the office and returned to the stall, where Megan sat in the dying light beside Halo, stroking the animal's neck. The horse didn't look any better, and Daniel wasn't sure she'd live to see the sunrise.

Too many strange things had happened on the ranch in the past few months. The main house had been robbed and his father's wife, Abra, had been attacked and left in a coma. Now someone had tried to kill one of his prize mares.

Daniel wasn't ready to give up on Halo, yet. And he still had to come up with a solution to Megan's problem or he'd lose her, too.

Megan smiled over her shoulder at him. "I kept Sleek from eating your sandwich."

The barn cat sat beside Megan, licking its paws. The stray had been an asset to the ranch and kept the mouse population down.

The sun had dipped below the horizon while Daniel talked on the phone with Kennedy. With his world tilted on its axis, Daniel wasn't sure what the next day would bring or how to keep everything he'd worked for from falling apart.

"You can go home. I'll stay with Halo," he said to Megan.

She shook her head. "If it's all the same to you, I'd rather stay. I know it doesn't make sense, but I feel like it's my fault Halo's in the shape she's in."

"Unless you purposely poisoned her, I don't see how it could be your fault."

"I should have realized something was terribly wrong with her and dealt with her immediately." She scratched behind the horse's ear. "Then you wouldn't be as sick as you are now, would you, baby?" Her tone was soothing, and Halo's ears twitched.

"We wouldn't have known anything sooner," Daniel said. "The lab had to make that determination. It wasn't until this morning that she went downhill."

"Still, I was the last one to ride her."

"Stop." Daniel held up a hand. "We'll both stay with her."

She gave him a crooked smile. "Thanks. I'd like that."

He left her in the stall and went about the task of feeding the other animals. When he returned to the stall, he carried several clean horse blankets and a section of hay. He spread out the hay on the ground.

Megan took one of the blankets from him, laid it over the hay and sat on one side of it, patting the spot next to her. "Sit and eat your supper."

Daniel sat and took the sandwich from Megan. When their hands touched, a spark of electricity shot up his arm, reminding him of that kiss and the subsequent dreams that had plagued his sleep the night before. At least if he stayed awake all night with Halo, he wouldn't be dreaming of lying naked with Megan.

"Was that Marshall Kennedy on the phone?" Megan gave him a half smile. "Sorry, I overheard a little."

Daniel chewed on a bite of deli meat, mentally going over his conversation with Kennedy. Megan had been with him when he'd researched the studs and breeders. She knew as well as he did what they needed at the Lucky C to make it a world-class operation, and she deserved to know the outcome of that conversation, even if she did quit in two days' time. "Yes."

"Well?" She leaned forward on her knees, her green eyes bright in the soft glow from the overhead lighting. "Is he going to deal with us or not?"

Daniel shook his head. "Jury's still out."

"Then why bother calling you?" She sat back, her excitement replaced by a frown. "Either he's going to sell to you or he's not."

"It's like I told Brett and Jack. The man has a thing about family. He looks at the lineage of the horses, but he's concerned about the family raising those horses."

"Then it should be a slam dunk. The Coltons are well respected as ranchers not only in Oklahoma but also across the United States."

"Ranching cattle. But we're new at horse breeding and not as well proven. That's not what he's concerned about, though. He wants to know his horses are going to a good family."

"Again, the Coltons are well respected. What could he be concerned about?"

"He's specifically worried about me. He called me a skeleton in the Colton closet. From what I've learned, the Kennedys are socially elite and proud of their status."

"Sounds like my parents. They would hate to have me mess up their standing by marrying beneath me." Megan shivered. "I've met too many of their social picks." She snorted. "No thanks. Do you think that's what's holding the Kennedys back?"

Daniel nodded. "I'm the stick in the man's craw. The bastard son of a Colton, and a Cherokee to boot."

Megan's face reddened and her eyes flashed. "Is he refusing to sell to you because you're half-Cherokee?"

"He didn't say that, but I'm betting he's not comfortable selling to the bastard son. I don't have the social status of a Kennedy."

"Daniel, you're just as much a Colton as any of your siblings."

"Not according to my stepmother."

"Abra is a bitter old woman who doesn't even like her own children. She's more interested in social status than love and family." Megan clapped a hand over her mouth and then sat back. "Sorry. I couldn't stop myself. I've seen how she treats you and your brothers and wanted to tell her what I thought about that. How can a woman dislike her own children?"

"It doesn't matter, and it doesn't bother me anymore." Not since he'd moved out of the main house. He didn't come into contact with Abra Colton as often and it suited him just fine.

"The point is, Kennedy can't hold an accident of birth against you. You're a good man. You're good with horses and have a great eye for quality. If he could only see that, he'd sell to you with no further questions asked."

"Well, that's just it. He'll get the chance. I meet with him face-to-face in exactly one and a half weeks."

"What?" Once again Megan sat forward. "When? Where? I'd love to be a fly on the wall at that meeting."

He wished Megan could be at his side. She'd be a

great asset because of her knowledge of horse breeding from the Triple Diamond and her pedigree from an impressive family tree with a long line of Talbots raising only the best Talbots and horses. Kennedy would fall in love with Megan's charm and capabilities just like he had.

She assured him, "Kennedy will see what a great program we have started here at the Lucky C." Her lips twisted. "I mean, the program you've started."

"I couldn't have even tempted the man without your help putting the data together to send to him. Why don't you come with me?" Then he remembered Megan was leaving the Lucky C to go home to California.

Megan sighed. "Unless I'm willing to let my horses be sold, I can't. I'm headed to California in the next week."

"Damn. I wish you didn't have to go." Daniel leaned forward and checked on Halo, racking his brain for a solution to both their problems. The horse lifted her head and stared at him with her big brown eyes as if to say she wished he could fix her problem, as well.

"You'll do fine," Megan said, leaning back against the wall. "The most important thing right now is to get Halo back on her feet."

"You're right." Daniel settled back against the wall beside Megan.

She closed her eyes, stifling a yawn behind her hand. "I don't know about you, but I didn't sleep worth a darn last night. My dad's threat and my ride on a sick horse weren't conducive to pleasant dreams." She yawned again and laughed. "Sorry. I'm supposed to stay awake all night with Halo. I won't be of much use if I fall asleep."

"Come here." Daniel slipped an arm around her shoulders and pulled her close. "Lean on me. I'll stay awake and let you know if there's any sign of change."

Megan snuggled up against him. "I thought you didn't mix business with pleasure?"

"You said it yourself. You quit." What could it hurt to hold her? It might give him a chance to come up with a plan to rescue her horses from being sold off, or find a way to impress Marshall Kennedy with his family when he wasn't even part of the official Colton line.

Megan closed her eyes again. "Mmm. This is much nicer. I should have quit sooner." Her breathing became deeper and her body relaxed against Daniel's.

If only she knew how hard it was for him to hold her and not kiss the tip of her nose or press his lips to her temple, she might not be so willing to fall asleep against him. All thoughts of being a good boss and not touching his employee flew out the barn door while he held Megan in his arms.

Halo stirred, lifting her head a little, her hooves kicking out just once before she settled back in the straw.

Daniel prayed that she'd make it through the night and he'd come up with a way to keep Megan. She'd been instrumental in his research and planning for his breeding program. She was good at what she did, and her parents would squander her assets, forcing her to go to social events she couldn't stand.

Sometime in the night, Halo shook out of the effects of the poison and got to her feet.

Daniel was so relieved, he almost woke Megan to tell her, but she was sleeping soundly and he hated to wake her. Instead, he lay down on the bed of straw and blankets and pulled her up against him. As he drifted into a deep sleep, he found himself wishing he could go to sleep every night with this amazing woman in his arms.

Megan woke to the soft thuds of hooves pawing at the dirt. She cracked an eyelid to see Halo standing in her stall, impatient for her feed and getting more impatient by the minute.

Joy filled her heart at the sight of the mare standing straight and proud, the effects of the poison worn off. Megan turned to tell Daniel, but he was asleep, his manly face softened in the gray light of dawn that snuck through the open door of the barn.

He must have been awake all night, worrying about Halo and wondering what to do about the meeting with the Kennedys.

Megan was loath to move away from the warmth of his body. It felt so firm and strong beside her.

One big obstacle had been cleared for Daniel. Halo would live. She was one of his best broodmares. Her loss would have been a big hit to his breeding program. Now all he had to do was impress the Kennedys. The irony of the situation wasn't lost on her.

Her family was among the socially elite of California. The Talbots' horse-breeding program at the Triple Diamond Ranch was nationally acknowledged. Daniel needed a boost on the social front in order for the Kennedys to consider him eligible for inclusion in their equine breeding efforts. What he needed was to marry into a family like the Talbots to give him social clout.

And if she and Daniel married, she'd satisfy the conditions of her grandmother's will and inherit a trust fund sufficient to purchase her horses from her father.

Megan could see herself married to a man like Daniel. He respected her mind and her ability to work with the horses, and he wasn't stiflingly overprotective. He'd worked hard to get where he was, earning his keep on the Lucky C, giving back to the family that provided him a home when his mother died. Yes, he was the kind of man she could easily fall in love with and probably already had.

If the ache that had settled in her chest when she thought of leaving the Lucky C and Daniel was any indication, she could see herself falling for this amazing man.

All her problems would be solved if only Daniel was interested in her as more than just his assistant.

"Do I have dirt on my nose?" Daniel stared up at her, a sleepy smile curling his lips.

"No," she answered. "Why?"

"You were staring at me and frowning." He swiped his hand across his face and sat up. "What were you thinking?"

How much she cared about him and wished he returned the feeling. Heat filled her cheeks, and she bit hard on her tongue to keep from blurting out her thoughts. To avoid answering, she turned to Halo. "When did she get up?"

"Around two in the morning. One minute she was lying as still as death, and the next she rolled to her feet as if she was done being sick."

Megan smiled. "I'm glad. I'll leave feeling much better knowing she is okay."

Daniel's brows dipped. "About that…" He stood and reached down for her hand. "I've been thinking."

Megan laid her fingers across his big palm, bracing herself for the rush of heated awareness to shoot from the point of contact throughout her body. And it did, leaving her feeling slightly breathless and off balance. Oh, yes, she was well on her way to loving this man, and he didn't have a clue.

If she were smart, she'd keep it to herself. He obviously wasn't of the same mind or he would have kissed her again. He'd had an opportunity while holding her through the night, and hadn't made a move.

Daniel pulled her to her feet. "You're frowning again, and I haven't even told you my idea."

"Oh, sorry." She slipped her hand free and stepped away from him to keep from making a fool of herself. "I guess I was thinking, too."

"Well, it's like this—and tell me I'm crazy if this sounds too insane to pursue—"

Megan watched as the man blushed and stumbled over his words. It wasn't like Daniel to be embarrassed. Nor was it like him to beat around the bush. Megan leaned back against the wall, enjoying this side of Daniel she hadn't seen. "It can't be all that bad. Your ideas are usually spot-on." She smiled, encouraging him to continue.

"You need the money to buy your horses."

Before he finished his sentence, she shook her head. "I told you, I won't take your money."

"That's good, because I don't have enough to buy the Triple Diamond breeding stock. But I might have a solution for both your problem and mine."

Megan's heart skipped several beats as Daniel's cheeks turned a ruddy red.

"You need a husband. I need an injection of social elitism that will impress Marshall Kennedy."

Her heart stopped. Her breath caught and held, refusing to move past the knot in her throat as she waited for what she'd only dreamed would come next.

Daniel shoved a hand through his dark hair and frowned. "I can't think of any other way to accomplish both, or I'd do it, but I'm fresh out of ideas."

"Daniel!" Megan said, her voice breathy. "Get to the point."

"Why don't we get married?"

Even though she'd known it was coming, it still hit her square in the chest. The air rushed from her lungs, and a tsunami of feelings washed over her. A surge of joy made her heart beat so fast she felt faint. She crested that wave and slid into the undertow of reality. "A marriage of convenience?"

"Exactly." He reached for her hands.

When she hid them behind her back, he dropped his arms. "It wouldn't have to be forever. Just long enough to satisfy the stipulations of your grandmother's will and keep your horses. That would help me get past the Kennedy gauntlet. We could leave today, find a chapel in Vegas and spend the night. It would be over in less than five minutes."

With her heart smarting, Megan forced a shaky smile. "Way to sweep a girl off her feet."

He waved his hand, and Halo tossed her head. "If you want, I can make an official announcement in front of my family."

Megan shook her head. "No."

"No, you won't marry me?"

"No." She pushed past him to pace down the center of the barn. "Your plan is insane."

"Do you have a better one?" he asked. "I'm all ears."

The plan was the same as the one she'd been thinking of before Daniel had woken up. Only when she'd dreamed it up, it didn't sound as cold and impersonal as Daniel's proposal. Somewhere in the back of her mind she'd hoped that a marriage to Daniel would be something more than one of convenience.

After yesterday's kiss, she wasn't sure she could be around Daniel for long periods without wanting another. And another.

"The problem is, my only other choice is to move home and live under my father's thumb."

"And you don't want to do that, do you?" he asked.

Megan faced Daniel, her back straight, her chin tilted up. "I'd rather die than live like my parents want me to. If it were just me, I'd stay and tell my father no thank you." Then her shoulders sagged. "But I can't abandon my horses."

"Is there anyone else who'd come to their rescue?"

"No." Megan glanced around, looking for the answer. Her gaze returned to Daniel. "If you're serious about your offer—" she paused, then went on "—I'm in."

As soon as she said the words, she wanted to take them back. This was not how a proposal was supposed to be. She should have been ecstatic, giddy with excitement for the man professing his love to her. Instead they'd hop a plane to Vegas and wham, bam, thank you, ma'am, they'd be married by some pathetic imitation of Elvis in a drive-through chapel on the Strip.

Daniel's lips quirked. "Why do I get the feeling you're not happy about this?"

"I don't know." She flung her hands in the air and fought back tears. "I guess I expected…well…not this."

"It's not as if it will be a real marriage. Once we're

both in the clear, we can get a quickie divorce, and you will be free to marry whomever you prefer."

Megan stared at the man. He really didn't have a clue that she was falling in love with him. "Yeah. But the man of my dreams would have to do a better job of proposing."

"You deserve the best, Megan. If he doesn't care enough to do it right, don't marry him."

She raised her brows. "And your proposal was the standard to measure by?"

"Oh, hell no." Daniel grasped her hands and pulled her closer. "If this were a real proposal, I'd have taken you out to dinner at a nice restaurant or, better yet, on a picnic to your favorite spot on the ranch, because I'd know you didn't give a damn about all that fancy stuff. You love being out in the fresh air, close to the animals you love."

Megan could picture this scenario. He'd take her out to the hill with the ancient oak tree near sunset and wait to ask until the bright orange globe settled at the edge of the horizon, brushing a glorious palette of colors across the clouds. She sniffed. "A picnic would have been nice."

"And I'd have brought along a bottle of wine."

She cocked her brows. "To get me liquored up?"

"Can't have my girl turning me down, now can I?" He grinned and pulled her closer. "Then at sunset, I'd have gone down on one knee."

Megan's breath caught in her throat just as it would have had he been performing according to his script. Her chest tight, she forced a chuckle, hoping to ease the tension rising inside.

Daniel's brows dipped. "What are you laughing about?"

"On a cattle ranch, you would have put your knee in a cow patty."

"Anything for the woman I was about to ask to marry me." Daniel held her hands, his gaze intense, the smile sliding away. "I'd have asked you properly, saying something flowery and sincere, like this. 'Megan, you outshine the stars in the sky and make my heart beat faster whenever you're around.'"

Megan laughed, the sound catching in her throat. "That would be a good start."

"'Would you marry me and make me the happiest man alive?'" He nodded to her. "And you would fall into my arms, crying happy tears, shouting yes at the top of your lungs."

A real tear slipped from the corner of her eye and trailed down her cheek.

Daniel caught it on the tip of his finger. "You've got the idea."

"A proposal like that would make it hard for a girl to refuse."

"That's where the liquor comes in to seal the deal." He curled his fingers around hers. "So, Megan Talbot, will you marry me for however long it takes to sort out our troubles?"

Her heart breaking just a little, Megan wanted to say no. Daniel still had a long way to go before he fell in love with her, if he ever did. Then again, if she wanted to save her horses, this option seemed to be her only recourse on her father's short deadline. If she married, she'd have the money she needed, and her father couldn't expect her to come home to California to live.

He let go of her hands and stepped back. "Want time to think about it? I know it sounds crazy. You might feel better if we put the agreement in writing. I don't want your inheritance, if that's what you're afraid of."

"No, I trust you, and no, I don't want time to think about it. My answer is yes." If she thought about it too long, she'd talk herself out of it, and she couldn't afford to pass up the offer. "For the horses."

"Right. For the horses."

Chapter 5

Daniel circled the single-engine Mooney as he went through his preflight checklist of the airplane. Flaps. Check. Horizontal stabilizer. Check. Ring?

Panic struck. He stopped in the middle of his inspection and dug into his pocket for his grandmother's wedding ring. He wished he'd had time to take it to a jeweler to have it sized properly and fitted into a pretty box for safekeeping. But after they'd made their decision, they'd agreed they had little time to dawdle.

In the past hour, he'd taken care of the animals and informed Jack he'd be leaving. Then he'd arranged for someone to take care of the breeder barn in his absence and check on Halo through her recovery.

He'd barely had time to pack a bag and file a flight plan with the Tulsa airport. In less than thirty minutes, he and Megan would be on their way to Vegas to get married.

Holy smokes! He was getting married.

Granted, it was a marriage of convenience, but it was no less nerve-racking. Megan came from a family far above Daniel's social class. Hell, for the first ten years of his life, he'd lived on the reservation in a trailer. Megan grew up in the lap of luxury, surrounded by people who took care of her every need. How could he compete with that?

He'd never truly been one of the elite Coltons, either. He'd never felt like he quite fit in.

Now he was marrying into a family known nationwide for their wealth and prestige. Megan's parents were often in the news attending various events.

Then he reminded himself that she'd given up that lifestyle to come to work for him. She was willing to muck stalls and get her hands into the dirty and not so pleasant tasks of raising horses. Her fancy upbringing hadn't slowed her down one bit. She was tough and fearless when it came to working with the large animals.

Megan had driven back to her apartment in Tulsa to throw some clothes into a suitcase and get back to the ranch. She'd be here any minute, ready to climb aboard the small plane the Coltons owned.

Damn. Where was that ring? When he couldn't find the pretty emerald-and-diamond ring, he nearly had a heart attack.

"Daniel!" Ryan Colton, Daniel's half brother, emerged from the darkness of the hangar into the bright Oklahoma sunlight. "Heard you were heading to Vegas."

"I am," he said, digging deeper into both front pockets.

Ryan's eyes narrowed. "Forget your key to the plane?" His lips twitched.

Daniel's fingers connected with metal, and the tension in his shoulders released. The ring was safe in his pocket. "No, thank goodness, I have it."

"Dude, the plane doesn't take a key."

His mind on the trip ahead, Daniel ignored Ryan's comment. "What brings you out to the hangar?"

"Jack informed me Halo was poisoned. What's going on?"

The tension returning for an entirely different reason, Daniel's chest tightened. "The lab reported they found poison in Halo's blood. We have no idea how it happened."

"Maybe she got hold of something in the barn or in the field."

"Megan and I went over the entire barn, thoroughly cleaned Halo's stall and couldn't find anything that would have poisoned her. We don't use rat poison in the barn."

Ryan smiled. "That's why we have Sleek."

"Right, and we have too much invested in the horses we keep in the breeder barn to risk storing anything poisonous there."

"Do you think someone might have given it to her?"

Daniel had considered that option. "Who would want to hurt Halo? She's one of the best mares in my breeding program, and she's got the best temperament."

"I don't know." Ryan scratched his chin. "Do you know of any competing breeders who'd go to the trouble of sabotaging your horses?"

Daniel shook his head. "It's not like she's a race horse with the potential to win a derby." He shrugged. "It makes no sense."

"I'll nose around and see if I can learn anything that'll shed some light."

"Thanks."

"Hey, on another topic, is Greta back from Oklahoma City?" Ryan asked.

His half sister, Greta, had been in Oklahoma City busily planning her wedding to Mark Stanton, the son of one of the wealthiest families in the state. He missed her expertise with the horses. She was one of the best trainers he'd known.

"Not that I know of." Daniel checked beneath the plane for any leaks. "Why do you ask?"

"I could swear I saw her at the hardware store yesterday." Ryan shrugged. "Must have been seeing things."

"I'll be glad when she's done with this wedding planning business." Daniel straightened.

"You and me both. It's not like her to get all girlie."

Megan emerged from the shadows of the hangar and out into the open, rolling a suitcase behind her. She wore jeans, boots and a green blouse that exactly matched her eyes. Her hair was damp but pulled back in her normal French braid. Other than the nice shirt, she looked like she was ready to go to work, not to her wedding in Vegas.

Daniel's heart skipped several beats. Megan could wear a feed sack and make it look great. With those long legs, the subtle sway of her hips and the way she smiled…his groin tightened, and he wanted to hold her close all over again. Keeping her at arm's length would be a challenge.

"Hey, Dan." Ryan waved a hand in front of Daniel's face.

Daniel barely saw the hand, his gaze on the woman walking toward them.

Ryan turned. "Ah, Megan. Are you going, too?"

Megan rolled her case to a stop, nodding. "Yes, I am." Her gaze shot from Daniel to Ryan and back.

Daniel took Megan's bag and loaded it into the plane. "I have a couple more checks. Then we'll be ready to go."

"So, what's in Vegas besides the usual—gambling, wedding chapels and shows? I haven't heard of any of those involving horses." Ryan stared at Daniel, then Megan.

A flush of pink rose in Megan's cheeks. She glanced at Daniel and gave him a slight shake of her head.

Taking Megan's cue, Daniel replied, "We're going to see a man about a horse. If the Kennedy Farms deal doesn't work out, we want to have a backup plan." Daniel didn't like lying to his brother, but Megan wasn't ready to announce their plans, and that was okay with him. He wasn't certain how he felt about what they were about to do.

"Well, then, I won't keep you." Ryan held out his hand. "Be careful. I understand there are some storms heading this way."

"I've already checked the weather. We're flying north of the system." Daniel took his brother's hand.

"Good. We kind of like having you two around." Ryan shook Daniel's hand and then pulled him into a hug. "See you in a day or two?"

"It might be closer to a week."

"A week?" Ryan stepped back, his eyes wide. "What kind of horses take a week to look at?"

Daniel's lips firmed. "After we stop in Vegas, we're going to California to check out more horses. I have a meeting scheduled with Marshall Kennedy in Reno in a week. We'll be back at the Lucky C long enough to regroup and head out again."

"Sounds like a nice vacation. Wish I could go along with you." Ryan nodded. "Again, you two take care and come back in one piece."

"We will."

Ryan stood back as Daniel helped Megan into the plane and climbed in after her. She settled in the copilot's seat and Daniel sat beside her, going over the remainder of his preflight check. When they were finally ready, he showed her how to wear the copilot's headset and slipped his headset over his ears.

"Ready?" he said into microphone.

"Ready." Her voice came to him over the sound system.

As they taxied down the grass runway and lifted off into a westerly breeze, Daniel gripped the yoke, his pulse racing as he thought about what lay ahead. In a few short hours, they'd be in Vegas getting married.

Megan's fingers curled around the armrests as the plane left the grass strip and climbed into the sky. When they were far enough away from the ground that she didn't have to worry about crashing, she settled back and relaxed.

"I knew the Coltons had a plane, but I didn't realize you all knew how to fly it."

"Not all of my brothers have learned."

"Just how long have you been flying?"

"Since I was about fifteen and Big J bought the plane. He paid for my flight lessons while he learned to fly, as well. It's always a good thing to have a copilot in case something happens to the pilot."

Megan's stomach fluttered as she stared at the yoke in front of her. "Just so you know, I don't have a clue how to fly this thing, but I'm willing to learn."

He smiled over at her. "It's not a requirement, but I'm glad to hear you're willing. Not many people are interested."

She liked it when he smiled at her. He had the faith in her to think she could learn to fly an airplane. She'd always been interested in flying, but her parents wouldn't have allowed her to take flying lessons any more than they wanted her working with large animals. To say they were overprotective would be a gross understatement. Hell, she'd learn to fly if it was something Daniel wanted.

"My parents are likely to flip when I come home with a husband. Just so you know. We're likely to incur resistance."

"I can handle it," Daniel assured her.

"I placed a call to the attorney who handled my grandmother's will and arranged an appointment with him in two days. I also arranged to meet with a horse broker."

"Good thinking. By this time a week from now, we should be sitting pretty. You with your horses, me with my breeder stock semen."

Megan nodded. "Sounds easy enough. However, I've never known anything to be that simple."

Daniel shot a glance her way. "True." He held out a hand. "We'll get through this together. We make a good team."

She took his hand, that same sharp crackle of electricity shooting through her. She had no doubt they'd make it, and she refused to think about what would happen afterward, when their marriage of convenience was no longer needed.

"Hey." Daniel squeezed her fingers. "It's going to work out."

She nodded, comforted by the gentle pressure on her hand.

"You didn't get much sleep last night. Why don't you relax and take a nap? I might need you later to spot me through the mountains."

Her heart leaped into her lungs. "Mountains?"

"Unless you want to take the long way around, we'll be flying just south of the Sangre de Cristo Mountains in New Mexico."

She bit on her bottom lip.

Daniel let go of her hand and brushed his thumb across her lip. "Don't worry. I've flown this route several times."

"I have, too. In a 747, not a crop duster." She stared out the window at the ground several thousand feet below them. "Something tells me it will be a lot different than flying over at thirty thousand feet."

"It is, but I think you'll like it."

Megan settled into her seat, letting the hum of the engine lull her into a trance while they were still over the flat terrain of Oklahoma and the Texas Panhandle. At least the danger of the flight took her mind off her coming nuptials.

She must have fallen asleep somewhere between thinking about crashing into the mountains and a cheesy wedding in Vegas, because the next thing she knew, they'd hit a speed bump on the Vegas Strip.

Megan's eyes popped open, and she stared around the interior of the airplane. It hadn't been a speed bump they'd hit. The little plane hit another pocket of air and jerked.

She sat up straight and stared out at a darkening sky. Thunderclouds rose high to her left, lightning flashing. "Is everything okay?"

"Should be," Daniel said through gritted teeth. His fingers gripped the yoke, his knuckles white. "Remember that storm my brother was talking about coming out of the southwest?"

"I thought we were going around it?"

"That's the idea. Only it's getting bigger as we speak. We won't be going through it, but we're getting some of the bumpy air around it."

Mountains rose ahead of them, their snow-covered peaks appearing beautifully dangerous. Megan's heart lodged in her throat. "I thought we wouldn't be going through the mountains on this trip."

"In order to go around the storm, I'm having to fly farther north. We're nearing the Sangre de Cristo mountain range."

Megan's pulse raced, her breathing becoming shallower. "Just how much experience do you have flying through mountains?"

He laughed, though it sounded strained through the headset. "Too late to ask now, isn't it? But for what it's worth, I have over two thousand hours flying this plane."

"That sounds like a lot. How many of those hours were in this kind of weather?"

"There are never enough hours flying in this kind of weather. The idea is to avoid these conditions."

"Should we put down?"

"Can't. Not here. The best we can hope for is to swing wide."

They hit more turbulence, and the plane dropped like someone had pulled the rug out from under them.

Megan swallowed a scream and held on.

Daniel moved his feet and scanned the instrument panel, his hands steady on the yoke. "Just a little farther and we should clear the side of this storm."

She caught and held her breath as they neared the snowy crags a lot lower than she liked.

Lightning flashed nearby. A rumble of thunder sounded over the roar of the engine and through the muffling of her headset.

Megan had never been so frightened in her life. But seeing Daniel in the pilot's seat, his jaw set, all his concentration on flying the airplane, made her feel a little safer.

Until the next big dip brought her even closer to the jagged peaks. Her stomach clenched, and she bit down hard on her tongue to keep from screaming again. Daniel didn't need a crying woman in the cockpit with him. She had to be strong, even though she shook from head to toe.

The clouds billowed higher, blocking the sun, making the sky ominous.

Megan found herself leaning away from the turbulence, willing the little plane to fly safely around the storm and up over the mountains.

They seemed to be heading straight into the mountains instead of flying over the top, and the storm appeared to be engulfing them in its fury.

Tearing her gaze away from the mountains, she risked a glance in Daniel's direction. His face was tense, a muscle flicked in his jaw and his knuckles were white on the yoke.

"It's going to be okay," she said softly, as if speaking the words out loud would make it so. She sent a silent prayer to the heavens to deliver them safely through the storm and over the mountains they were racing toward.

"Hold on," Daniel said in her ears.

Her fingers dug into the leather of the armrest. She closed her eyes, trusting Daniel to deliver her safely over to the other side of the storm and the mountain.

Another drastic drop forced her eyes open in time to see the ragged peaks directly in front of them.

Daniel struggled with the small plane, pulling back on the yoke at the last minute, narrowly missing the edges of a giant outcropping.

Once over the top of the mountain, the clouds parted, and they blew through as if spit out by the storm. Slowly the turbulence subsided, and they flew out of the black clouds, into an entirely different world of sunshine and blue skies.

"Wow." Megan pressed her hand to her heart and drew in a long, steadying breath, then let it out. "You were amazing."

Daniel scrubbed a hand down his face. Beneath his Cherokee complexion, his face had paled.

Megan reached out and placed her hand over his on the controls.

Eventually he unwound his grip, transferring it to her hand. "I'm sorry. I shouldn't have tried to outrun the storm. We could have been killed."

"But we weren't, thanks to your superb flying skills."

"I feel like we should find a place to land and rent a car for the rest of the journey."

"No way. I've never flown into the sunset in a single-engine airplane. And it appears as if we're going to have an outstanding display."

"As long as you're okay."

"I'll admit, I was shaking in my boots about the time we hit that last really bad dip."

"You and me both." He squeezed her hand. "But from here to Vegas it should be smooth."

"As long as you're flying, I'm okay." She smiled across at him and settled back, refusing to release his hand unless they hit another intense storm.

Megan figured if they could survive something as insanely intense and dangerous as braving that storm and nearly crashing into the mountain, things could only get easier. They'd land, check into a hotel, find a twenty-four-hour wedding chapel and tie the temporary knot.

What could be hard about that compared with the flight over?

Chapter 6

"We're sorry, but the hotel is booked for the weekend," said the clerk behind the counter of the newest of the big casino hotels.

"Every room?" Megan asked.

"There's a huge techie convention going on. I've had to call several hotels to find rooms for walk-in guests. There just aren't any available. I'm sorry, ma'am, but I can't help you."

Megan couldn't believe their luck. The one weekend they decided to fly to Vegas to get married and every hotel they'd been to thus far had been completely sold out.

"Come on. We'll walk next door." She hooked Daniel's arm and dragged him to the exit. "I have a feeling there will be a vacancy there."

"We've been walking the Strip for over an hour

with no luck." Daniel covered her hand on his arm and glanced down at her with a crooked smile. "We might have to sleep in the plane at this rate."

"It'll be okay. There has to be a room in one of these hotels. I'm determined to have a shower. I still smell like the barn, and that's no way to go to a wedding." She winked up at him.

"Which reminds me." Daniel's lips firmed. "We still have to find a chapel."

"Excuse me, sir," someone said behind them.

The clerk they'd been speaking with ran to catch them at the door. "I just got off the phone with a cancellation. Our special honeymoon suite is available."

Megan was already shaking her head. "A suite? Isn't that expensive?"

Daniel stepped toward the clerk. "We'll take it."

"But, Daniel, we don't know how much they're asking."

"I don't care. It might be the only room available in all of Las Vegas, and we have a wedding to go to. It only seems fitting."

Daniel followed the clerk back to the desk and slapped his credit card on the counter. A bellboy appeared and collected their bags.

Soon they were shown to a large penthouse suite with floor-to-ceiling windows overlooking the brightly lit Las Vegas Strip.

Megan walked to the window and stared out at the glitzy lights of the city, worried that Daniel was spending too much of his own money to make this farce of a wedding happen. "I would have been fine sleeping in the plane."

Daniel stepped up behind her and rested his hands

on her shoulders. "This is better. And we need to take a few pictures of us in this suite when we return after the wedding to show your parents."

Megan leaned back against him, the solid strength of Daniel easing her misgivings and stirring in her a deep longing to be held in his arms for longer than a temporary arrangement. "You're right. I just hate spending your money for my troubles."

"You're helping me, too, so we're even."

Megan turned back to the spacious living room with a table and chairs for intimate dining and a sofa for two in the middle of the sitting area. A door opened into a bedroom with a king-size bed made up in crisp white sheets and a classic white comforter. One bed. Two people.

"We can worry about sleeping arrangements when we get back from the chapel," Daniel said. "I'd like to take a quick shower. How long do you need to get ready?"

"About twenty minutes. I want to shower, too, but you can go first."

Alone with Daniel in the hotel suite, Megan tried to keep it all businesslike, but one look at the bed and her pulse kicked up. A second look and her core heated. If this were a real wedding between two people in love, the room would be perfect for consummating the marriage.

For the hundredth time since Daniel had made the suggestion of getting hitched, she reminded herself it was temporary. Daniel had shown little interest in a relationship between the two of them over the past few months she'd been working for him. And he'd been pretty adamant about their marriage being a business arrangement, nothing else.

Daniel set Megan's bag on the luggage stand. "You

know, maybe we should revisit the idea of a prenuptial agreement."

His statement hit her square in the chest. "What?" She faced him, frowning.

He paced away from her and back, raking a hand through his thick, dark hair. "You're a potentially wealthy woman. You need to protect your assets."

"Isn't it a bit late to get an attorney to draw up a prenuptial agreement? We're getting married as soon as we can get showered and dressed."

"At the very least, we could write it out on a piece of paper and each sign it in front of a witness."

"My grandmother's trust fund isn't a huge amount."

"Megan, you don't have any siblings you haven't told me about, do you?"

She shook her head.

"You're an only child. You stand to inherit everything your parents own."

"I don't want what they have," she insisted. "I would rather they spent it all before they die." She'd left California to get away from that life and had no need of their money or land holdings. "I couldn't give a damn about my inheritance as long as we save those horses. If my parents should pass away before we end our relationship, I'd give all their money and property to charity. You could have it."

Daniel's lips thinned. "I don't want your parents' money. I prefer to make my own way in life."

Her back stiff, her chin held high, Megan said, "Same here."

"But you'll have a fiduciary responsibility to their wealth should they leave it all to you. I'm sure they have people who depend on them for their livelihoods. You want to protect them."

Megan's mind flew to their housekeeper, Mrs. Gibson, who'd been with the Talbot family since Megan could remember. She'd practically raised Megan when her parents were off to all corners of the world. Then there were the groundskeeper and the ranch foreman, both of whom had worked for the Talbots for decades.

"Okay, so I can't just walk away from it. But we don't have time for a formal agreement and all the attorneys who should be involved."

Daniel rested his hands on her arms. "Let me get my shower, and while you're getting yours, I'll write up something. We can both sign it and have a bellboy witness it."

"I think it's a lot of trouble. I know you are a good man and you wouldn't do anything to jeopardize my horses. Otherwise, I wouldn't consider marrying you, even if it is temporary." She cupped his cheek, rose up on her toes and dared to kiss him. "But thank you for thinking of it."

Daniel stepped around her, unzipped his suitcase and dragged out a garment bag and his toiletries. "I'll only be a few minutes." He entered the bathroom and shut the door behind him.

Megan opened her suitcase, removed the dress she'd packed and stared at it with a critical eye. She hadn't kept many items from the vast wardrobe her mother had insisted on buying for her on Rodeo Drive in California. But she'd brought a couple of her favorite dresses to Tulsa when she'd packed up and left home.

When she'd stood in the little bedroom in her apartment going through her closet, she'd almost wished she'd brought more. Then she'd found the simple white cock-tail dress she'd purchased with her own money on sale in a shop in downtown Tulsa. It had been marked down significantly and looked good on her. The best part about the dress was that she'd bought it with her own money. She hadn't paid a ridiculous amount, and it fit and looked as good as anything she'd left behind.

She shook out the wrinkles and hung the dress in the closet, trying to ignore the sound of water running in the bathroom. A door separated her from a very naked, very wet Daniel. She didn't have to use much of her imagination to envision him nude.

On many occasions through the heat of summer at the Lucky C, he'd gone shirtless while he worked on the ranch. His chiseled chest and taut abs glistened with sweat in the sunshine.

For a moment, she leaned her cheek against the bathroom door and closed her eyes. Water would be streaming over his broad shoulders, down his thickly muscled chest and lower. What would it feel like to touch his naked skin, to run her hands over the hard planes of his body?

Her blood burning through her veins, she reached for the doorknob before she realized what she was doing. The cold, hard metal woke her. Her breath hitched and she jerked upright, her eyes wide. Why torture herself? The man wasn't interested.

Megan left the bedroom and wandered around the suite, counting the minutes until the faucet shut off and Daniel emerged from the shower.

She was standing at the floor-to-ceiling window in the sitting room when a sound behind her alerted her to his presence.

"The shower's all yours."

When Megan turned to face him, her stomach fluttered and blood rushed south to her core.

Daniel wore dark trousers and a white shirt open at the neck. He worked the buttons on his sleeves. "Damned buttons weren't made for big hands."

Her throat dry, Megan stepped forward. "Let me." She nudged his hands away, her skin tingling where it brushed against his. She made quick work of the buttons, finding it hard to breathe. With him standing so close, she was surrounded by the potent scent of his aftershave.

"You smell good," she said and quickly stepped away.

He dug in his pocket and pulled out a bow tie. "You don't happen to know how to tie one of these, do you?"

She smiled, her heart thudding hard in her chest. She should have told him no and walked away. Instead, she took the tie from his hand and wrapped it around his neck. She was so close to him, their breaths mingled. "I used to tie my father's neckties." Her fingers fumbled with the cloth, but managed to knot the tie perfectly.

Almost faint from not daring to breathe while she stood so close, Megan started to back away. Now she really wanted to kiss Daniel.

His hands captured the back of her head. "This is going to be harder than I thought." Then he bent, his lips crashing down on hers in a bone-melting kiss.

With his tongue he traced the seam of her lips, and she opened to let him in. He swept past her defenses and conquered her, caressing the length of her tongue in smooth, dangerously sensual strokes. One of his hands slid down her back and cupped her bottom, pressing her closer.

Megan leaned into Daniel, the hard ridge beneath the

fly of his trousers pressing into her belly. The urge shot through her to rip the bow tie from around his neck and loosen all the buttons of his shirt. Her entire body burned with the need to feel his body against hers.

At last he pushed her to arm's length and stared down at her with enigmatic brown-black eyes. "You should get your shower."

Her knees shook as she stepped away from him. Her arms slipped down his chest to fall to her sides. Then she turned and stumbled through the bedroom. She didn't stop until she was in the bathroom with the door closed between her and Daniel.

Her heart racing, Megan leaned her back against the door and pressed her fist against her pulsing lips. How could this arrangement remain all business when there was nothing businesslike about the way they'd just kissed?

If Megan hadn't run when he'd told her to get her shower, Daniel might not have been able to let her go. That kiss had shaken him more than he cared to admit. Dragging in several deep breaths, he forced himself to focus on what needed to be done.

While the shower ran, Daniel found a sheet of hotel stationery and wrote out a statement that, once married to Megan Talbot, he would not retain any rights to her inheritance. He'd have someone witness him signing the paper later. He folded the paper, slipped it into his pocket, grabbed the room key card and left.

He took the elevator down to the lobby and went in search of the concierge. The man at the counter helped him call around to the marriage registration office and nearby wedding chapels to find one that could fit them in for a quickie wedding.

The first one didn't answer. The second chapel was booked until the following day at two in the afternoon.

The third was booked through the next week, and the fourth had one opening if they could make it there in five minutes. Otherwise they would have to wait until the following morning at nine. Daniel thanked the woman and called the next number the concierge offered.

The receptionist on the other end of the call answered, "This is the Graceland Wedding Chapel. You bring the bride and groom, we provide everything else."

"Do you have any openings for wedding ceremonies tonight?" Daniel asked.

"Yes, sir. We're open 24-7."

"I'd like to make a reservation for an hour from now."

"I'm afraid we can't do that," the receptionist said.

Daniel's hopes slid into his boots. What the hell? This was the town of gambling, partying and the wedding destination of people wanting to tie a quick knot. So far, things hadn't gone as smoothly as he would have liked. The near-death experience in the Sangre de Cristo Mountains, then the almost failed attempt to secure a hotel room and four calls with no wedding chapel were wearing on him. If he were as superstitious as his ancestors, he would have read it as a sign the wedding wasn't meant to be.

"We've only had one cancellation, sir. The time will be thirty minutes from now, and there might be a wait."

His heart lightening, Daniel gripped the phone, his optimism returning. "Will it be a long wait?"

"Depends on when our Elvis shows up."

Daniel ground his teeth at the vagueness of her answer. "How many couples are waiting on him?"

"There are two couples waiting right now."

Wanting to reach through the phone, throttle and then hug the young woman, Daniel asked for the address, committed it to memory and ended the call.

He made arrangements to have champagne and roses delivered to the room while they were out. By that time, he'd been gone long enough that Megan should have been showered and ready to go.

Daniel entered the elevator. Before the doors could close, two women entered wearing skimpy black dresses and impossible leopard-print stilettos. They giggled and leaned on each other, and they reeked of perfume and alcohol.

"Oh, baby, aren't you the handsome devil?" the brunette cooed, letting go of her friend to drape herself on Daniel's arm. "Please tell me you're in Vegas to have fun."

He smiled and peeled the woman off his arm. "I'm in Vegas to get married."

"Oh, well, now. Isn't that sweet?" the brunette said. No sooner had he untangled himself from her than she wrapped her hands around his arm again. "So you aren't married yet?"

"Headed in that direction now." Daniel prayed they'd hurry and stop on the woman's floor.

"The important item to note is that you aren't married, yet." She leaned across and pecked his cheek. "You still have time to back out."

"I'm not backing out," he assured her.

The blonde with too much hairspray poofing her hair out at strange distances, took her friend's arm. "Denise, sweetie, you need to leave this poor man alone. He's not going out with you when he's got his own honey waiting for him at the altar."

"You look good enough to eat. Don't get married. It only destroys your waistline and makes you bitter." Denise poked a thumb toward her chest. "Ask me. I know all about crappy marriages. Celebrating my freedom tonight. Ditch the bride and come with us for the night. No regrets. No divorce attorneys."

Her friend nodded. "Trust her on that one. It can get ugly."

The elevator bell dinged and the door slid open. "I believe this is your floor." Daniel held the door open.

"If you change your mind, join us." Denise gave him her room number and stumbled out of the car.

Daniel was glad when the door closed and continued up to the penthouse. He had no reservations about Megan. In the few short months he'd known her, he'd learned she was trustworthy and had a big heart. Possibly too big a heart, as evidenced with her agreement to marry him only to save a few horses from being sold.

He'd marry her even if he didn't need the social clout, just to foil her family's attempt at extortion. What kind of father would threaten to sell the horses his daughter loved just to get her to come home and live by his rules?

The elevator arrived at his floor and he got out, more convinced they were doing the right thing. He swiped his key in the lock and entered.

The sitting room was empty, and he didn't hear the sound of a shower or blow-dryer. Silence greeted him and made his heart skip several beats before racing to catch up.

"Megan?"

No answer.

Daniel stepped toward the bedroom and came to an abrupt halt.

Megan appeared in the doorway, wearing a white dress that plunged low between her breasts, hugged her waist and hips and then floated out around her thighs to the tops of her pretty knees. She'd pulled her hair up and away from her face, the long strawberry blond tresses cascading down her back in soft, loose curls he wanted to bury his hands in. Her eyes widened, her cheeks flushed and her full, lush lips curved upward in a smile.

"Wow. You look amazing." Daniel swallowed hard and clenched his fists to keep from reaching out and taking her into his arms. Remaining platonic would be the biggest challenge he'd ever faced when she looked so damned gorgeous and kissable.

Her brows furrowed and her smile slipped as she glanced down at her dress. "Too much?"

He shook his head. "No, you're perfect." God, he wanted to pull her close and hold her until his pulse slowed and he could get a grip on the rising passion threatening to overwhelm him. But he knew that if he succumbed to his desire, his pulse wouldn't slow until he'd stripped her naked and made love to her all night long. Only when he fell into an exhausted sleep would his heartbeat return to anywhere near normal.

Megan touched his arm. "If you've had second thoughts, we don't have to go through with this. My problems aren't yours. I can figure out something that doesn't involve you giving up your freedom to save a few horses."

Daniel nearly groaned. Standing before her, he inhaled the fresh scent of Megan. She had to be nearly naked beneath that dress. All he had to do was pull her into his arms, wrap those legs around his waist and...

He dragged in a deep, fortifying breath and let it out. "Unless you've changed your mind, we're going through with the plan."

"You just seem so tense."

A short, hard laugh erupted from his throat. "I promised to keep this arrangement purely business." He leaned back and raked her with his gaze. "But I'm finding it difficult. Now, if you're ready, I have the address of the wedding registration office and a chapel. But we have to rush."

He offered her his arm, bracing himself for that electric jolt he received each time she touched him.

Her hand curled around his elbow, sending that spark of sensations shooting through him, straight to his groin. Yup, keeping this marriage platonic would either prove he was a saint or kill him. Daniel suspected it would kill him. "Let's go get married."

Chapter 7

Megan sat in the backseat of the taxi beside Daniel, her heart pounding, her mouth dry and more nervous than she'd been when she'd left home to strike out on her own. Though this was a marriage of convenience, she couldn't help but feel as though it was a particularly momentous occasion.

After taking them to get their marriage license, the taxi stopped in front of a little white wedding chapel, the blue sign lit up with white neon lights. A smaller sign below had an image of a dancing Elvis Presley painted on it.

Daniel leaned forward. "Are you sure this is the address?"

"Yes, sir. This is the place."

Megan fought back a giggle at the scowl that settled on Daniel's face as he paid the taxi driver and he helped her out onto the sidewalk.

"I don't know," he said, staring at the dancing Elvis. "This isn't quite what I had in mind."

Megan squeezed his hand. "It's exactly what I had in mind."

"Are you sure?" He didn't look convinced.

"Absolutely. It's Vegas, baby." She winked. "Lighten up. If the certificate is valid, that's all that matters."

Still frowning, Daniel led her into the lobby of the little chapel. Against either wall was a couple seated on a bench. One pair wore black jeans and leather jackets. The young man's hair was shaved in a Mohawk, and he sported a one-inch gauge in each ear. The woman had piercings in her lip, nose and eyebrow, and her ears were rimmed in studs. Her hair was shaved on one side and long and black on the other.

Megan gulped and shifted her attention to the other couple. They appeared to be in their late forties or early fifties. She wore a short sequined dress and spike heels. The man with her wore a suit and tie.

"We can look elsewhere," Daniel whispered close to her ear, causing tingles to spread throughout her body.

"No," she said, her voice breathy. "This will be fine."

They were met at the front desk by a woman wearing a '60s miniskirt and go-go boots. Her lips were painted a pale pink and she chewed gum, smacking it loud enough to echo in the room. "Welcome to the Graceland Wedding Chapel. How can I help you?"

Daniel stepped forward. "We want to get married."

The woman pointed to what appeared to be a menu. "Which package would you like? The Las Vegas Elvis Wedding Package or one of our traditional wedding packages?"

Though afraid to ask, Daniel did. "What's in the packages?"

"All of the packages include use of the chapel, photography, music and wedding services. The officiant fee and marriage certificate are separate. If you select the Las Vegas Elvis Wedding, the bride may choose to have Elvis walk her down the aisle."

Daniel stared at the different options and turned to Megan. "Really, we can go somewhere else."

Her heart warmed at his concern, and she squeezed his arm. "I love this chapel. It's quaint and we don't need much. We could do the basic traditional package."

At that moment, the Elvis impersonator entered the building, wearing a dark, bedazzled shirt, open down the front. He displayed a significant amount of chest hair. He wore sunglasses and tight black pants. His dark hair was slicked back with the signature lock falling across his forehead.

"Anyone here for a wedding?" he called out and pulled Megan into a bear hug. "How about you two?" He pointed to Daniel. "Is this your hunka-hunka burnin' love?"

Megan's cheeks flamed, and she was happy to see Daniel's turn ruddy. "Yes, he's my fiancé. But these people were here first." She glanced at the older couple and the pierced pair.

"Let's get these weddings rollin'."

An hour later, Elvis had performed the ceremonies for the older couple and the pierced one.

"If you'll give me a few minutes, I'll get out of the Elvis gear and we can perform your ceremony."

Megan glanced at Daniel. "If it's all the same to you,

I'd rather just get started. No need for the minister to change. Are you okay with that, Daniel?"

Daniel's brows twisted and he stared hard at her, then sighed. "If you're okay, I'm okay."

The receptionist handed a modest bouquet of red and white roses to Daniel and a boutonniere to Megan.

Megan attached the flower to Daniel's lapel and patted his chest. "It's going to be okay."

His brow cocked as he handed her the bouquet. "If you say so."

"I do."

"Sweetheart, save the *I do*'s for the ceremony." Elvis nodded toward the front of the chapel. "Now if the groom will take his place at the altar, I'll escort the bride down the aisle."

Megan's hand shook as she laid it on Elvis's arm and waited for Daniel to take his position at the front of the chapel. When he turned to face her, the music started and Megan's heart squeezed hard in her chest.

The receptionist handed Elvis a microphone and he sang "Can't Help Falling in Love."

Slowly, Megan and Elvis walked down the aisle in time to the music, the words bringing a lump into Megan's throat and making her eyes sting. The closer she came to Daniel, the more she realized just how the words to the song fit the way she felt.

This half-Cherokee man who loved horses as much as she did and who didn't quite fit in, just like her, was the only man she could imagine spending the rest of her life with. If this wasn't love, she was even more on her way to falling in love with him.

As Elvis ended the song, he handed her off to Daniel and took his position in front of them.

"Megan, do you promise to love Daniel tender and love him true for all of your days?"

Megan gulped hard to clear the knot from her vocal chords and answered, "I do."

"And, Daniel, do you promise to love Megan tender and love her true for all of your days?"

He held Megan's hands in his and answered in his deep, resonant tone, "I do."

"Do you have a ring?" Elvis asked.

Megan gasped. "I didn't even think about rings."

Daniel smiled and dug in his pocket, pulling out a beautiful ring with an emerald center stone surrounded by white diamonds. "I did. This was my grandmother's wedding ring. It's not much, but it meant a lot to her."

He slid the ring onto her finger, echoing the words Elvis prompted him with. Megan wished she'd had something to give to him, but then, this wasn't a real wedding and this wasn't going to be a real marriage. But still…

"I'm sorry I didn't have time to get it fitted," he whispered. "We can do it when we get back to Tulsa."

The ring fit a little loose, but Megan didn't care. The ring had belonged to his grandmother and was something he obviously cared about.

"By the power vested in me by the state of Nevada and the Graceland Wedding Chapel, I pronounce you husband and wife. You may kiss the bride." Elvis sang "Love Me Tender."

For a moment, Daniel hesitated. Megan held her breath. Then he bent, gathered her in his arms and kissed her.

The photographer's flash blinked close by, but nothing penetrated their embrace until Elvis's song ended and he cleared his throat.

"All you two need is the certificate and you can commence with the wedding night." Elvis escorted them back to the receptionist's desk, where they signed the marriage certificate and the photographer snapped more pictures. Then they were on their way with a marriage certificate and a DVD documenting their nuptials.

A white limousine stood at the curb, the driver holding the door for them.

Daniel handed Megan in, gave the address to the driver and slid in beside her with a huge sigh.

She shifted the bouquet to her other hand and touched Daniel's shoulder. "Tired?"

"I don't know what I feel. That was the most bizarre wedding ceremony I've ever seen."

"I don't know. I thought the Elvis impersonator did an excellent job with the accent and the songs." She held up the DVD. "If I thought my parents would come unhinged by my marrying, wait until they see these wedding photos."

Daniel took her hand in his. "I'm sorry. Your wedding should have been more…"

Megan raised her eyebrows. "Boring?"

"I don't know." He shook his head. "Classier."

"Personally, I liked the Elvis touch. I promised myself I'd never marry a man who lacked a sense of humor."

Daniel couldn't resist Megan's smile and grinned himself. "I almost laughed out loud when he first walked in the door."

"And how perfect were the song choices for a wedding?" Megan giggled and hummed "Love Me Tender."

The sparkle in her green eyes captured and held him as they drove between the brightly lit casinos.

"Do you want to go dancing?"

"You dance?"

Daniel frowned. "I've been known to two-step on occasion."

"I'd love to dance. But not tonight. I'm pretty tired from all that's happened in the past forty-eight hours." She leaned against his arm. "You sure know how to show a girl a little excitement."

When he helped her out of the limousine, she didn't release his hand until he had to get the key card out of his pocket to open the door to their room.

When she started to walk through the doorway, he tugged her back. "We have to do things right, even if they are only temporary." He swept her off her feet, crushing her against his chest. "Now, Mrs. Colton, welcome to the honeymoon suite."

She draped an arm around his neck and stared around the room. "It looks different." Then her eyes brightened and her smile grew wider. "Flowers and champagne? You shouldn't have." Her arm tightened and she kissed his cheek. "But I'm glad you did."

"You deserve so much more. I hope that one day when you marry for real, your husband does it right."

Her smile slipped and she sighed. "You've set the bar high, Daniel. I don't know how any man can come close. Thank you for giving me an unforgettable wedding day."

Daniel couldn't think of a reason to hold her in his arms longer, so he lowered her feet to the ground and stepped away. Then he crossed to the table, where an ice bucket held a bottle of champagne. Two champagne flutes stood beside it.

He popped the cork and sparkling liquid spilled onto

the table. Quickly filling the two flutes, he held one out to her. "To us."

She shook her head and winked. "No. To wedded bliss, however long it might last."

Daniel's chest tightened as he stared across his glass at Megan. She made a beautiful bride with her cheeks flushed and her hair tumbling over her shoulders in long, loose curls. The dress hugged her figure like it was a part of her, swirling around her legs when she moved.

Daniel drank the liquid all in one gulp, wishing it were whiskey, something with a bit more of a kick to take the edge off his desire. But it might have had the opposite effect, lowering his inhibitions, making him forget his promise to keep this marriage a strictly business relationship.

At that moment, as Megan stood in her white dress with her back to the dark sky and bright lights of Vegas, there was nothing businesslike about the way Daniel felt.

"You can have the bedroom. I'll take the sofa," he said, his voice gruff.

Megan glanced at the sofa and shook her head. "That's not even a real sofa. It's more like a love seat." She turned to him, settling her hands on her hips. "I'm smaller. You can have the bed. I'll sleep out here."

When he opened his mouth to protest, she raised her hand. "You're doing me a great favor by marrying me. The least I can do is let you have a decent night's sleep. You'll need that to get through the interrogation my parents will put you through in a couple days."

"I won't make you sleep on the sofa."

"Then are we both sleeping in the bed? Because you are not sleeping on that." She pointed to the sofa. "Don't even bother to argue."

He shrugged. "Then I guess you can have the bathroom first."

"Damn right I will." Her lips quirked and her eyes flashed as she marched past him into the bedroom with its adjoining bathroom.

Scrubbing a hand over his face, he realized just how tired he was. But when Megan was in the room, his body seemed to go into hyperdrive, the adrenaline powering his blood, keeping him alert to her every move.

The woman was playful, resilient and amazing. Most women would never consider an Elvis wedding appropriate. Megan showed her ability to adapt and her sense of humor, smiling and humming to the music the impersonator sang.

Her parents had no idea what a treasure she was. They should have just let her live her own life. The more Daniel was around her, the more he suspected he was falling in love with her. But he couldn't.

Megan came from money.

Daniel came from the res and a single-wide mobile home that had seen its better days two decades before he and his mother lived there.

He wasn't really a part of the Colton family even though Big J had taken him in. He didn't have the family tree his other siblings could claim, coming from both Big J and Abra Colton's lineage.

Megan deserved a better man with a better family. A man who knew how to act in public and wouldn't embarrass her or her parents.

His stomach knotted at the thought of meeting her parents for the first time and announcing they'd been married. He was without a single doubt that they'd be disappointed in Megan's choice of a husband.

Daniel poured more champagne and drank it, the bubbly fizz not his drink of choice. He stood in the door frame of the bedroom, staring toward the bathroom.

"Daniel?" Megan chose that moment to crack the bathroom door and peek out, her hair falling forward over a very naked shoulder. "Could you hand me my bag?"

His heart stood still as he stared at her.

"Please?" she prompted, pushing him out of his stupor.

Daniel grabbed her bag from the floor and handed it to her. When her fingers touched his, jolts of fire rippled through his veins, sending heat throughout his body and south.

"I'm headed out for a few minutes," Daniel muttered, backing away from her. "Don't wait up for me."

Her eyes widened. "Where are you going?"

"It's Vegas. I thought I'd get in some gambling."

"Oh." The disappointment on her face almost made him change his mind. He couldn't. If he stayed in the suite with Megan, he'd forgo his promise, pull her into his arms and make love to her the rest of the night and well into the next day.

"I'll have my cell phone if you need me." Daniel left the room and hurried down the hallway to the elevator. If he had to stay up all night gambling, so be it. He couldn't go back to the room when he wanted to kiss his new wife and make mad, passionate love to her.

Chapter 8

Megan left the bathroom wearing a pale blue baby-doll nightgown. A lot of good it would do her. Daniel had run out of the room so fast, he left skid marks on the carpet.

He definitely wasn't interested in her or in making their marriage real.

Megan wandered around the bedroom, her hand skimming across the comforter, wondering what it would be like to lie naked beside Daniel in the king-size bed. She ached so badly inside that she wouldn't be able to keep her hands off him for long. Maybe that's why he'd agreed to sleep in the bedroom, where he could close and lock the door to keep her out.

Megan found a blanket in the closet and took one of the pillows off the bed. At least she could get a good night's sleep, even if Daniel didn't. She spread the blanket, plumped the already fluffed pillow and lay down, bending her legs to get all of her on the sofa. The settee was much too small for either her or Daniel.

She lay for a long time staring up at the high ceilings and out at the Las Vegas night sky.

Where was Daniel? Megan checked her cell phone just in case she'd accidently turned it off or set it on silent. No calls, texts or voice mails. An hour passed and she couldn't sleep, not knowing when he'd come back.

Pushing to her feet, Megan returned to the bedroom and entered the bathroom, closing the door behind her. All the effort she'd put into looking good in her nightgown had been wasted. She pulled her hair back into a high ponytail to get it out of her face.

A noise in the other room made her catch her breath. Had he come back? Would he want to kiss her? *Please let him want to take me in his arms and make love to me.* "Daniel? Are you back?" She flung open the door and scanned the bedroom and the room beyond.

Megan stood perfectly still in the doorway, her heart beating hard against her ribs. "Daniel?"

Again, no answer.

Her pulse picked up, thrumming through her veins—not in anticipatory excitement but because of the creepy feeling she had someone other than Daniel was in the living room.

Megan stepped backward, closed the bathroom door and quietly turned the lock. If Daniel spoke up and let her know he was in the room, she'd unlock it quickly. But Daniel hadn't responded, and there was definitely someone out there.

The plush carpeted floor muffled even the heaviest footfalls.

She'd carried her cell phone through the suite and

into the bathroom earlier, hoping Daniel would call. If she had to, she could call 9-1-1. With someone already in her room, would anyone arrive in time to save her?

When the doorknob turned, Megan nearly fainted. Whoever was out there wanted in. Megan curled her hand around the knob and held it, keeping it from turning, just in case the lock didn't keep the intruder out.

The knob stilled.

Megan backed away from the door, dove for the cell phone on the counter and hit Daniel's number. It rang four times while Megan held her breath, praying he would pick up before whoever had come into their suite got creative and jimmied the lock.

At last Daniel answered, "Megan. Are you okay?"

She pressed the phone to her ear and whispered into the receiver. "There's someone in our room."

"What do you mean?"

"I'm locked in the bathroom and there is someone in the room."

"I'm on my way. Stay on the phone with me."

"I will." She clutched the phone like a lifeline, listening to Daniel's reassuring voice, while her other ear strained to hear movement beyond the door. "You didn't order room service, did you?"

"No."

She bit down on her lip to keep it from trembling. "Me, either."

She stood in the middle of the bathroom, staring in horror at the door, her thoughts running the gamut of self-defense classes she'd taken as the child of a wealthy family. All her life she'd been taught not to trust anyone and beware of strangers who could commit random acts of violence or people who might want to kidnap her. Now all those lessons flew out the window with her nerves.

The knob twisted again.

This time Megan wasn't near. It wiggled as if someone was jimmying the lock. She stared at the door, willing it to hold back whoever was on the other side. "He's turning the knob," Megan said, her voice shaking.

"Yell out loud that you're calling 9-1-1," Daniel said. "I'm in the elevator now."

Megan held the phone away from her mouth and yelled, "I'm calling 9-1-1!"

The knob stilled.

"Help, someone is breaking into my room," Megan said loudly and clearly enough that whoever was on the other side of the door would hear and leave. She recited the details of her hotel and room number to make it sound official.

"Good," Daniel reassured her. "Is there anything in the bathroom you could use as a weapon?"

Her heart hammering, Megan glanced around at the towels, tiny plastic bottles of shampoo and a small bar of soap. All of her toiletries were in the other room. "Not really." She grabbed a towel from the rail and held it in front of her, ready to throw it in the intruder's face if he should break through the door.

"I'm almost to our floor."

"Good," she said. Something hit the door hard. Megan yelped.

"What happened?"

"He's trying to break down the door." She yelled more loudly, "Hotel security is on its way up, and the police are less than two minutes away!"

Another loud thump and the door rattled on its hinges, but held.

Megan's instinct was to get as far away from the door as possible, but she figured if he burst through, his momentum would throw him into the bathroom. She could toss the towel over his head and duck past him while he untangled himself from the terry cloth.

Sure. And pigs could fly.

Into the phone she whispered, "I'm putting you on speaker and setting the phone on the counter in case I have to run."

"Okay," Daniel said. "I'm just one floor short. Hang in there. I'm almost there."

She held her breath and braced herself for the next blow to the door.

A moment or two passed and nothing. She strained to hear any movement on the other side of the panel. Her heart stood still as she waited, holding the huge luxury towel in front of her, spread like a fisherman's net.

Something slammed against the bathroom door so hard, the door frame splintered. Another slam and the door crashed open. A man in dark clothes and a ski mask fell into the room.

Megan tossed the towel in the man's face and ducked past him.

She had almost cleared the door when a hand reached out and snagged her arm, jerking her back. Megan twisted, employing one of the escape techniques she'd learned long ago. She freed her arm and ran through the bedroom, into the sitting area and straight for the exit, footsteps pounding behind her.

A sob rising up in her throat, she reached for the door and yanked it open. Before she could run through, a hand hit her hard in the back, slamming her onto the floor. She landed on her hands and knees and rolled to the side, away from her attacker. At that exact moment, the elevator dinged, indicating the arrival of the car.

"Daniel!" Megan screamed.

The man in the ski mask leaped over her sprawled form and ran for the stairwell at the opposite end of the hall.

The elevator door opened and Daniel leaped out. "Megan?" He ran to her and dropped to his haunches. "Oh, baby, are you okay?" His hands skimmed her body, her arms and legs, his assessing gaze sweeping across her.

Tears pooled in her eyes as she pushed to a sitting position. "I'm okay. He went that way." She pointed to the stairwell.

Daniel paused. "Did he hurt you?"

"No. I'm fine."

Daniel held out his hand and helped her to her feet. "Go into the room and lock the door, chains and all. Call hotel security and wait for me to return. Don't let anyone in but me or security."

Her heart racing all over again, she touched his arm. "Where are you going?"

"After your attacker." He ushered her to the door and bent to brush a quick kiss across her lips. "Lock it." Then he was gone, racing down the hall to the stairwell. As he ran, he shot a glance over his shoulder. "By the way, I love the outfit." With a wink he pushed through the door.

Warmed by his comment, Megan watched until he disappeared. Once he was out of sight, a chill shivered across her skin. She ducked back into her room and closed and locked the door as promised. She hurried over to the phone on an end table and dialed the operator. "Hotel security."

"One moment while I connect you," the operator said.

"Security."

Megan sighed. "Someone just broke into my room." She gave the details, assured them the intruder was gone and then hung up to wait for their arrival.

All through the call, her mind was on Daniel, praying he was okay. Part of her wanted him to catch the intruder while the other part of her didn't want him to get hurt in the process. She paced to the door and looked through the peephole into the empty hallway, wishing Daniel would come back. She turned and leaned against the door, her gaze panning the room. Why had someone broken in? They didn't have anything worth stealing.

She walked through the sitting area, through the bedroom and into the bathroom. Nothing appeared disturbed. In the bedroom, again, nothing seemed out of place. No drawers were opened. Her purse sat on the dresser in the same position she'd left it. In the bathroom, she slipped into the fluffy white hotel bathrobe. She grabbed her phone and held it, willing Daniel to call and let her know what was happening in the stairwell.

A knock at the door made her jump and yelp.

"Hotel security."

Megan hurried to the door and peered through the peephole. Two men wearing the uniforms she'd seen in the casino stood outside her door.

She slid the chain off and unlocked the dead bolt. Her hand shook as she opened the door.

"Ma'am, we understand you've had a break-in. We notified the police, and they are on their way. We're here to protect you until they arrive."

"Thanks." Megan stood in the robe, wishing she'd taken the time to get dressed, feeling uncomfortable in a bathrobe with nothing more than a sexy nightgown beneath it. Where was Daniel?

Daniel ran down the stairs, leaped over the railing and dropped to the next level. He stopped and listened. Below he heard footsteps pounding on the stairs. He leaned over the railing and caught a glimpse of someone in black three or four floors below. Fueled by the sound and the sight of his prey, Daniel continued downward.

The metal clink sounded of a stairwell door opening and closing. Daniel leaned over the railing again but didn't see anything. He was still several floors from ground level.

His heart beating rapidly, he continued downward from the penthouse level until he reached the ground and burst through the door.

Multicolored lights flashed, and the constant ringing of bells and the musical cacophony of the casino assailed his senses. He scanned the immediate vicinity for a man in black. There were a couple of older men wearing black shirts, standing at the slot machines, but no one appeared to have been running down multiple flights of stairs.

Daniel hurried past row after row of slot and video poker machines. At one point he thought he saw a man in black duck around a group of people at a roulette table. Upon closer investigation, he discovered a woman with dark hair and a black blouse drinking a martini and laughing up at her date.

As large and confusing as the casino was, Daniel knew it was a lost cause to continue his search. The longer he was away from Megan, the more he wanted to return to her and make certain she was okay.

He took the elevator back to the penthouse level and hurried toward their room. The door was open, and a couple of security guards stood inside.

When he entered through the open doorway, the guards blocked his path.

Daniel held up his hands and nodded toward Megan. "That's my wife." The words rolled off his lips, feeling so natural and right.

Megan's cheeks reddened. "You can let him in. He's with me."

Daniel slipped around the security guards and pulled her into his arms. "Are you okay?"

"Yeah. More importantly, are you?" She pushed to arm's length and stared up into his eyes. "Did you catch him?"

He frowned and shook his head. "He must have gotten off on one of the higher floors. I went all the way down to the bottom and never saw him." Glancing over her shoulder, he asked, "Anything missing or disturbed?"

"Nothing. He was in the room long enough to grab my purse, but he didn't even touch it."

A minute later, the police, the hotel manager and the assistant manager arrived, filling the room. The police took Megan's statement, dusted for prints and looked around, leaving shortly afterward.

The hotel manager and assistant manager stood in the hallway with Megan and Daniel until the police left. When they were gone, hotel maintenance staff entered and wiped away all traces of fingerprint dust and splintered wood from the door frame. "We'll have someone fix the frame tomorrow," said the manager. "Please accept our apologies. Your room will be comped and our security staff will be working closely with the police, going over the video footage to help them identify your intruder. We'll have guards on the floor for the remainder of the night."

"Thank you." Daniel held the door for the hotel manager and his assistant. When they'd passed through, he closed it and turned to Megan.

Her face was pale and her eyes were rounded, with dark circles beneath.

Daniel opened his arms. "Come here."

Megan fell against him, burying her face against his chest.

He held her close, resting his cheek against her soft hair, breathing in the scent of her. After the insane race to get to her before the intruder did and then the race down the stairwell to catch the bastard, Daniel didn't think his heart would ever slow. Who the hell would attack an innocent woman? Was it a random event or had he targeted Megan?

"I've never been more scared in my life," she muttered against his shirt, her fingers curling into the fabric.

Daniel's jaw hardened, his arms tightening around Megan. "I'm here now. I won't let anyone hurt you."

She slipped her arms around his waist, her body shaking against his. "I didn't think you'd get here in time."

Daniel hadn't, either. He'd prayed all the way up in the elevator, watching the numbers tick at the pace of molasses dripping. "Did he hurt you?"

"He pushed me down. Other than a little rug burn on my hands and knees, I'm fine. I'm just glad *you're* okay."

He shook his head. She'd been the one attacked, and yet she was concerned about him. His chest swelled.

Megan was an amazing woman. "Come on. You must be exhausted." Tucking her in the curve of his arm, he walked her toward the bedroom. "You can have the bed. I'll take the sofa."

Her arm clamped around his waist. "The sofa is too small."

"I'll make do."

"You'll be uncomfortable and won't sleep."

"It won't hurt me for one night." He stopped beside the bed and let his arm fall from around her.

Megan didn't let go of his waist, nor did she move from where she stood beside him. "Stay with me," she whispered.

The softly spoken words went straight to Daniel's heart. He wanted to wrap his arms around her and hold her until all the bad in the world turned good, but if he lay down beside her, he wasn't sure he could stop at a hug. "I can't."

"At least until I go to sleep." Her head dipped. "I'll understand if you don't want to."

Daniel closed his eyes, his fists clenching. "It's not that I don't want to."

Megan turned her face up to his, her brow creased. "What do you mean?"

He shook his head and gripped her arms. "I want to. Hell, I want *you* and that's the problem."

Her chuckle made his groin tighten, the sound soft and sexy, stirring his blood. "Daniel, we're married."

"Only in name." He let go of her and shoved a hand through his hair to keep from dragging her into his arms and kissing her like there might not be a tomorrow.

She touched his chest, sending warning signals throughout his body. "It doesn't have to be in name only."

"This is supposed to be temporary. You have your life. I have mine." He forced himself to take a step backward. "I don't belong in yours."

Her frown deepened. "My life is at the Lucky C Ranch and so is yours. How different are our lives?"

He shook his head. "You are the daughter of a very wealthy man. I'm a bastard son of a Colton. We're worlds apart."

Megan planted her fists on her hips. The image of her in her fluffy terry-cloth bathrobe, her trim legs peeking out from the hem, and her pretty little feet bare against the carpeted floor almost undid Daniel. She tossed her ponytail back over her shoulder. "You make it sound like I'm stuck up, when in actuality, you're the one who's stuck up."

"I'm not stuck up."

"Look, Daniel, I don't judge you based on your family or where you came from. I take you for the man you are now. The least you could do is give me the same benefit of the doubt."

"It's different."

"The hell it is." Megan pointed to the door. "Go. Sleep on the sofa. I'll be just fine on my own." She reached for the sash around her waist and untied it, letting the robe drop to the ground around her ankles. Then she tipped up her chin and pushed her shoulders back, making her breasts rise in the sexiest sheer nightgown Daniel had ever seen in his life. The garment revealed more than it covered and sent his pulse rampaging through his veins. "Too bad you won't be along on this honeymoon."

When she started to turn away, Daniel grasped her elbow and yanked her back and into his arms. "What are you trying to do, damn it?"

"Nothing," she said. "Absolutely nothing."

He swept his hand along the side of her face and up to pull out the elastic band around her hair, letting it fall down around her shoulders. "Well, you're doing a whole lotta something to me, and I can only take so much."

She stared up into his face, the anger melting from her eyes, her tongue coming out to wet her lips. "That's your problem," she said, her voice soft and breathy.

"No, it's our problem." He cupped the back of her head with one hand and bent until his lips were a hairbreadth from hers. "This is so damned wrong." He fought to keep from taking it a step further, knowing he was losing this battle and fast.

"Then why do it?" she asked, her words warm against his lips.

"Because it feels so right." He lowered his mouth to hers, intending only a light brush, telling himself he'd just get a little taste of her and go away. Control flew out the window when their lips touched. He could no sooner back away than stop breathing.

Daniel crushed her body against his, the soft curve of her breasts pressing against his hard chest, her thighs straddling one of his, her arms circling his neck to bring him closer. This was where he wanted to be. Not in the other room, lying cramped on the impossibly small sofa.

She opened her mouth on a sigh, and he swept in to claim her tongue in a long, hot, wet caress.

He slid his hand down her back to cup her bottom, pulling her closer until his straining member rubbed against her belly. The kiss went on, the heat building between them, the need to feel her skin against his becoming a physical ache.

Megan broke the kiss and stepped away.

Daniel groaned, reaching out to bring her back within his embrace.

She shook her head and reached for the buttons of his shirt, flicking them free one at a time all the way down to where they disappeared into the waistband of his trousers. Gripping the fabric, she pulled it loose and freed the remaining buttons with quick, deft strokes of her dexterous fingers.

Impatience sent Daniel over the edge. He shoved her hands aside, unbuckled his belt and jerked it out of the loops, slinging it across the floor. Then he grabbed the hem of her gown and yanked it over her head, tossing it aside. He swept her with his gaze, lingering on her perky breasts, the nipples puckered and beaded into tight little buds.

A slow flush rose up her neck and into her cheeks. With exaggerated care, Megan loosened the top button of his trousers and slid the zipper down, unleashing his straining member into the palm of her hand. Her lips curled upward and her brows cocked. "Commando?"

"Always." He toed off his cowboy boots and his trousers slid down his legs.

Once he stood naked in front of her, he sucked in a deep breath and let it out in an attempt to rein in his galloping pulse. "If you want, you can back out now."

"You're wrong," she said, gently squeezing his hard staff. "I couldn't back out even if I wanted to. I need you. Now. Inside me." Tugging gently, she backed toward the bed. "Don't fight it."

"I'm past fighting. I concede this round to you and your gorgeous body."

Chapter 9

A thrill shivered across Megan's body. "Victory at last," she murmured, aroused beyond reason, barely able to form a coherent thought.

Daniel scooped her legs up and laid her on the bed. He hooked his finger in the elastic band of her panties and dragged them down her legs.

Now we're getting somewhere. She ran her hand up her torso and plumped one of her breasts, hoping to entice him into moving this along a little faster. Her core on fire, she needed him to quench the blaze.

He crawled onto the bed, leaning over her, his arms bulging, his member nestling in the mound of curls over her sex. "I didn't go into this deal with sex in mind."

"Consider it a bonus." Megan wrapped her legs around his waist and urged him closer.

"Uh-uh. Not yet." With one hand he reached back

and disengaged her legs. "I want this to be as good for you as it will be for me."

Was he kidding? Any more excited and she'd burst into flames. "Oh, I have no doubt it'll be good," she said, her voice low and husky.

"Shh. Anyone ever tell you that you talk too much?"

"Sometimes—" He cut off her words with a kiss, darting his tongue into her mouth. He tasted of mint and coffee and smelled of the outdoors and aftershave. She opened to him, offering him everything in exchange for one night of passion.

After ravaging her lips and mouth, he trailed hot kisses along her jaw and down her neck.

Megan tilted her head back to allow him better access to all those sensitive places in his path. When he reached her breast, her back arched automatically, her body taking over, reacting to his every touch.

Daniel tongued her nipple, flicking the tip and rolling it around between his teeth.

She cupped the back of his head, running her hands through his thick, dark hair, urging him to take more. When he switched to the other nipple, the cool air across the first one only made her more aware of her nakedness.

Though she wasn't a virgin, she had never been so very aroused and aware of a man's body as she was with Daniel. His huge frame, thick muscles and hard staff made her want to get even closer. She wanted him inside her.

Daniel abandoned her breasts and seared a path with his tongue and lips down her torso, dipping briefly into her belly button but not stopping for long. He finally reached the apex of her thighs and parted her folds with his thumbs.

Megan stiffened, waiting for his next move, her breath hitched in her throat, her fingers knotting the sheets at her sides.

His head lowered, and he tapped his tongue to that strip of flesh alive with nerves. The touch sent sparks of electricity shooting through her body. A tingling sensation built at her center, radiating outward. "Do you know what you're doing to me?"

His chuckle blew warm over her wet entrance. "I hope I do."

"Don't stop," she cried.

"Yes, ma'am." He tapped her center again.

Megan moaned and reached for his head, digging her fingers into his hair, pulling him to her.

His wet tongue stroked her again and again, then moved down to her damp entrance, swirling around in her juices before returning to her aching, needy flesh. While he tongued her, he slipped a finger into her channel, her wetness coating him, making it easy for him to slide another inside, and another.

She writhed, her body moving to the rhythm of his tongue and fingers, the heat building, her insides tensing, rising to that peak she reached for with all her might.

One final flick sent her rocketing for the heavens like Fourth of July fireworks in sudden, glorious bursts, shooting out in all directions.

Megan rode the rocket to the moon and back, her hips moving to the pulsing beat of blood hammering in her veins.

As she returned to the earth and her senses, another ache filled her, and she urged Daniel up her body, dragging at his hair.

"Hey, that's attached." He laughed and complied, sliding his body over her torso and breasts until his lips hovered over hers. "Are you ready?"

"Oh, you have no idea."

"I think I have a little bit of an idea. But first…" He leaned over the side of the bed, reaching for his trousers and the wallet in the back pocket.

Thankful he'd had the wherewithal to remember protection, Megan grabbed the foil packet from his hands and ripped it open, then slid the contents over his rock-hard member. She tossed the empty packet to the side. "We aren't done yet."

"Are you always this insatiable?" He smiled, his eyes darker than dark, his lips wet from pleasuring her.

"Baby, it's you." She gripped his bottom and brought his staff to her entrance. "I can't seem to get enough."

"It goes both ways, sweetheart."

"Then don't let anything stop you now."

He nudged her opening.

"Oh, please, don't take it slow," she begged.

Hot and wet from the most incredible foreplay she'd ever experienced, she was ready.

Daniel drove into her, burying himself hard and deep.

Megan raised her hips to take him even deeper.

He withdrew and entered her again. His length and girth filled her, stretching her channel in the most glorious, sensual way. Megan bucked beneath him, digging her heels into the mattress to meet him thrust for thrust.

He rode her hard and fast, his long, steady strokes building speed, the friction inside heating her, sending her back up to the top of the peak.

One last time he powered into her, all the way until he could go no more. There he held her, his body rigid, his member so thick and solid, yet throbbing and warm, pulsing inside her to the rhythm of her own heartbeat.

When at last his muscles relaxed, he collapsed on top of her and rolled over, taking her with him, retaining their intimate connection.

Megan lay with her cheek against his naked chest, her body limp and replete after the most mind-blowing sex she'd ever experienced.

Daniel pulled her into his arms and rested his chin against her temple. "That was amazing."

"I have no words, except…wow."

He stroked a hand down her arm and along the swell of her hip. "We should get some sleep."

"I haven't even thought about tomorrow."

"We have an entire day of honeymooning and another night here. You don't have to think beyond that. Not yet." He kissed the top of her hair, then pressed his lips to the tip of her nose and finally her lips.

Megan wove her fingers into his hair and deepened the kiss, holding on for as long as she could before breathing became a necessity.

Her body stirred against him, and his flaccid member grew hard all over again.

"I assume sleep is not on your mind," she teased him, her finger trailing down his chest and belly to the tip of his shaft which pressed against her stomach.

"Not now. And not for the rest of the night if you keep doing that."

"Is that all it takes?" She circled him with her finger. This time she rose up over him, straddling his hips, her knees sinking into the mattress, her warm wetness easing down over him.

"Who needs sleep, anyway?" Daniel thrust up into

her. Holding her hips in his big, calloused hands, he guided her up and down in a hot, rapid ascent until they climaxed together, calling out each other's names.

Megan lay over his bare chest, her racing heartbeat matching his. Exhaustion melted her into him, and she could barely move enough to slip onto the bed next to the big Oklahoman. "Sorry, that's all I had in me. Give me a couple hours of sleep and I could do it all over again."

"Is that so?"

"You bet." She looked into his eyes. "Promise me one thing."

"What's that?"

"Tomorrow." She yawned and closed eyelids so heavy she could barely keep them open. "No regrets."

Daniel lay awake for a long time after Megan fell to sleep, staring into her fresh, beautiful face. Her strawberry blond hair fanned out over his arm in burnished-gold, silken strands. Her full, soft lips were swollen from his kisses, and her fingers rested against his chest, curling ever so slightly as if to hold on to him.

No regrets.

As soon as she'd said it, a dozen thoughts had powered through his head, every one of them a strong reason for him to step away from her as fast as he could. He was a good man, but he wasn't the kind of man who strove for wealth and power. He liked living on the ranch and taking care of horses.

His goal was to establish a viable horse-breeding program, not to conquer the world one corporation at a time. He had no desire to be a big shot in an office. Horses were his passion, and no matter how little he made at what he was doing, he wouldn't want to do anything else. He loved the animals, felt most comfortable around them. More so than around humans.

Except Megan. She'd fit right into his life without so much as a bump in the road. Her passion for horses equaled his, and her desire to live simply paralleled his own. Then why did he think she was a debutante to be coddled and protected until the day her parents handed her off to some rich playboy? He'd provide for her, protect her and see to it she never lacked for the most beautiful things money could buy. But would he let her do the things she loved? Would he love her like she deserved to be loved?

No regrets?

Daniel's only regret was Megan's accident of birth. If she had not been born of insanely wealthy parents, he could have seen being with her for the long haul. But he didn't have enough to offer her.

He must have drifted off in the wee hours of the morning. When he opened his eyes, sun streamed through the curtains of the honeymoon suite.

Megan stirred beside him, rolling onto her back.

Daniel slipped his arm out from beneath her and propped himself up on his elbow to stare down at the beautiful woman. Tall, slender and curvy in all the right places, she was absolutely gorgeous. Never in all the time she'd worked for Daniel had she expressed an interest in him, nor had he encouraged it. He respected her as his employee. Though he'd considered her hands-off, he couldn't change the way his body reacted to hers when they worked in tight quarters.

Even now, as she lay sleeping in the bed, his breath quickened and his member hardened.

If he didn't move immediately, he'd be touching her again like some sex-starved teen.

Daniel eased off the mattress and stood. They needed at least one day in Vegas to make it look like a proper honeymoon before heading on to California to meet with her grandmother's attorney. The sooner they got the ball rolling on her inheritance, the sooner she'd be able to purchase her horses.

While in California, they'd meet with her parents, an encounter he didn't look forward to. They'd be upset she'd married beneath her. Daniel hoped they didn't make a big deal out of it.

Megan was old enough to make her own decisions and live life the way she planned, not the way her parents felt she should. The least he could do was show her a proper honeymoon for an unusual wedding. He stepped into the bathroom, past the jagged edges of the busted door frame.

His heart stilled for a moment. If the attacker had been successful, what would have happened to Megan? Had he been there to hurt, kidnap or kill her?

And why? What did Megan have that an intruder would want? Kidnapping made more sense. Her parents were rich. If they loved her, they'd pay anything to get her back alive. Killing her made no sense whatsoever, unless it had been a random break-in and the burglar was on an insane mission to murder.

Daniel glanced at the sleeping Megan through the doorway and decided to leave the door open enough that he could hear if anyone were to break in and attack again. He'd keep her close until they returned to Oklahoma. For that matter, had her horse been poisoned in order to cause injury to Megan? Perhaps he was putting two and two together and coming up with five.

He switched on the shower and stepped beneath the cool spray, hoping the water would wash away the fog of uncertainty and make his thoughts clearer. The danger they'd encountered had to stop before Megan got hurt.

Whatever he did that day, he needed to keep his hands off his bride. This was supposed to be a marriage of convenience, not the real deal. As soon as she acquired her grandmother's inheritance, she wouldn't need him anymore. Daniel had to remind himself of that fact. Megan would be his ex-wife and, if she chose to stay at the Lucky C, she'd be his employee again. He had to keep their relationship on a business level. No more making love into the dark hours of the morning.

The cool spray of the shower did nothing to tone down his rising desire. Just the thought of a naked Megan lying in the bed made his insides heat. The water warmed as he lathered a bar of soap, spread it over his face and body and then stepped beneath the showerhead to rinse off.

Cool air fanned across his backside. Slender fingers circled his waist, and a warm body pressed against him.

Daniel's body reacted immediately and with profound lust. He leaned his hands against the cool tiles and let the water wash over his head and shoulders as he gathered his wits and held tight to his slipping control. "You are making it extremely difficult to remain hands-off in this marriage," he grumbled.

"You were the one who wanted this marriage to be hands-off." Megan pressed her cheek and other, more interesting parts against his back. "How's that working for you?" Her hands slid lower to fondle his hard staff.

"I'm failing miserably." He sighed and turned to face

her, gathering her in his arms. "Especially when you look so damned beautiful in nothing but water and soap."

Her brows rose. "I don't have any soap on me."

"Guess we'll have to fix that." He lathered his hands with the bar and set it aside. Starting at her neck, Daniel spread the suds across her shoulders and over the swell of her breasts. He stopped to tweak each of her puckered nipples, swirling the slippery bubbles around and around until Megan captured one of his wrists and guided his hand lower to the tuft of hair over the apex of her thighs.

"There's no soap here," she said, her voice gravelly and sexy.

Daniel cupped her sex and slid a finger between her folds.

Megan's breasts rose on a long, indrawn breath. "Yesss." She gripped his upper arms and closed her eyes, holding on while he touched her again.

Daniel studied her face as he toyed with the special place that made her crazy when he stroked her. He liked watching her eyelids flicker, her tongue dart out to wet her lips and her hips gyrate with every movement of his finger. Her response made him ready to take her there against the cool tiled wall.

He slipped his soapy hands around to her back and down over the rounded swells of her bottom. Then he lifted her, and she wrapped her legs around his waist. Poised at her opening, he was sorely tempted to thrust up inside her.

With her hands braced on his shoulders, she tried to lower herself, but his hands on her hips stayed her descent.

"No. We can't do this."

She drew in a deep breath, her breasts within reach of his lips. "Protection?"

"It's in the other room."

"Then let's go into the other room." She cupped his chin and smiled down into his face, the shower pelting her chest, the water dripping off the tips of her breasts.

Daniel groaned. "It's more than just protection. We can't keep doing this. When the charade is over, we have to go back to being us."

"And this isn't us?" Her fingers raked through his hair, and she tipped his head toward hers. "It could be."

"It shouldn't be," Daniel said. "I promised I wouldn't take advantage of you."

"What if I want you to?"

His lips quirked on the corners. "It doesn't make it right."

Her mouth pressed into a thin line. "I swear, Daniel Colton, you have the hardest head of any of the Coltons. What does it take to get you to look past the nose at the end of your face?"

"What do you mean?"

"Nothing." She loosened her legs around him. "Let me down."

Now that she'd asked him to put her down, he was certain he didn't want to. But he complied.

Megan stepped out of the shower onto the mat and slid the curtain shut in his face, fire flashing in her green eyes.

Daniel didn't like that she was mad, but perhaps it would be better if she stayed that way. The less she liked him, the easier it would be to go back to their former way of getting along.

Staring down at his erection, he doubted they'd ever

go back to the way it was before they were married. Who was he trying to kid?

He rinsed under the lukewarm water and switched it off. When he pulled the shower curtain back, Megan had left the bathroom and closed the door behind her.

His pulse leaped at the thought of her in the bedroom alone with a possible intruder. Daniel dove for the door, his wet foot slipping on the tile floor. Instead of opening the door silently to check on her, he crashed into it headfirst and slid to the floor.

His head throbbing, he pushed to his feet and regrouped. He flung open the door, throwing a towel around his naked waist.

Megan was halfway across the room, headed in his direction, a frown denting her brow. She wore a black lacy bra and matching panties, the darkness of the scraps of material enhancing the paleness of her skin. "I thought I heard something fall in there."

"You did." He straightened, his pulse settling into an uneven rhythm with her almost naked in front of him, the undergarments almost as enticing as her nude body. "I just—" he cleared his throat "—wanted to make sure you were alone."

Her brows lifted, and she glanced around the room. "I believe we are the only two people in the suite at this time."

"Good." He marched into the room, grabbed his clothes and kept going into the sitting area, thus avoiding temptation.

"Hey, cowboy." Megan leaned in the doorway, her arms crossed, her lips quirked. "You can run, but you can't hide from the way you feel."

"It's not right. We're only in this for a short while."

Megan dipped her head. "So why not enjoy each other's company in the meantime?"

"It's not right. My mother and father did that, and what did it buy them?" He jammed his legs into his blue jeans. "A bastard child."

Megan's arms dropped to her sides, and she crossed the floor to where he stood pulling his shirt over his shoulders. She laid her hand on his arm, all amusement wiped from her face. "Daniel, a child of ours wouldn't be a bastard." She nodded toward the papers on the end table. "We're legally married."

"For show."

"It's legal."

He shook off her hand. "You deserve a better match."

Her frown returned, and she spun away from him. "For the love of God. You sound like my parents." Megan disappeared into the bedroom. Drawers slamming and the rasp of a suitcase zipper were the only sounds coming through the open door. Then she appeared, pulling a dress down over her head. "That marriage license has to be legal for me to collect my inheritance."

"I realize that."

"Fine," she said, straightening the hem of her dress. She turned and gave him her back. "Zip me."

A chuckle rose up his chest, and he crossed to where she stood in her stiff, fiery anger.

He dragged the zipper up the back of the dress. Before she could get away, he turned her to face him. "Look, let's make this day a good one, no matter what happens in the coming days. We have all of Vegas to explore and no one to please but ourselves." He held out his hand. "Deal?"

She stared at it, her eyes narrowed. Then she relaxed

and slid her hand into his, her frown easing. "Deal. We'll make it a day." Letting go of his hand, she glanced up at him, her eyes narrowing again for just a moment. "But I still think you're discriminating against me because of my family." She poked him in the chest with a finger. "I. Am. Not. My. Family." She reentered the bedroom, calling out, "The sooner you get that, the better." Slinging her purse over her shoulder, she emerged in the doorway. "Ready to paint this town red?"

He grinned. "Let's do it." Daniel pushed aside all his misgivings about this marriage of convenience for the day and concentrated on showing Megan a good time, while keeping a close eye on her in case the man who'd broken into their room showed up again.

Chapter 10

Megan smiled and laughed through the day, walking along the broad sidewalks of the Vegas Strip. She and Daniel toured several of the more notable casinos from the pyramid of the Luxor to the MGM Grand. They ate a sumptuous lunch at the Eiffel Tower Restaurant in the Paris Las Vegas Hotel and Casino and walked beneath the sky-painted ceilings of Caesars Palace.

The day passed in a whirl of activity and fun. Megan hadn't realized how entertaining Daniel could be and how special he made her feel, always opening doors for her and holding her hand everywhere they went.

At The Venetian, Daniel hired a gondola to take them through the beautiful canal winding its way through the spacious hotel and casino. The oarsman paused long enough to use Daniel's smartphone to snap a picture of them in each other's arms, drifting beneath an arched bridge.

Despite the nature of their agreement, Daniel went above and beyond what was necessary to make the day special. If she hadn't known better, Megan could almost have believed they were truly on their honeymoon.

At the end of the day, they stopped in front of the Bellagio in time for the spectacular musical light show. Daniel slipped his arm around her and she leaned in to him, tired but happy. Their fake honeymoon had been everything she could hope for in a real one. And she'd spent it with the man she was falling madly in love with. Her heart swelled with the last strains of music.

"Ready to get dinner?" Daniel asked. "Or would you rather go back to the hotel and order room service?"

Megan didn't have to think twice. "Room service." Back in their hotel room, she wouldn't have to share Daniel with a thousand other people. Even if he didn't want to be intimate, he would be with her. She would be happy with any scraps he threw her way. But she'd be beyond ecstatic if he carried her back to the bed and made sweet love to her through the night.

On the walk back to the hotel, the lights of the city shone all around them, neon illuminating the night sky, masking the stars she knew were just beyond the halo of garish brightness. "Though Vegas is fun, I'll be glad to go home to Oklahoma. I like my nights filled with stars."

Daniel reached out and grasped her hand, pulling it through the crook of his arm. "You and me both. Nothing makes me happier than to lie on the ground and stare up at a clear night sky and count the stars until I fall asleep."

"My father's ranch is over fifty miles north of San Francisco, but the lights from the city fade the stars." She leaned against his shoulder. "I much prefer the nights on the Lucky C."

Cars moved past them on the street, and a steady stream of humanity passed them on the still-warm concrete sidewalks.

Daniel pulled her to a halt at a crosswalk and pressed the button for the pedestrian light. "We can cross here."

Their hotel was on the other side of the busy thoroughfare. Just a few more feet before she had Daniel all to herself.

The light changed and the traffic pulled to a halt, the little walking man figure lighting on the crosswalk sign.

Megan stepped out on Daniel's arm, ready to be back in their room, with all the possibilities of how the rest of the evening might go racing through her mind.

Screeching tires made her turn to glance at one of the cars waiting at the intersection. It jerked forward, the scent of rubber burning against the pavement as whoever was driving floored the accelerator.

The car careened toward Megan and Daniel.

People scattered, screaming.

Daniel shoved her hard, sending her flying out of the way of the oncoming vehicle. She hit the ground and rolled to the side, the tires barely missing her as it raced by.

A loud thump made her blood run cold. Megan stumbled to her feet, her heart lodged in her throat. "Daniel!" she cried out.

The vehicle sped on, disappearing into a red sea of taillights. On the ground before her, Daniel lay on his back.

"Daniel!" Megan rushed forward and fell on her knees on the pavement.

"I'm okay." He lifted a hand as if to prove it, though he didn't get up immediately. "Just bruised my backside.

Give me a minute to feel if anything is broken." Slowly he moved his legs and arms. Finally he sat up.

People gathered around them even as the light changed to green for the waiting cars.

"Hey, mister, are you all right?" A woman stepped up to them. "I'm a nurse. You should stay down until an ambulance arrives." She held a phone to her ear. "I'm calling 9-1-1 now."

Daniel was already shaking his head. "No. Don't. I'm okay. Just a little shaken up."

"We saw that car hit you, dude," a teen said. "I swear he did it on purpose."

"Yeah," another teen said. "If you hadn't rolled over the hood, you'd be a dead man."

Daniel pushed to his feet and gave the teens a wry smile. "Thanks. I think I get the picture." He hooked Megan's arm and led her out of the street to the relative safety of the sidewalk.

"At least go to the hospital and let the ER doctor check you out for a concussion," Megan urged him.

The nurse had followed them and stood beside Megan, nodding. "He really should. Sometimes you think you're okay, but you could have head trauma and intracranial bleeding."

Megan's stomach lurched. "You're going to the hospital." She turned to wave down a cab. When one pulled up to the curb, she opened the door and pointed. "Get in."

"Really, I'm fine," Daniel insisted. "I jumped up on the hood. The vehicle didn't hit me."

"You landed on your back and probably hit your head in the fall. Which would explain why you can't seem to focus enough to get into the cab." Megan tapped her toe. "Are you going to get in, or are two women going to have to manhandle you into the car?"

Daniel glanced from Megan to the nurse and back before he raised his hands in surrender. "Okay, okay. I'm getting in."

The nurse sighed. "Good. Just let a doctor check you out. I'm sure you're fine, but it doesn't hurt to have the doctor confirm."

Megan turned to the nurse and held out her hand. "Thank you."

The nurse smiled and shook her hand with a wink. "Your husband is too cute to lose to a freak accident. Take care."

Megan climbed in beside Daniel and told the cab driver to take them to the hospital.

Daniel sat beside her, rubbing a hand over the back of his head. "We could be ordering room service," he grumbled.

"We can still order room service when we get back. They serve 24/7." Megan scanned his face and body for injuries. Other than a scuffed elbow, he looked fine. "Let me feel the back of your head."

He leaned forward. "I've got a knot from the fall."

"Where?" She leaned close. He captured her hand and guided it to the spot, where she felt a chicken-egg-sized bump. "You did get a bump, poor baby."

He removed her hand from his head and used it to pull her close to him. "Mmm, you smell good."

"After a day tromping around Vegas, I shouldn't."

"Damn, Megan." He set her away from him and stared down at her hands. "Your hands are raw." He leaned back and studied the rest of her, including her skinned knees. "How did you get those?"

She smiled. "A certain cowboy shoved me out of the way of a speeding car."

"Oh, baby, sorry I pushed you too hard."

She shook her head. "I'm okay. If you hadn't pushed me as hard as you did, we would both have been hit. I'm just sorry you took the brunt of that maniac's bad driving skills."

"Good thing we're going to the hospital. The doctor should be able to help you."

"I've only got skinned knees and hands. My head didn't connect to the ground. How did you keep from getting crushed by that car?"

"I was pretty good on the vault in high school. I planted my hands on the hood of the car and swung my legs to the side. A great vault, but a terrible landing."

"You're alive. That's what matters." She wrapped her arms around him, the sound of his body thumping against the metal of the vehicle replaying in her mind. "Wow, you could have been so messed up."

He chuckled and winced. "Ouch. Careful how hard you squeeze. I suspect a bruised rib."

"Sorry." She sat up straight and carefully moved away. "What's happening here? First the attack in our room, now a hit-and-run."

Daniel's lips thinned. "It can't be a coincidence."

Megan shook her head, her hands trembling. "It's as if one or both of us are being targeted."

The cab drove up to the ER entrance. Megan got out and extended her hand to help Daniel.

He ignored her hand and climbed out on his own. "Thanks, but I really am okay."

"If it's all the same to you, I'd rather hear the doctor

say that." Megan led him into the hospital and up to the registration desk.

An hour later, after Daniel had his head scanned and Megan had her knees cleaned and bandaged, they left in another cab. When they arrived back at the hotel, they looked pretty banged up and hurried to their room.

"You can have the shower first," Megan offered. "I'll order room service."

"If they come before I'm out of the shower, don't answer the door," Daniel warned her.

Megan's heart warmed at his concern. "Not everyone is out to get me."

"Maybe not, but that's three near misses in as many days. If you're not getting a persecution complex by now, I'll get one for you." He pointed at her. "Don't open that door for anyone. I'll answer it when I get out."

"Yes, sir." Megan popped a smart salute and smiled. "You can answer the door. In the meantime, I'll call in a dinner order."

Daniel entered the bathroom and left the door propped open.

Megan couldn't help peeking as he dropped his jeans and shed his shirt.

He turned, caught her staring and winked. Then he stepped into the shower, closing the curtain between them.

Megan's cheeks heated. "Tease!" she called out.

"Peeping Tom!" he shouted back.

Still smiling, she lifted the phone and called room service, ordering a couple of steaks and a bottle of wine.

When she hung up, she entered the bedroom and scrounged through her suitcase for something to wear. She settled on an oversize T-shirt and a pair of shorts.

Not exactly a sex goddess outfit, but she wasn't planning on seducing Daniel after he'd been knocked around.

Her cell phone rang in the other room. By the time she reached it, it had stopped. Checking the caller ID, she noted it was her parents. Rather than spoil the rest of her evening, she decided not to return the call.

The choice was taken out of her hands when her phone rang again and startled her enough that she pressed the receive button.

"Megan?" her mother's voice sounded in her ear.

"Hi, Mother."

"Why didn't you answer the first time I rang? Is everything okay?"

Megan sighed. Her mother worried far too much about her, to the point of obsessing. "I'm fine, Mother." If *fine* meant almost being thrown from a horse, having her room broken into and nearly being run over by a crazed driver, she was just dandy.

"You don't sound fine. When are you coming home?"

Her heart thumping against her ribs, Megan took a deep breath and dove in. "As a matter of fact, I'll be home tomorrow."

Her mother gasped. "Tomorrow? Why didn't you tell us sooner?"

"I only knew myself today," she fibbed just a little. She'd known since the day before, but one day's difference didn't matter that much.

"What if I'd had an appointment or a meeting to go to? Fortunately, my calendar is free tomorrow, so I can pick you up from the airport in San Francisco."

"I won't be flying into San Francisco, Mother." Megan bit her bottom lip and forged on. "I'll be flying into the airport at Santa Rosa."

"In a regional jet?" Her mother had a fear of small air-craft, almost as strong as her fear of her daughter riding horses. "I wish you'd come in something much larger."

"I'm flying into Santa Rosa in a four-seater. We want to rent a car from there, so no need to meet us."

"A four-seater? Oh, baby, that's worse than I thought."

"I'll be fine. My pilot is exceptional."

"But it's such a long way from Oklahoma to California in something that small."

"I'm not flying directly from Oklahoma, Mother."

"You'll be stopping along the way?"

"Stopped. We flew into Las Vegas yesterday. We're flying out tomorrow. I'm not sure what time we'll be leaving, so don't wait at the airport for me. I'll call when we're on our way out to the Triple Diamond."

"Your father won't be happy to know you're flying in a death trap."

"It's not a death trap, Mother. I'll be safer than if I drove out to California."

"Oh, dear." Megan could picture the normally unflap-pable Josephine Talbot wringing her hands and clutch-ing the phone in a white-knuckle grip.

She hated worrying her mother, but she hated worse being smothered by her mother's fears for her. "Mother, my phone battery is about to die."

"Charge it. I'm sure your father will want to talk you out of flying tomorrow."

"It's not his decision. I have to go now. The battery light is blinking. Bye, Mother." She ended the call and turned off her telephone.

"Your parents?" Daniel asked from the doorway. He had a towel slung over his bare shoulders, and he wore a pair of clean blue jeans and nothing else.

Megan's breath caught in her throat, and her belly tightened. The man had no right to look that deliciously sexy. "Yes, that was my mother. She thinks flying in anything less than a 777 is a—how'd she put it?" Megan tapped a finger to her chin. "Ah, yes—death trap." She smiled up at him. "What do you say to that?"

"Sounds like she worries about her daughter." He raised the towel and rubbed it through his dark hair, standing it on end. Then he turned and strode back into the bathroom to deposit the towel. "The shower's all yours."

"Thanks." She gathered her shirt, shorts and panties. "The steak's on the way. I'd like to meet with the lawyer in Santa Rosa before we go to my parents' home. They live farther out." Megan turned her back to him. "Unzip, please."

"Are you always this demanding?"

"Don't worry. I won't demand you do anything you don't want to." She glanced over her shoulder, forcing an innocent look. "You do want to unzip my dress, don't you?" Megan fluttered her lashes for effect.

Daniel groaned. "Now who's being the tease?" He unzipped the dress and then slapped her bottom. "Go on. I'm not waiting for you if the food comes before you're out."

"I wouldn't expect you to." She marched into the bathroom and purposely left the door open as she pushed the dress off her shoulders, letting it float to the floor around her ankles. When she stepped out of her panties and straightened, naked, she cast a glance toward Daniel.

"Tease," he said.

"Peeping Tom." Megan winked and stepped into the shower, proud of herself for daring to flaunt her naked body. The cowboy had a huge complex about the difference between his background and hers, and she meant to pick that complex apart and get down to their similarities. She loved horses. Daniel loved horses. She loved seeing him naked. Apparently, Daniel wasn't immune to seeing her naked. Score one for the debutante.

Unfortunately, this battle had yet to be won. Tomorrow would be a huge skirmish with her parents. One she hoped they'd come out of unscathed and with her precious horses intact.

Daniel continued to stare at the closed shower curtain even after Megan disappeared behind it. He could imagine the water running over her pale skin, dripping off the tips of her breasts and down to that tuft of hair between her legs. He groaned.

Megan poked her head around the curtain, exposing a wet breast. "Did you say something?"

"No." Daniel choked on his response and turned away from the enticing view, his member hardening beneath the denim of his jeans. How was he supposed to keep his promise to himself and to her when she was so damned beautiful and sexy and, well, hell—Megan was everything a man could want in a woman. Soft skin. Silky, long, strawberry blond hair. A body a model would envy. And she was good with horses, wasn't afraid to get dirty and loved staring up at the stars at night.

He glanced out the window of the sitting room at the bright lights of the big city and wished he was back at the Lucky C Ranch in Oklahoma. Life was simpler there, and he didn't have to worry about cars running over him or his wife.

Wife.

He wasn't used to that word where Megan was concerned. But the more he said it, the better it sounded. And his grandmother's ring looked beautiful on her hand.

"It's gorgeous, isn't it?" Megan came to stand beside him, wearing a softly worn T-shirt and a pair of jersey knit shorts that hugged her buttocks and thighs like a second skin. Her hair hung halfway down her back in long, straight, damp tresses, a few strands curling as they dried.

Without makeup and dressed like a college student with bare feet and her bare breasts pressing against the cotton T-shirt, she was even more desirable than in the sheer teddy she'd worn the night before.

Who was he kidding? She could wear a paper sack and he'd be turned on.

A knock on the door forced him to focus on something other than the way her distended nipples formed tiny tents in the cotton shirt.

Daniel grabbed a five from his wallet and hurried to the door.

A man in a hotel uniform wheeled a cart in with two covered dishes, wineglasses and a shining bucket with a bottle of wine chilling in ice. Daniel tipped the man and held the door as he exited. He closed and locked the door, turning the dead bolt and sliding the chain in place.

Megan arranged the plate on the bistro table in the corner and smiled across at him. "Ready?"

He was ready for so much more than food, but he forced himself to take a seat across from her.

"Did you tell your parents why you were in Vegas?"

"My mother was more concerned about what I was flying in than why I was in Vegas. I guess it didn't occur to her I might be eloping. Now, if my father had been the one on the phone, that would have been his first question."

"Tell me about your father."

"My father is a taciturn man used to getting his way on the ranch and in the boardroom. He doesn't suffer fools well, and he can tell when someone is blowing smoke. So our stories have to match perfectly, or he'll figure it out."

"No pressure, right?" Daniel cut a slice of steak and popped it into his mouth, chewing on the food and the information Megan was feeding him. He swallowed. "Your father likes it best when you march to his beat, I take it."

"He does. I believe he thinks I'm an adolescent still in need of his protection. I'm surprised he didn't try to stop me when I moved to Oklahoma. He probably would have if I hadn't told him I was going out to visit an old college friend. I guess he couldn't conceive of the idea that I wouldn't come home." Megan glanced down at her plate, the food untouched. "I couldn't stay in California."

"Because of your father?"

"Mostly."

Daniel figured there was more to her story than her father's overbearing ways. When she was ready to tell him, he'd be there to listen.

They finished their meal in silence, sharing the bottle of wine. The alcohol took the edge off Daniel's desire and eased the tension between them. When they were done, they brushed their teeth at the double sink in the bathroom. For a moment, Daniel felt as though they were an old married couple, sharing the simple moments of married life. Megan finished before him and left the room.

When he was ready to call it a night, he walked into the bedroom, fully expecting to see Megan in the bed. It was empty.

He frowned and went to find her in the sitting room, curled up on the sofa, a pillow beneath her head and the comforter from the bed wrapped around her. She'd closed her eyes, but Daniel could tell she wasn't asleep.

"You can have the bed."

"I'm fine," she said and stuck one of her legs out from under the comforter, laying it on top. "Just a little hot."

Daniel stared at the long, slender leg as if willing her to cover it. Finally he stepped back and turned for the bedroom door, his rib hurting and a few other aches making themselves known from his tussle with the speeding car. "Good night."

"I hope you sleep well," she called out.

He could swear he heard a muffled chuckle, but when he turned back, she was lying still, her eyes closed. He must have been imagining the chuckle.

As he stretched out on the king-size bed, his arm fell over the empty space beside him, and he wished she was filling it. Daniel had to remind himself they were from two completely different worlds, and though she had assimilated well into his, he didn't belong in hers. The next day would prove that more than he cared to admit. Meeting her parents would help to keep him on track and focused on getting through this ordeal and back to his life at the Lucky C. There he and Megan would go back to being boss and employee, if she even wanted to return with him.

Daniel couldn't fall asleep knowing Megan was in the other room. Fear kept him awake—fear that he wouldn't hear if the door to the suite opened and the attackers returned. After fifteen minutes of straining his ears to hear every movement, he got up, marched into the sitting room and scooped Megan off the sofa.

"Hey," she cried. "What are you doing?"

"Getting a good-night's sleep." With her pressed against his body, he doubted that would happen, but he'd rest easier knowing he could protect her if she was in the same room as he was.

"What if I don't want to sleep with you?" She crossed her arms over her chest. "Put me down. I can walk."

He shook his head. "We're already halfway there," he said as he entered the bedroom and tossed her on the bed.

Megan landed with a grunt. "You don't have to be such a caveman," she groused, sliding over the mattress to the far side, away from Daniel. "I was perfectly fine in the other room." She pulled the sheet and blanket up over her arms and chest.

"Yeah, you might have been all right, but I wasn't." He lay down beside her and turned his back to her. "Just go to sleep, will you?"

"Sure." The bed moved, the blanket shifted and then her bottom bumped against his. "If that's what you want."

"It is." He swallowed hard to keep the groan rising in his throat from escaping. Sleep was the last thing on his mind. Making love to Megan was foremost in his thoughts and every nerve in his body.

A soft snort sounded from the other side of the bed. She knew.

Daniel gritted his teeth and forced his eyes closed. He'd keep his hands to himself if it killed him. And it likely would.

For a long time he lay there trying not to feel every

move Megan made. Making love to her in the first place had been a big mistake. Now that he knew what it was like to hold her in his arms and thrust deep inside her...

His member thickened, and he started all over trying to turn off that part of his body. It was a battle he was destined to lose. One he would stay awake into the small hours of the morning fighting.

The best he could do was think about his bruises and the pain they gave him, along with the terror of seeing that vehicle coming straight at Megan. For the entire day he'd been out with her, he'd sensed something wasn't right, as if someone was watching them. Every time he'd turned around, no one stood out.

As he finally drifted off to sleep, Daniel was assailed by a sense of impending doom. The same feeling he'd had the moment before the car's engine revved and the driver barreled toward him and Megan.

Chapter 11

Megan woke before Daniel and slipped into a designer dress she knew was one of her mother's favorites, hoping to soften the shock of her daughter's elopement.

Her mother would protest, but deep down, she cared about Megan. To a fault.

Frank Talbot was another matter altogether. He'd be furious and ready to call in the lawyers to annul their union. The man was a complete control freak. If the deed wasn't his idea, it wasn't worth the legal documents it was written on.

Megan had to convince him that her marriage was what she wanted and that she loved Daniel with all her heart. Hopefully her father would buy it and leave it at that.

Megan buckled the strap of her stilettos and stood, teetering. God, she hated heels. She preferred wearing her boots every day instead of the trappings of a debutante. When she'd left California, she'd vowed never to wear high heels again. And here she was, ready to break an ankle climbing in and out of an airplane in them.

She had to remind herself she was doing all of this for the horses. A thrill of excitement rippled through her at the thought of seeing her beautiful horses again.

"Do you want to eat breakfast before we go?" Daniel emerged from the bedroom, wearing blue jeans, a crisp white button-down shirt and a brown leather jacket. His dark hair hung longish, nearly to his shoulders, and one errant strand dipped down over his forehead, giving him a roguish flare.

Megan's heart fluttered over Daniel Colton. He was a beautiful man with his high cheekbones, rich complexion and eyes so dark a woman could fall into them and never want to come out.

His sooty brows sank. "Are you okay?"

Megan shook herself out of her lust-fest over the half-Cherokee man. It was *his* fault she couldn't concentrate. She was almost certain that if he'd given in and made love to her last night, she wouldn't have been so off-kilter now. Focusing on his words, she answered, "I'm fine. Why do you ask?"

"I also asked if you wanted to have breakfast before we left, or would you prefer to wait until we get to Santa Rosa?"

"I prefer to wait. My stomach is knotted."

Daniel held out his hand. "Everything is going to work according to plan."

She laid hers in his. "I hope so."

He squeezed gently and then released it. "Let's go. I can file our flight plan once I get to the airport."

"How long is the flight?" Megan asked.

"An hour and a half."

That would put them in around lunchtime. "I'll call the attorney's office and see if we can get in right away."

"Good." He reentered the bedroom and came back out carrying his bag and hers. "Did you sleep all right?"

She smiled brightly and lied, "I did, thank you. How about you? Did you sleep okay?"

"Yes." The dark shadows under his eyes and the firmness of his jaw told a different story. Megan had felt his every move through the night and had chosen to let him suffer as much as she did. She'd been sure to bump up against him on purpose so that he'd be reminded of what he was missing. She'd thought maybe, just maybe, he'd turn over, pull her into his arms and make love to her.

That hadn't happened, shaking Megan's belief that he was as aroused as she had been. But seeing how tired he was gave her a thrill she wouldn't admit to Daniel.

He'd have to get over his prejudice against her for her lineage. To her, its only advantage was to provide a little leverage in Daniel's negotiation with Kennedy Farms.

It had been a wake-up call to her, reminding her of why she didn't belong in the fast-moving, big-spending limelight of her family's wealth and notoriety. Had Chase lived and they had gone through with the wedding, their marriage wouldn't have lasted an entire year.

Chase Buchannan was charming and sexy. He lived life in the fast lane. Having grown up the son of a high-powered movie producer, he'd been everywhere and done everything, including drugs and racing. He loved his cars fast and his women faster. Why he'd asked Megan to marry him was a mystery to her.

She had accepted his proposal to shock her parents. Unfortunately, her desire to shock had backfired. Chase's connections met with her father's approval, if not her mother's. Megan had hoped Chase loved her for herself. Only later did she realize she'd desperately wanted to be loved to the point she would have married a man completely wrong for her. Chase was more in love with living on the edge than he ever was in love with her.

Megan gathered her purse and followed Daniel out of the hotel room, studying the man who'd offered to marry her to help her save the horses she loved so much.

If Daniel was as passionate about a woman as he was about his horses, he'd be a man who would love her completely and sacrifice everything to protect her and make her happy.

He worried that his heritage made him a bad match. In Megan's view, it made him even more appealing because he had to work hard to prove himself. The boys Megan grew up with tended to be lazy and took everything for granted, including their friends.

Daniel was as loyal to his friends as he was to his family. If only he could see that he was not inferior stock. His Cherokee blood made him even more appealing to Megan along with his lack of pedigree. He wouldn't always be targeted by the paparazzi, his life on display for everyone to see and criticize. Married to Daniel, Megan could live her life the way she wanted. The way she'd done for the past four months.

She loved it and had learned so much from Daniel about breeding horses and caring for the animals and people he loved.

Daniel hailed a cab that took them to the airport where the Colton plane was parked.

After a thorough preflight check, he filed his flight

plan, loaded their luggage and helped her up into the plane.

A short taxi on the runway and they were in the air, flying west to face her parents and the attorney with the real marriage certificate for their fake marriage.

Feeling a little let down by the entire affair, Megan sat silently for the majority of the ride, speaking only when she had a question about the plane's instruments. She enjoyed the scenery from the small windows, marveling at how close the plane flew to the mountaintops.

Daniel piloted the craft with skill and confidence. By the time they cleared the Sierra Nevada Mountains and descended into the Santa Rosa Airport, Megan had gone over every possible scenario that could happen when she introduced Daniel to her parents. Her nerves were stretched taut as the landing gear kissed the runway.

Daniel brought the plane to a halt at one of the general aviation hangars and shut down the engine. He turned to her and smiled. "You look like you're about to face the firing squad."

"I feel like I am."

He sighed and held out his hand. "It'll be all right. The marriage certificate is legal. We've consummated the marriage. Your parents can't undo what's been done."

Megan shook her head. "You don't know my father. He has the most expensive attorneys with the most clout on retainer. The man can do anything he wants to do."

"Except order you around. That's what I'm for." He winked at her and reached across to unbuckle her safety harness, his knuckles brushing against her belly, sending flickers of electricity shooting across her body. "Come on. We have an appointment with your grandmother's attorney. One step at a time will get you through this."

Megan held on to his hand when he would have pulled it free. "In case I haven't told you, thank you for doing this for me. You didn't have to marry me."

"Remember, I'm getting something out of this marriage, too. I should be thanking you."

"Don't thank me until you get Kennedy to agree to sell you the semen for your breeding program." She let him help her out of the plane and onto the ground, liking the feel of his hand on the small of her back as they caught a shuttle to the rental car companies.

A half hour later, they were driving away from the airport in a sleek black SUV.

Megan used her cell phone's GPS to get them to the office of her grandmother's attorney, Lloyd Young. A receptionist showed them into a conference room and offered them bottled water or coffee. When they declined, she left.

An older gentleman with graying temples strode into the room. Megan recognized him. He'd read her grandmother's will four years ago. He greeted her with a warm handshake. "Megan, it's good to see you." He held out his hand to Daniel.

"Mr. Young, this is Daniel Colton. My husband." Megan stumbled on the word. It was so new to her.

Daniel held out his hand and shook the lawyer's.

Mr. Young's brows rose. "This is a surprise." He grinned and glanced back at Megan. "Congratulations. When was the happy occasion?"

"Two days ago," Megan answered. She hooked her arm through Daniel's.

The attorney nodded. "I take it you didn't come to pay a social call."

"Not really," Megan admitted. "I've come to claim the trust fund my grandmother left me."

The attorney nodded. "Let me check the wording in the will. Seems to me the trust wasn't released until your thirtieth birthday or until you married, whichever came first."

Megan dug in her purse for the marriage certificate and handed it over to the lawyer. "Seems I met the marriage clause first."

Mr. Young took the certificate. "I'll have a copy made and return it to you. Please, make yourselves comfortable while I go over the will. My secretary will see to your needs."

"Thank you." As soon as the attorney left the conference room, Megan's shoulders sagged. "I hope this doesn't take too long. I'm sure it's been four years since Mr. Young looked at that will. I can't remember the exact wording. I know I had to be married. But I'm not sure there wasn't another stipulation associated with the trust."

"We'll know soon enough," Daniel said.

"Either way, we won't get the money today. It's probably tied up in a bank, and I'll have to sign for it."

"Once you have it, you'll be closer to purchasing your horses from your father."

Megan smiled. "I think you'll like them. They're good quality stock. Some of the best the Triple Diamond has to offer."

"I look forward to seeing them."

"If my father and mother let us." She faced a large painting of Northern California's craggy coastline, her stomach as churned up as the sea splashing against the rocky shore.

"You're a grown woman. Why would they keep you from them?"

"My mother still thinks I'm too fragile to be around such large animals. Even though that's all I've done since I moved to Oklahoma." Megan paced the length of the conference table and paused at the window, staring out at the bright blue sky. "I wish my parents didn't feel like they have to control me."

"No one can control you." Daniel stepped up behind her and rested his hands on her shoulders, the warmth and firmness helping to steady her nerves. "You're your own individual, with the right to make your own decisions."

She snorted. "Yeah, thus the reason I'm here."

Daniel's hands slid down to her hips and he pulled her back against him, his arms circling her waist. "We'll get through this. Your horses will not be sold."

"I hope you're right." She rested her hands over his and leaned against him. Though she valued her independence, she loved how protected she felt in Daniel's arms. Too bad it was all for show.

The sound of a man clearing his throat made her jump, and she spun out of Daniel's arms to face Mr. Young. Heat suffused her cheeks, and she pushed her hair back from her face.

"I hope I'm not intruding." The attorney smiled and waved toward the conference table. "I took a moment to read through the wording. It seems you will have access to some of your money immediately upon your marriage, and the rest of the trust fund will be transferred over in full upon the six-month anniversary of your wedding."

Megan's heart dipped into her belly. This part she hadn't remembered. If she couldn't get all the money, she might not be able to afford all seven horses. "How much will be released now?"

"One hundred thousand dollars." He pointed to the document.

Megan read it, her chest tightening when she got to the part about being married six months before the remainder of the funds would be released. She couldn't look up and face Daniel without revealing her tears.

A hand slid into her lap and squeezed her knee. Even with the disappointing news, he was there to reassure her that all would be well. More tears welled up in her eyes.

Mr. Young pushed a box of tissues under her nose.

"Thank you." Megan grabbed a tissue and pressed it to her face.

"Your grandmother loved you very much and wanted to protect you against fortune hunters." Mr. Young held up a hand. "Not that I think your new husband will take advantage of you."

Daniel's hand stilled on her knee. Megan slid hers over his. "My husband doesn't want my money."

Daniel pulled a sheet of paper out of his pocket and handed it to Mr. Young. "Although it hasn't been filed with the courts, I wrote out a prenuptial agreement and had it witnessed by one of the hotel staff in Vegas before our wedding."

Megan frowned. "When did you do that?"

"While you were getting dressed for the ceremony."

"You didn't have to do that."

"Yes. I did." He cupped her cheek. "I didn't want anyone, including you, to think that I wanted anything other than the pleasure of having you as my wife."

She gave him a watery smile and swallowed hard

to dislodge the lump in her throat. If only his words were true.

"If you don't mind, I'd like to make a copy of it for our records." Mr. Young took the paper from Daniel and stepped out of the office for a moment, leaving Megan alone with Daniel.

Still reeling from Daniel's words and the fact that she wouldn't have access to all the money in her grandmother's trust fund, Megan stared at the papers in front of her. "One hundred thousand dollars might not be enough to buy all of the horses if they go for auction to other breeders."

"If he plans to sell them to a glue factory, it will be more than enough."

Mr. Young returned, handed the prenuptial agreement to Daniel and turned to Megan. "It will take a couple days to get these documents through the system. Where will you be in the meantime?"

"If her parents will have us, we'll stay at the Triple Diamond Ranch."

"Good. I'll let you know when you can access the money."

Megan stood and held out her hand to the attorney. "My grandmother had a lot of faith in you. Thank you for taking care of her and her assets."

"She was a good woman, and she only wanted the best for you." Mr. Young held out his hand to Daniel. "Take care of her. Her family cares a great deal for her."

"I'll do my very best," Daniel answered, shaking the man's hand.

As Megan stepped out into the sunshine, she drew in a deep breath and let it out. "I'm sorry."

"For what?"

"I'd forgotten about the six-month stipulation. I didn't pay much attention at the reading four years ago."

"I'm sure you were still grieving for your grandmother."

Megan smiled. "She encouraged me to be the person I wanted to be. Not the person my parents thought I should be. It was because of her that I finally moved away from California."

"She sounds like a wonderful woman."

"Just so you know, I don't expect you to stay married to me for six months. If I can make the money last long enough to purchase my horses and move them somewhere safe, that will be enough for me."

"We'll worry about the six months later. Right now, let's concentrate on getting your horses from your father."

"Are you ready to meet my parents?" She glanced up at him, trying to read his face for any sign that he'd had enough of playing charades.

"I'm ready. I think the real question is, are you ready?" He held out his hand.

She laughed and took his. "As ready as I'll ever be. Let's go to the Triple Diamond Ranch."

Chapter 12

Daniel followed the GPS on his smartphone to the address Megan gave him. Forty-five minutes later, he pulled up to a large stone-and-iron gate with an arched sign over the top indicating the Triple Diamond Ranch.

In the seat beside him, Megan stiffened, her hands clenched in her lap. She gave him the code for the keypad without turning toward him.

After entering the code, Daniel waited as the gate swung open.

Megan leaned forward, her gaze sweeping the pastures to the left and right of the long drive. "I don't see any of the horses."

"Perhaps they have them in another pasture."

"Perhaps." She pulled her bottom lip between her teeth and continued to scan the fields between the stands of trees blocking visibility from the SUV's windows.

The drive curved and angled up an incline lined with tall trees. When they emerged from the forest, a huge, sprawling mansion spread out before them.

"Home, sweet home," Megan muttered, looking anything but excited about the prospect of visiting the beautiful house with the French-vanilla stucco, arched entrance and Roman columns. Surrounded by lush landscaping and bright blue skies, the home was something most people only dreamed of.

"It's beautiful."

"My mother had a hand in the design. They built it when I was a toddler."

Daniel mentally compared the mansion to the single-wide mobile home he and his mother lived in for the first ten years of his life. He had nothing in common with this lifestyle, which made anything permanent between him and Megan even more impossible.

"Did you call ahead to let your parents know what time to expect us?"

"No. They just know it's today. Maybe they will have a prior commitment and we can let ourselves in."

The front door opened, and a woman stepped through. She wore a tailored dress and high heels, and her red hair was twisted into an elegant knot at the back of her head.

She was followed by a man with a shock of neatly combed white hair and smoothly tanned skin.

"Your parents?" Daniel asked.

"That's them."

"You look a lot like your mother."

"I've been told that." Megan glanced around the circular drive. "You can leave the vehicle here. Someone will move it to the garage."

Daniel shifted the SUV into Park, climbed out of the

vehicle and rounded the hood to the other side. Thankfully Megan waited for him to open the door. He held out his arm and she accepted it, letting him help her out of the SUV.

She hooked her hand through his elbow and pasted a smile on her face.

Daniel could see the strain in her expression as she faced her parents.

"Megan." Her mother moved forward, her face wreathed in smiles. She engulfed her daughter in a fierce hug. "I'm so glad you decided to come home."

Her father stood on the top step, his brows angling downward in a V. He was a big man, but not quite as tall as Daniel. His face was lined with experience. Permanent creases were engraved in his brow, probably from years of frowning. Though tanned, his skin had a slightly gray tint to it, and the whites of his eyes were tinged yellow.

Megan hugged her mother and glanced up at her father. "Father."

He nodded. "I shouldn't have to threaten you to get you to return to where you belong."

Megan's frown equaled her father's. "I'm here for now. Can't you be happy?"

The man's scowl deepened. "Your mother has been beside herself."

"Oh, don't let him scare you, dear. I'm just happy you're here." Josephine Talbot clasped her daughter's hand and tugged her toward the house. "Come inside and get unpacked. You must be exhausted."

"No, Mother." Megan pulled her arm from her mother's grasp and leaned into Daniel. "This is Daniel Colton."

"Daniel Colton." Mrs. Talbot's brows wrinkled. "Megan's boss, right?"

"Yes, ma'am."

She pressed her hand to her chest. "How nice of you to see Megan safely home."

"Mother, he's not just my boss anymore." Megan's cheeks reddened.

Daniel felt sorry for her and stepped forward. "What she's trying to tell you is that Megan and I got married two days ago. We're husband and wife." He lifted Megan's hand and pressed a kiss to the backs of her knuckles.

"What the hell do you mean? Married?" Daniel's announcement made Frank Talbot leave his position towering over the rest of them and march down the stairs to confront Daniel and Megan. "Is this true?"

Megan nodded and held up her left hand with the simple ring Daniel had slid onto her finger. Standing in front of a multimillion-dollar mansion, Daniel figured the ring appeared cheap, despite how rich it was in memories and the love his grandmother had shared with his grandfather.

Mrs. Talbot's eyes widened. "You got married?"

Megan nodded. "We did."

"I had such plans for a beautiful wedding for you."

"A wedding with someone we knew," her father grumbled, glaring at Daniel. "Someone suitable."

Megan's back stiffened and she took a step, placing her body between her father and Daniel. "Daniel is more than suitable. He loves me, and I love him. That's all that matters."

"I'm sure he loves you, and every cent you stand to

inherit." Her father's face turned ruddy. "I won't stand for this."

Megan threw back her shoulders, her green eyes flashing. "You don't have to stand for it. It was my choice, and I chose Daniel. Besides, he doesn't want my money or yours."

Daniel chuckled at the fierceness of her defense. "Sweetheart, I can stand up for myself." He gripped her shoulders and moved her back to his side. Daniel stuck out his hand. "Mr. Talbot, I'm Daniel Colton, and I'm happy to make your acquaintance as the father of my bride. If we aren't welcome here, we will be on our way." He stood for a long moment, his hand held out, waiting.

"Frank," Mrs. Talbot said sharply.

Megan's father finally took Daniel's hand and squeezed it with a bone-crunching grip.

Daniel was used to sturdy handshakes, but Frank Talbot was making a point. Pasting a smile on his face, Daniel squeezed back.

Despite the man's recent sickness, he had a killer grip, and he was letting Daniel know he wasn't a wimp.

Though he could swear his bones were breaking, Daniel refused to be the first to release. He bit down on his tongue to keep from yelling out.

Josephine Talbot clucked her tongue. "Come, Megan. Let me help you carry our bags into the house, while those two strut." She rolled her eyes and stepped around her husband. "Men."

Megan cleared her throat. "Father, Daniel. Are you two going to let us carry our things into the house?"

Frank's gaze met Daniel's. "Of course not."

Daniel stared at the man a moment longer and then loosened his grip at the same time as Frank.

He wanted to shake the blood back into his fingers, but he didn't dare show a single sign of weakness in front of Megan's father. Instead, he used his left hand to click the release on the back of the vehicle and unloaded his and Megan's bags.

"You didn't bring much with you," Mrs. Talbot said.

"We're not staying long," Megan announced. "We only stopped by to check on how you and Father are doing. And we wanted to let you know of our marriage."

Her father crossed his arms over his chest. "I haven't approved this union."

"Father, I'm twenty-eight, I don't need your approval to marry whom I want."

Her father's chest puffed out. "As a Talbot, you have certain obligations."

"Well, I'm not a Talbot anymore, now, am I?" She pushed her shoulders back and lifted her chin. "My last name is Colton."

Her father opened his mouth and then snapped it shut, his lips thinning into a straight line. "We'll see."

"Father—" Megan said with a warning frown.

"Megan? Is that you?" a voice called out from the front door. A woman with light blond hair and blue eyes ran down the steps and hugged Megan. "I haven't seen you in forever." She hugged her again and stepped back to examine her. "You look good. Oklahoma sunshine must agree with you."

"Hey, Christine. I didn't know you were here." She looked to Daniel. "This is my cousin."

"Christine has been living at the Triple Diamond for the past month. She apparently cares what happens to us," Frank said.

Megan's green eyes flared. "I care about you, Father. I love you very much, but I won't let you live my life for me."

"Obviously. You moved to Oklahoma without so much as a goodbye, and now this." He waved his hand at Daniel.

"This is my husband. I would hope you'd treat him with some respect."

Daniel almost smiled at how natural the word *husband* rolled off Megan's lips, and he had the sudden urge to pull her into his arms and kiss her.

"Frank," Mrs. Talbot's entreaty pierced the anger in Frank's attack.

A muscle ticked in the older man's jaw. "My apologies."

"Husband?" Christine's eyes widened. "You got married?"

Megan nodded. "We did."

"Let me see the ring." Christine grabbed her hand and lifted it to the light. "Oh, the ring is so pretty and old-fashioned. I simply love it. Aren't you going to introduce me to your hunky husband?"

Megan turned to Daniel. "Daniel Colton, meet my cousin, Christine. She's my father's niece. Christine and I are the last of the Talbots, since our fathers only had one daughter each."

"Oh, don't be so stuffy. All this heritage stuff is silly, anyway." Christine held out her hand and Daniel took it.

"My thoughts exactly," Megan muttered.

"It's just like you to beat me to the draw." Christine laughed. "I thought for sure I'd be next to the altar and here you go and get married." Her cousin raised her left hand, flashing a large marquis diamond. "I'm engaged!"

Daniel's chest tightened at yet another reminder of the difference between his and Megan's worlds.

Megan's smile was tight, but she managed to say, "That's wonderful, Christine. Who is he?"

"Josh Townsend. He's a real estate agent in LA. You'll get to meet him. He'll be here late this afternoon."

"Let's go inside out of the hot sun," Mrs. Talbot said, ushering the group into the cool interior of the mansion.

He'd thought the outside of the house was ostentatious, but the inside outdid the exterior in luxury. White marble floors stretched across the immense foyer. Two carved staircases rose up on either side to the second floor with dark mahogany railings and richly carpeted steps.

The ceiling rose high overhead with bright skylights letting in ample sunlight.

"Where do you want us to put our things?" Megan asked her mother.

"Why, in your old room, of course." Mrs. Talbot waved to a servant. "Let Manny carry them up for you. I'll have our housekeeper, Maggie, bring tea into the sitting room."

"I'd like to wash my hands first," Megan said.

"Me, too." Daniel smiled at Mrs. Talbot. "Thank you."

"You can show Daniel to your room."

Frank Talbot growled beneath his breath.

Mrs. Talbot turned on her husband. "If you can't be nice, go fiddle with your horses or something. I want to spend time with my daughter, even if you don't." She softened her demand with, "But don't push yourself. You're still recovering."

"I'm perfectly fine," Frank insisted.

"For a man who had prostate surgery less than a month ago."

Frank Talbot left the house, grumbling, "Woman has no right to throw my illness around like a weapon."

Mrs. Talbot turned to Daniel and Megan. "Now, you two go on. I'll have something cold to drink waiting for you when you come down."

"If you don't mind, we've been cooped up for a long time in an airplane. After tea, we'd like to stretch our legs."

"Oh, by all means. We can catch up more at supper." Mrs. Talbot smiled. "You can walk in the garden if you like."

"Daniel and I would prefer to go down to the barn and see the horses," Megan said, her gaze following her father out the door. "That is, if they haven't been sold off yet."

Josephine Talbot shook her head. "Your father is all bark."

Megan's lips thinned. "I never know when he will actually bite."

Her mother touched her arm. "Darling, not as often as you think."

Megan turned to face her mother. "Are you saying he was bluffing about selling my horses?"

"Yes and no." Her mother sighed. "He is determined to sell them eventually, and I want him to."

"Mother!" Megan shook her head, her eyes filling with tears. "I love those horses."

"And your father loves you and me. He would do anything to have you closer." Mrs. Talbot touched her daughter's arm. "Please don't hate him."

Daniel's belly tightened. He could see the love and

concern in her mother's eyes. The woman was caught between two very independent and stubborn people and was trying to play mediator to keep her family together.

"Go upstairs and wash up. We'll talk in a few minutes." Mrs. Talbot laid a hand on Daniel's shoulder as he walked by. "I promise we're not always this difficult."

Daniel smiled at the woman, liking her in that instant. "I'll reserve judgment."

"That's all I ask." The older Talbot woman nodded and walked away.

Megan paused, halfway up the stairs, her gaze moved from her mother to Daniel. "Are you coming?"

"Just because we're married doesn't mean you get to boss me around." He took the stairs two at a time to catch up with her and patted her on the bottom.

"Hey." She slapped at his hand, her cheeks reddening. "That's mine."

"We're married now. What's mine is yours and what's yours is mine."

"You could have gone along with that rule last night," she muttered.

He grabbed her, cupped the back of her head and nibbled on her ear. "Hey, babe, it's all about the show." Oh, but his body wasn't getting the picture. Holding her this close, touching her bottom and kissing the side of her neck made him forget they were playing a game of charades. He wanted to take her the rest of the way up the stairs, find the nearest bedroom and make use of the bed.

But her mother was waiting, and her father was livid. This game wasn't going to be a dunk.

Megan's blood sizzled through her veins, her neck tingling with the touch of Daniel's lips. Once she had him in her room and shut the door behind her, she rounded on him, her hands on her hips. "This is not going to work."

"No? Your parents seem to think it's all real."

"I'm not talking about what my parents are thinking. I'm talking about you touching me, kissing me and patting my butt."

"Liked that added touch of reality?" He winked. "I thought you'd want me to show a little PDA in front of your family."

"PDA?"

"Public display of affection." He entered the bathroom and switched on the water faucet. "Most newlyweds can't keep their hands off each other. We're supposed to be madly in love, thus the quickie wedding in Vegas. That would be one of the two reasons for getting married so fast."

Megan leaned against the bathroom door frame. "And the other?"

"One of us being pregnant." Daniel leaned over the sink and splashed water in his face.

If Megan wasn't mistaken, Daniel was grinning beneath his hands. She grabbed a hand towel from the cabinet and slung it at him. "Well, we both know that isn't going to happen." Her eyes widened. "But my parents don't know that. Crap. Do you think they think we're…you know." The thought of carrying Daniel's baby warmed her insides at the same time it left an empty ache in her womb.

Daniel straightened, wiping his face with a towel. "I have no idea what your parents are thinking, other than my hand hurts and your dad hates me."

"He doesn't hate you. He hates the idea he's not the main man in my life anymore. Did he crush your hand?"

Megan shook her head. "He did that to every one of my dates. Scared them off."

"I can see why." Daniel shook his hand.

"How did you keep a straight face and not yell?"

Daniel twirled the towel and popped her with it. "I'm not a teenaged weakling. I work with my hands."

"Sorry. I have nightmares about my father's attitude toward the boys I met."

"You're twenty-eight. You can't tell me he chased away all of them."

"No." Megan didn't offer more. She didn't see a need in enlightening Daniel about her prior engagement. Instead, she raised her brows. "Are you done? Think I might have a chance at that sink?"

"All yours." He tossed the towel on the counter and stepped around her. The doorway was too tight for both of them to fit through at once.

Megan refused to give way. If he wanted by, he'd have to touch her, and to hell with his hands-off approach to their marriage.

Daniel turned sideways and started through the doorway. When his hip touched hers, she stared up into his eyes, challenging him. Yes, she wanted him, and she'd bet her best thong panties he could see it in her eyes.

Daniel paused, his hips pressed to hers. "You're playing with fire, woman."

"Yeah. Unfortunately, there's no one here willing to put out the flame."

For a moment, she thought he'd move past. But his hands shot out and grabbed her wrists, pinning them above her head. Her breath caught in her throat and her breasts jutted out, the nipples hardening against his chest.

"You're making this more difficult than it has to be," he grumbled.

"I know." She swiveled her hips, her pelvis rubbing over the hard evidence of his desire. "That was the idea."

"Damn, woman." He bent, his lips crashing down on hers, stealing her breath away.

His tongue lashed out, darted between her parted lips and claimed her mouth, her tongue and her soul.

She tugged against his hold on her wrists, wanting to wrap her arms around his neck.

Daniel held firm, refusing to release her.

The frustration of not being able to touch him made her even hotter and more desperate to be one with the man. When he finally allowed her to breathe again, she was on fire with a need only he could satisfy.

"Wash up, sweetheart. Your mother is waiting." He turned her toward the bathroom and swatted her behind.

Megan didn't protest. She couldn't. Her mind was in a lust-induced fog, too befuddled to let a coherent thought surface. She'd gotten what she wanted. A kiss to douse the flames. Only it had backfired and fanned the blaze instead, leaving her wanting more of the same.

Megan splashed water on her face and dried off with a towel, staring at herself in the mirror. Her lips were full and swollen from Daniel's kiss. What was she going to do? The more she was with him, the more deeply she fell in love with her husband.

How long would they have to keep up the pretense of a loving marriage? And when it was all over, how would she continue to work with the man knowing what it was like to be married to him?

Megan pulled her hair back, secured it in a loose, messy bun and shook her head. Her mother was a fastidious dresser. Every hair had to be in place and her makeup perfect before she left her room each day. Though her mother tried to instill the same sense of style and confidence in her looks, Megan always fell short, opting out of wearing makeup and refusing to go to great lengths to fix her hair. She could be seen with a ponytail and a clean face most often.

Daniel didn't seem to mind, and the horses didn't care. Why should she?

Megan smoothed the wrinkles out of her dress and left the bathroom.

Daniel held out his arm. "Ready?"

"As ready as I'll ever be." They descended the staircase and entered the sitting room in which her mother had entertained many of the social elite including several political figures and movie stars. The Talbots were as well-known in California as the Coltons were in Oklahoma.

Christine sat on the sofa beside Megan's mother, chattering away about a mutual acquaintance.

"Oh, there you are." Mrs. Talbot rose and waved a hand toward another sofa facing the one she and Christine sat on.

It didn't strike Megan as odd that Christine was so chummy with her mother. Close in age, Megan and Christine had spent quite a few summers together on the Triple Diamond Ranch. They both loved the horses, and they enjoyed the outdoors. Christine's father had taken her and her mother to New York City to live. Not until her mother died of cancer and her father in a car wreck four years ago had she returned to California for good.

Mrs. Talbot took her seat on the sofa and lifted a pitcher of lemonade. "I have hot tea, but I thought as warm as it is outside, you might prefer iced lemonade. And I had the cook make up a tray of sandwiches in case you two are hungry."

"Thank you, Mother. We didn't stop for lunch on the way over."

Daniel helped himself to a triangle of bread and deli meat. "Thank you for thinking of it."

Her mother's smile filled the room. "We're just happy you're finally here."

Megan bit into a sandwich and chewed. She wanted to get outside and check on her horses, but she didn't want her parents to think that was the only reason she'd come home. She didn't want her father to know how much his threat had shaken her.

"Christine was regaling me with stories of her life in LA," Mrs. Talbot said.

"How is your acting career taking off?" Megan asked politely.

Her cousin smiled. "I had a callback from a commercial audition last week. I'm waiting for my agent to contact me."

"Are you going to continue acting after you're married, dear?" Mrs. Talbot asked.

"Yes, of course." Christine glanced at Megan. "Josh is behind me."

"Will he have a decent job to support you while you're pursuing your career?" Megan's mother asked.

"He's in real estate. He's quite good at it. Right now he's on his way back from a convention in Nevada. He should be here for dinner, so you can meet him."

"That will be nice," Megan said, wishing her cousin wasn't there and feeling bad that she had such thoughts. What she wanted was time alone with her mother so she could question her about her father. Alas, Christine was there to stay and completely oblivious to a mother and daughter's need for a private conversation.

Daniel polished off another triangular sandwich and drank a glass of lemonade.

Megan picked at a sandwich and sipped at the lemonade, counting the minutes until she could politely escape.

"Mrs. Talbot, like Megan mentioned, we have been cooped up in a plane for the last few hours. Would you mind if we went outside to stretch our legs?" Daniel asked.

"But of course you should. You can stroll in the garden behind the house or see the horses."

"Megan tells me the Triple Diamond Ranch has some of the best quarter horses in the country," Daniel said.

Her mother shrugged. "That's Frank's pet project. I wish he'd just sell them and concentrate on staying well and healthy."

"Daniel is a horse breeder. He's working on his own breeding program in Oklahoma." Megan rose to her feet, glad of Daniel's segue into getting out of the house. "I'd like to show him the barn."

"Oh, darling, should you be out there? Those horses are so big and spirited."

"I'm a biologist. I work with animals." When Megan's mother wasn't swayed from her fears, Megan sighed and added, "Daniel will be there to protect me, Mother."

Something akin to a snort erupted from Daniel, and a smile tilted his lips upward on the corners.

Megan elbowed him in the side. "Besides, I want to check on Father."

Daniel wiped the smile off his face and offered, "I'll

keep your daughter from undue harm caused by the horses, Mrs. Talbot."

"It's just that Megan is our only daughter and, well, I don't want her to be harmed."

"Mother, I'll be fine with Daniel," Megan assured her mother again.

"Oh, let them go." Christine stood beside Mrs. Talbot and slipped an arm around her aunt. "They're newlyweds. They probably just want time alone together."

Megan gave Christine a smile. "That's right. We want some time alone. And I want to make sure Father is okay."

Megan led Daniel out through the back of the house. They skirted the glistening swimming pool and a pool house and followed a stone path through a rose garden before they emerged on a paved road leading to the stables.

"The last time I was here, my father had been in the hospital for prostate cancer. They think they got all of it, but he's been going through chemotherapy to kill any remaining cells," Megan said.

"I'm sure he's happy to have you here," Daniel said.

She smiled, her chest swelling for the handsome man beside her. He was the kind of man her father couldn't scare easily, and for that she was grateful. "I'm happy you're here with me." Her attention returned to the stable and the surrounding fields. "I don't see any of the horses."

"Don't borrow trouble. They're probably inside or out behind the stable."

"I hope so." She hated to think her father had made good on his threat and sold her horses. Then her marriage to Daniel might still help snag him a deal with the Kennedys, but on her end, it would have been for nothing.

The door to the stable stood wide-open, the interior dark compared with the bright sunshine outside.

Megan stepped through the door and inhaled the familiar scents of hay, horses and manure. A whinny sounded from one of the stalls and another answered, followed by several more.

Daniel leaned close to whisper in her ear, "Seems your horses are here and they remember you."

Joy filled Megan's heart and she ran to the first stall, long ago designated as Misty Rein's. The beautiful bay mare tossed her head above the gate and whinnied again.

Thank God. Her father hadn't sold her horses, yet.

Daniel followed Megan to the first stall and ran an appreciative gaze over the animal. She had good conformation, and from what he could see of her teeth and her coat, she was healthy and well taken care of.

His belly tightened at the smile spreading across Megan's face.

She ran her hand along the mare's nose and pressed her tear-stained cheek to the side of the animal's face. "They're still here."

"Of course, they're still here." Her father appeared out of the shadows. "They were my only bargaining chip to get you back to the Triple Diamond."

Megan turned toward her father, color rising in her cheeks. "You tricked me into coming back?"

"I had to do something. You broke your mother's heart when you left."

"I never wanted to hurt you two. I just couldn't live

the way you wanted me to. I'm happy in Oklahoma. Happier than I've ever been."

Frank Talbot's eyes narrowed. "Then I guess you didn't come home to stay."

"No. I came home to tell you of my marriage to Daniel." She slipped her arm around Daniel's waist and leaned into him.

Daniel liked the feel of her body next to his. The casual hug warmed his heart and heated other places inside. But mostly, it made him feel good, and he wanted that feeling to go on forever.

Mr. Talbot shook his head. "I wish you had told us before."

Megan tensed. "Before I got married? Why? So that you could talk me out of it?" She reached for her father's hands. "I love Daniel. He understands me, and we have the same dreams."

"And what are those?"

Daniel straightened at the man's challenge. "I'm building a horse-breeding program at the Lucky C Ranch."

"It's hard to make a living with horses."

"Daniel is doing great. His horses are receiving national attention."

Daniel squeezed her arm. "But you're right, sir."

Megan glanced toward him, her brows puckered.

"It is hard to make a living at breeding horses. But I have acquired some excellent stock, and I'm hoping to improve my herd by investing in semen from a national champion stud from Kennedy Farms."

Megan's father's brows rose briefly and then lowered. "You talk the talk, but Kennedy isn't an easy man to work with."

Daniel forced himself to relax. "I've noticed. But I'm working on him. I have a meeting scheduled with him at the Symposium on Equine Reproduction in Reno in a few days."

"He granted you a meeting?" Talbot shot a glance at his daughter. "Are you going?"

Megan nodded. "I am."

Her father scowled. "Your mother never wanted you working around the horses."

Megan gave him a soft smile. "You knew I was all along, didn't you?"

"Someone had to keep an eye on you. You had a mind of your own and a tree far too close to your bedroom window."

Her eyes widened. "You knew I was sneaking out?"

He nodded. "I'd have done it, too."

"Then why didn't you just give me permission to be around the horses?"

"Your mother never knew, and it was better that way." Her father reached out to run his hand along the mare's neck. "Your mother had three miscarriages before she was able to carry a baby almost to full term."

"And I was a preemie." Megan's face softened.

Her father's hand stilled on the horse. "She almost lost you, too. I have to tell you, I don't ever want to see your mother that sad ever again."

Megan's arm tightened around Daniel. "How awful to lose three children and almost the fourth. No wonder she's overprotective. I can't imagine losing even one child." Her eyes misted.

Daniel hugged her close.

"Well, now you know why I had to get you back. Your

mother was sad." Frank Talbot shook his head. "I will not allow her to be sad."

"But, Dad, I can't stay. My life is in Oklahoma."

"Now that she knows you are happily married, she might be okay with you living so far away." Mr. Talbot stared hard between Megan and Daniel. "You are happy, aren't you? This man didn't twist your arm to marry him, did he?"

Megan laughed. "Not at all. We're…" She ducked her head, her cheeks suffusing with color.

"I asked Megan to marry me because I couldn't imagine life without her. We love each other," Daniel finished, leaning down to kiss her temple.

For a long moment Mr. Talbot studied them, and then he nodded. "Okay. But please don't tell your mother you're working with the horses in Oklahoma. She'll be hard-pressed to come to grips with the fact that you're happily married. Sure as I breathe, she'll worry herself into an early grave if she thinks you're going back to work with the breeding program."

"But that's what I do," Megan protested. "There's a bigger chance of my dying in a car wreck than of being hurt by one of the horses at the Lucky C."

"You let me work it out with your mother. In the meantime, she wants me to sell all of the horses." He stroked the mare's neck.

Megan touched her father's arm. "But the horses were always your project."

"True. But the cancer has taken a lot out of me, and I can't give the animals as much of my time as I used to."

"I thought the doctor said he got all of the cancer."

"So far, that's what it looks like. But ten horses is a

lot to keep up with. I promised I'd sell seven of the ten, only keeping a few to ride for pleasure."

"And where will you sell the seven?" Megan's fingers dug into Daniel's shirt and all the way to his skin.

"I hand-selected all of my horses based on their pedigree. They are equal to the ones at Kennedy Farms. If you have need of more breeding stock in Oklahoma," her father said, "I'll give them to you for a wedding gift."

Daniel nodded. "From what I see of them, they would be an excellent addition to the ranch, either as breeders or as working stock."

Her father glanced at Megan. "Do you want the horses?"

"Yes!" Megan flung her arms around her father's neck. "Thank you, Dad."

Her father's cheeks reddened. "Well, I'd better get back to the house before your mother calls an ambulance."

"Thank you, sir." Daniel held out his hand to Mr. Talbot. "The horses mean a lot to your daughter."

"I wonder if they don't mean more than her family," Talbot groused. He took Daniel's hand and shook it without crushing it this time.

When he let go, Megan grabbed her father's hand and squeezed. "I'll always love you and Mother, but I'm all grown up and want to live my life my way."

Mr. Talbot drew in a deep breath and let it out. "It's hard to let go, not only for your mother but also for me."

"I know." She lifted his hand to her cheek. "You like to control everything around you."

Her father's shoulders sagged. "That has been the hardest thing to learn these past few months. Some things are out of my control."

Megan hugged her father again. "I love you."

He patted her back. "I love you, too. Now, don't be late for dinner. It makes your mother nuts."

Frank Talbot left the barn, and silence reigned for a couple of minutes following his departure. Megan turned to the mare and pressed her forehead to the horse's nose. "You're going to be okay."

Daniel touched her shoulder. "So are you."

She laughed. "I get to keep my horses."

"And you don't have to spend all of your grandmother's inheritance to get them."

"I can use that money to pay for their upkeep."

"You can stable them at the Lucky C."

"I'll pay you for boarding. And if you approve of their bloodlines, we could consider them in your breeding program. I know you are being very selective. I've seen the lineage charts on the horses you have. Mine could be of value to you."

"We'll look into it when we get back to Oklahoma. Hopefully your father won't be in a hurry to get them off his farm."

"I'll speak with him. Perhaps we can use his trailers to transport them." Megan turned to him and wrapped her arms around his waist, burying her face in his chest. "Thank you."

"For what?"

"For suggesting the marriage of convenience. My father would not have been so easily swayed had I come on my own or brought a man he couldn't see eye to eye with."

"Your parents only want you to be happy and cared for."

Megan nodded. "I knew I'd been born premature and spent a month in the hospital before my mother could take me home. But I didn't know she had miscarried three times before me. She must have been heartbroken each time and terrified when I came along." Megan glanced up at Daniel. "I can only imagine how devastating it would be to lose a child."

"You have to appreciate the people in your life while you have them. Tomorrow is never guaranteed." Daniel pressed a kiss to her forehead.

"You lost your mother when you were ten?"

He nodded, his memories going back to the single-wide mobile home he'd shared with his mother. "She did her best to give me a good life. I didn't realize until after she was gone that I had all I needed. I had her love."

"She must have been a wonderful mother." Megan cupped his face, her hand warm against his cheek. "What about Big J? Didn't he love you?"

"He took me in, despite his wife's objection. What man takes in his bastard son and gives him a home and his love? I never felt like his love for me was any less than his love for Abra's children."

"You were fortunate to have him as a father."

"Yes, I was." Abra had been the thorn in his side, never accepting him as one of the family. He fit in nicely with his siblings, but never with Abra. He couldn't blame her. He was the product of her husband's adultery.

"The proof of his love is that you turned out okay. From an orphan to a Colton, you've made a place for yourself at the Lucky C Ranch."

He shook his head. "The horse-breeding program has to prove itself as another way to make the ranch produce. If it doesn't work, I'll have to move out and find a job that will support me and any family that comes along."

"And you don't want to leave the Lucky C?"

He shook his head. "It's my home. The horses have been the one constant in my life. I love working with them."

The mare whinnied beside him as if to add her consensus. She nudged Daniel's shoulder, pushing the two of them off balance.

Megan laughed and held on to Daniel's arms. "Misty agrees. She's usually not so friendly to male strangers."

"Do I pass her test?"

Megan hooked her arm through his. "Yes. You passed her test and my father's. Now, we'd better get back to the house and dressed for dinner to pass my mother's test."

"Dressed for dinner?"

"She insists on formal attire for dinner."

"I should have packed my tux."

"Not that formal, but slacks and a blazer. Did you bring a blazer?" she asked. "If not, maybe one of my father's will fit you."

"Relax. I brought a jacket." He clasped her hand in his and led her out of the stable and back along the path to the house. "Your family has a beautiful ranch."

"You think so?"

"Yes."

"It's a lot different from the Lucky C." She pointed toward the vineyards and the pastures. "In California, most farms are a mix of cattle, vineyards and orchards, unlike the ranches of Oklahoma."

"I think it's important to diversify."

"Right." She grinned up at him. "Thus the horse-breeding program on a cattle ranch."

"Right." Daniel stopped to stare out over the vineyard-covered hillside. The setting sun bathed the hills of grapevines in a golden haze.

"You should talk with my father. He's the one who made this place a success."

"I will. Perhaps he has more ideas we can transfer to the Lucky C."

As they neared the house, Christine, wearing a long halter dress in a deep royal blue, rose from a chair beside the pool. "There you are. I'd like to introduce you to my fiancé, Josh."

A man stood from the chair beside her and extended his hand. "Megan, I've heard a lot about you from Christine and your parents."

"Nice to meet you." Megan shook the man's hand and turned to Daniel. "This is my...husband, Daniel."

Josh turned to Daniel. "Congratulations. You've married into a very special family." Josh curled an arm around Christine. "I look forward to the day Christine and I will be married."

"And when will that be?" Megan asked.

"Soon, I hope." He winked at Christine.

"I'm holding out for a big wedding," Christine said. "Not that eloping to Vegas hasn't crossed my mind. That sounds so romantic."

Josh's handshake was less than firm, and he let go quickly. Daniel had no desire for a repeat performance of Frank's bone-crushing grip, but he had a tendency to gauge a man's character by the way he shook hands.

"I understand you raise horses for a living," Josh said. "How's that working for you?"

Daniel tensed. "Yes, I raise horses." He wanted to tell Josh it was none of his business how it went for him. Instead, he answered with his own question. "What is it you do?"

"I'm into acquiring and selling real property."

"How's that going for you?"

Megan coughed into her hand.

Josh didn't take offense to Daniel's question. Quite the opposite. "I have a knack for finding treasures, tweaking them and reselling for a huge profit. I have a talent for seeing the potential."

"I suppose you could say that's what Daniel does, as well," Megan said. "He can spot an excellent prospect in a horse from a hundred yards away."

"Very interesting." Josh tilted his head. "I would think working with horses would not be very profitable."

Megan hooked Daniel's arm. "Some things aren't about the money but about the passion. Daniel and I love working with horses much more than with people."

"Horses can be very unpredictable and difficult to work with," Josh pointed out.

"With patience and understanding, you learn each animal." Megan's lips twisted. "People can be even more unpredictable than horses at times. And sometimes even less trustworthy."

"You have a point. But most people don't weigh a ton. Seems horses can be a lot more dangerous."

Megan's jaw tightened. "A person with a ton of metal around him can be a lot more dangerous than a horse, especially if that person has an addiction to speed and excitement."

Christine nodded. "Like your former fiancé?"

Megan nodded, her face pale, her lips firming.

Josh turned to Christine. "You mean Chase Buchannan? The Academy Award–winning actor who died in a car wreck a year ago?"

Christine touched his arm. "Yes. Megan was almost

killed in that same car accident." Megan's cousin grimaced. "I'm sorry about what happened to you and him."

Megan didn't respond, her body stiff, her green eyes dark.

Daniel hadn't heard this story from her, and it brought home to him just how much he didn't know about Megan Talbot. She'd been engaged to a movie star. His chest tightened.

"Ah, here you all are." Mrs. Talbot appeared in the back entrance to the house. She wore a long dress the color of champagne. Her hair swept up in a twist at the back of her head, the sides sleek. Her ears were adorned with long, shimmering diamond earrings. "Dinner is almost served."

The two couples followed Megan's mother into the house.

Once inside, Daniel turned to Megan's mother. "If you'll excuse us, we'll go change for dinner."

Mrs. Talbot smiled. "Certainly."

Megan took his hand, and they ascended the staircase together. Daniel knew she held his hand for show, but it was warm in his, and he squeezed it reassuringly.

Once in the bedroom, Megan opened a door leading into a huge walk-in closet. "I can dress in here and give you privacy." She handed his suit to him. "You might need this."

"How did it get in there?"

"The maid unpacked your case for you."

He wasn't sure he liked someone unpacking for him. It wasn't something a boy who grew up in a trailer park got used to. Even when he'd moved to the Coltons' main house, he'd insisted on hanging his own clothing and cleaning up after himself.

When Daniel reached for the suit, he caught a glimpse of the closet's interior. It was as big as his bedroom in the Coltons' house. An entire wall filled with dresses. "Holy smokes, you could open your own dress shop."

Megan grimaced, her cheeks reddening. "My mother insisted I have all the latest fashions. She was annoyed when I wore my jeans and boots every day. It's part of the reason she insisted on formal dining. Just to get me into a dress." She closed the door between them. "I'll be ready in a minute."

While she was in the closet, Daniel stripped out of his clothes and slipped into his suit trousers. "I didn't know you were engaged."

"It wasn't relevant when I applied for the job at the Lucky C," she answered through the wood-paneled door.

"What happened to make him wreck his car?"

"He liked going fast," Megan said.

Daniel stuck his arms into the button-up shirt and pulled it over his shoulders, vaguely noticing that the wrinkles had been ironed out of it and the suit. His thoughts were on the car wreck and the fact Megan had almost lost her life. "Why would he drive that fast with you in the vehicle with him?"

Megan opened the door to the closet and stepped out, wearing a long black dress that hugged all her curves like a second skin. "I think he was impressed with his Porsche, and he wanted me to be impressed with the car and his driving skills." She glanced to the side. "I just wanted him to stop and let me out." Megan snorted softly. "He did both by slamming into a telephone pole, which fortunately ejected me, throwing me clear of the vehicle. Unfortunately, it killed him instantly."

Daniel took her hands in his and held them while he

stared into her eyes, trying to read the emotion there. "I'm sorry for your loss."

"Yeah, well, it's been almost a year." She pulled her hands free of his. "Are you ready?"

Daniel shook his head. "I can see why your mother wanted you to wear dresses." He swept her from head to toe with his gaze. "You're absolutely stunning."

"Thank you." She dipped her head, color rising up her neck. "You don't have to compliment me when we're in the privacy of my room."

"Yes. I do." Daniel touched a finger to her chin and raised her face so that she was forced to look him in the eye. "You're a beautiful woman. And though I'm not a poet, beauty, whether it's scenery, a painting, a horse or a woman should be recognized. I'm recognizing you."

She stared up at him, her green eyes filling with tears. "That is perhaps the loveliest compliment I've ever received."

For a long moment he stood, enchanted by her shining eyes, her body, the dress—hell, everything about Megan. Then nothing could stop him from lowering his lips and claiming her lush mouth.

At first his kiss was gentle, a skimming of his lips over hers. Within a moment, desire overwhelmed him and his arm slipped around her, bringing her body flush against his. He crushed her mouth with his, his tongue caressing hers in a long, sensual glide.

She tasted so sweet, warm and wet. He could hold her forever and kiss her even longer and it wouldn't be enough. When at last he was forced to draw air into his lungs, he raised his head and pressed his forehead against hers. "We'd better go down before your mother comes up to find us."

"What mother?" She clutched his arms. "You're right. We should go down. My mother has been known to climb the stairs looking for me."

Daniel shrugged into his suit jacket, glad for the extra clothing to hide the evidence of the effect she had on him. The next day or two would be torture. He didn't know how he'd keep his hands off her, but he had to. If not for her protection, then for his. He suspected he was losing his heart to this amazing woman.

Megan hooked her arm through Daniel's and walked with him down the curved staircase, wishing they had insisted on staying in a hotel. Then at least they could claim they were still on their honeymoon and wanted their privacy. She'd lock the door and refuse to leave until he made mad, passionate love to her. Oh, hell, once would never be enough.

She was so totally in love with Daniel Colton, there was no going back. At the end of their agreement… She didn't want to think about the end when her emotions were tied up in him already. Megan vowed to take one day at a time. With Chase, she'd learned there might not be more days to follow.

"Oh, good." Her mother appeared in the foyer. "I was about to come up and find you. We're waiting on you two."

"Sorry to keep you, Mrs. Talbot." Daniel kissed Megan's temple. "Your daughter is so gorgeous, I can't seem to stop kissing her. And I can see where she gets her beauty." He lifted the older woman's hand and kissed her knuckles.

Megan's cheeks flamed and her heart warmed.

Her mother smiled at her. "He is a charming man, isn't he?"

"Yes, he is." Megan glanced up at Daniel.

He winked.

"Come into the dining room. I'm sure you're hungry." Her mother led the way into the formal dining room and indicated where they should be seated.

"Thank you, Josh and Christine, for helping to set the table and gather the dishes. I sent Maria home. She wasn't feeling well, and I didn't want her to work when she was sick."

"Anything you need. We appreciate that you're allowing us to stay here for the next few days." Josh laid a hand on Mrs. Talbot's arm. "Your hospitality always makes us feel comfortable and at home."

"It's the least I can do when you've come all the way out here to visit us. And I'm so happy you were able to be here when Megan brought her new husband home."

Daniel nodded. "Thank you for letting us stay, Mrs. Talbot. Especially on such short notice."

Frank appeared in the doorway, dressed in a tailored suit. "What are we waiting for? Let's eat."

Megan and Daniel sat across from Josh and Christine. Frank and Josephine sat at either end of the table.

A servant filled wineglasses around the table, while another placed small bowls of soup in front of each person.

Daniel sipped his soup and played the part of the doting newlywed. Soon the soup dishes were cleared and replaced with plates laden with shrimp scampi smothered in garlic sauce, lobster tails dripping with butter and lush green spears of asparagus.

"Your father has officially retired as CEO of Talbot

Enterprises," Megan's mother announced. "He will remain on the board of directors for at least a year until he decides what he wants to do with it after that."

Megan's gaze shot to her father. "I can't imagine you letting anyone else run the company you built from the ground up."

Her father nodded. "Neither could I until my health took a nosedive. I'd rather putter around on the Triple Diamond than spend every waking hour worrying about my business. Perhaps I'll sell it and be completely done with it."

Megan frowned. "I thought you had the cancer licked."

Her father nodded. "For now. But you never know. I didn't want to die with too many regrets."

Her mother sighed. "He's taking me on that trip to Europe I always wanted to go on."

"But you've been to Europe many times," Megan said.

"On business," Frank corrected her. "Your mother was always good to come along and keep me company."

"We never went to explore or enjoy the culture. I was left to wander around on my own. This time your father is going to take me. No phones. No laptops. No business associates. Just the two of us." She smiled at her husband. "Like the honeymoon we never had."

"How very sweet," Christine said. "A toast to the honeymooners." She lifted her glass.

Megan, Daniel and Josh lifted their glasses to her parents.

The look her parents exchanged was one Megan had seldom seen in all the time she'd lived under their roof. Love shone from their eyes, and it warmed Megan's heart.

"Well, I'm glad," Megan said. "I always thought you spent too much time at work."

Her father nodded. "I should have spent more time with you and your mother. I realize that now. I should have been there for your mother more than I was."

Her mother smiled. "We're going to make up for lost time."

"That's right." Her father clapped his hands together. "Don't be surprised if we spend all of your inheritance in the meantime." Then his brows dipped. "But don't worry. We'll keep the Triple Diamond, and it will be yours when your mother and I are gone. You can keep it or sell it. Now that you're married and living in Oklahoma, you might not want the responsibility of owning a ranch in California."

"I would rather you spent all the money you earned. It's yours and Mother's. I'll make my own."

Her father's chest puffed out. "That's my girl."

"And I'll just have to get used to the fact you're working with large animals." Her mother bit her lip. "But please be careful. You are our only child, and we want grandchildren. Lots of grandchildren."

Megan's cheeks heated. "Mother, we only just got married."

Frank nodded from Daniel to Megan. "Of course. But I hope you will at least consider having children."

"We wanted more." Her mother's eyes glazed with moisture. "We were lucky to have Megan. I always wanted grandchildren. Do you two plan on having children?"

Megan shrugged, her gaze going to Daniel. "We haven't thought past our wedding." She didn't even know if Daniel liked children.

"Do you like children, Daniel?" her father asked.

Megan cringed for the man. He'd volunteered to marry her to save her beloved horses. Now he was stuck in an interrogation about his views on children.

"I love children and hope to have half a dozen. You see, I grew up with my half brothers and half sister. I can't imagine my life without them now."

Her mother let out the breath she'd been holding in a nervous laugh. "Thank goodness." A smile spread across her face. "You two seem perfect for each other. Any child would be lucky to have you as parents."

Her heart ached at the joy in her mother's face. Guilt sat like a lead weight in the pit of Megan's belly. The lies they were telling her parents would eventually have to be unraveled into disappointment when she and Daniel announced their divorce. Those grandchildren they so desperately wanted would not happen with Daniel. And at the rate Megan was going with doomed relationships, they'd never have those grandchildren.

Perhaps she'd overreacted to her father's threat to sell her horses. Unfortunately the damage had been done, and now she had to continue the lie or further distress her parents. And with her father just pushing past the danger of cancer, the truth might set him back on his road to recovery.

"Do you two see yourselves moving to California to take over the Triple Diamond Ranch?" Josh asked and popped a bite of shrimp into his mouth.

"Not anytime soon." Megan looked from her mother to her father. "I'm learning so much at the Lucky C Ranch. As long as Daniel will let me, I plan on working with his horse-breeding program."

"Oh, darling." Her mother reached out to touch her

arm. "I hope you will reconsider when you become pregnant."

"Josephine, leave her alone. She's a smart woman, and I'm sure she wouldn't put a child of her own in harm's way."

Her mother nodded. "Of course."

Megan could sense her mother wanted to say more, but she didn't. After what her father had revealed in the barn that day, Megan could understand better her mother's overprotectiveness and desire to wrap her only daughter in a protective cocoon.

She wished she'd known this sooner. Knowing wouldn't have made her quit riding horses or sneaking out her window. But it might have made her less inclined to accept Chase's proposal to punish her parents for their stranglehold on her life.

Megan turned to her cousin, shifting the focus off her and Daniel. "So, when is the big day for the two of you?"

Christine blushed. "We haven't actually set a date. I'd like to be married at Christmas. I've always liked the idea of a snowy setting."

"Perhaps we'll be as spontaneous as you and Daniel and elope. Tahoe, perhaps?" Josh smiled at Christine. "A winter wedding at Tahoe." He reached for her hand and raised it to kiss her knuckles.

Christine's eyes glowed. "I'd love that."

"That would be nice," Megan's mother said. "I would have enjoyed throwing a huge wedding for Megan, but I shall be content as long as she promises me some grandchildren."

"Mother." Megan shook her head.

"I know. I know." Her mother grinned. "Shall we adjourn to the patio? I can have coffee served there. It's supposed to be a clear night."

Megan pushed to her feet. "That sounds great."

Josh stood. "If you don't mind, I have a few phone calls to make, and then I'll join you."

"Of course." Christine turned to follow Megan's parents out to the patio.

"I'd like to walk off some of that delicious dinner." Daniel held out his arm to Megan. "Care to join me?"

She took his arm. "The garden is pretty at night. Mother had a landscaper commissioned to design it with subtle lighting and smooth paths. I think you'll like it."

"I'm sure I will, as long as I'm with you."

"You two go on. We'll be here when you get back," her father said.

Megan couldn't get away fast enough, her guilt gnawing at her insides. As soon as they were out of earshot, she let go of a long sigh. "I'm sorry you got caught up in the inquisition." They passed through a beautiful rose garden, the roses illuminated by soft white lighting pointed up from the ground.

"What inquisition? Your parents are concerned about their only daughter and living vicariously through you. I think all parents live a little through their children. Even their grown children."

"Since when did you become a philosopher? I didn't even think you liked people. You are always so wrapped up in your horses, I rarely see you interact with other people besides your family."

He slipped his hand down her arm to clasp her fingers in his. "There is a lot you don't know about me, and vice versa."

"You're right." She leaned against his shoulder. "I'm

really sorry I got you into this mess. And now that I know why my parents are so overprotective, it makes me feel terrible about lying to them."

They arrived at an arched walkway covered in ivy vines, creating a tunnel through the darkness. Lighting at their feet guided them to the other side and out into the open.

"I know what you mean. The bottom line is that they love you and will do anything to protect you."

"To the point of driving me nuts." She shook her head. "And all it took was telling them I'm married now, and they're backing off. I'm convinced Dad would have sold the horses eventually if I hadn't taken action, though. With my father's health problems, he has had to reposition his life and his involvement in his various interests."

"He has it right. No one goes to his grave saying 'I wish I had spent more time in the office.' Your father might live five, ten, twenty years or more. But there are no guarantees."

"And he finally understands family is more important."

"So does this mean you'll be spending more time with your parents? Possibly moving back to California? Will I be losing my assistant?"

"No, I love Oklahoma. I'm going back. As for this marriage, since my father is giving me the horses, I don't have to stay to arrange for a buyer. I can work with my grandmother's attorney over the phone and fax. We can leave tomorrow."

"I thought you wanted to stay for your family."

"I only came to convince my mother and father that I'm not coming home to stay. I think they get the point."

"What's your hurry to leave?"

"I feel almost as heavily invested in the negotiations with Kennedy Farms as you are. I'd like to be prepared for the meeting with them in Reno, and I'm worried about Halo. She's one of your broodmares. What if the poison had an effect on her kidneys or liver?"

"My brothers are having the vet check her over while we're gone. However, I'd like to get back to find out what poisoned her. Or, God forbid, who."

Megan nodded. "Exactly. I can visit my parents again when we have everything settled."

"What about our marriage?" Daniel asked.

Megan's muscles clenched. "I still need my grand-mother's trust fund to support my horses without my father becoming suspicious. If all you're willing to do is the minimum until I get the initial release of funds, I won't hold you to the six months."

"I don't mind holding out for six months. It might get sticky with my family."

"Do we have to tell them?"

"If we want the Kennedys to buy into it, we have to get the Coltons to believe we really did it."

"It's not as if we didn't. We have a certificate to prove it."

"Exactly. But when it's all over, wouldn't you rather come back to California?" He waved his hand. "All of this will one day be yours—a beautiful house, a diversified ranch and servants to take care of you."

Megan shook her head. "My father built this. I want to make it on my own. And as long as my father and mother are here, they would constantly be questioning my involvement with the animals."

"I can see that would be hard to deal with. But it's an easier life than the one you have in Oklahoma."

"I don't want easy. I would be bored and get lazy."

Daniel snorted. "I can't imagine you lazy."

A smile quirked at the corners of her mouth. "If I didn't know better, I'd think you were trying to talk me into staying here. Don't you like me as your assistant?"

He chuckled, the sound warming her heart. "You're the best assistant I've ever had."

She backhanded him gently in the chest, loving how they could tease each other so easily. "I'm the *only* assistant you've ever had. Besides, I love working at the Lucky C with the horses."

"Just the horses?" Daniel stopped and turned her to face him. "What about me?"

Megan's heart lurched, and her breath caught in her throat. "Of course. I love working for you. You've been patient teaching me what you know about breeding horses for their best qualities. You've taught me all the hands-on kinds of things they don't teach in the university labs."

Facing Daniel, Megan couldn't stop talking. Her stomach bunched and her breathing became labored as she stood so close to him without touching him. With moonlight reflecting the darkness of his eyes, a soft breeze blowing through the leaves and the scent of roses in the air, the setting was ripe for love, if only he was so inclined. "It's a lot different working with microscopes and lab rats than with live animals the size of horses," she said, her voice fading, her need to kiss him finally stalling the words.

He pressed a finger to her lips. "Sometimes you talk too much."

"I do. Especially when I'm nervous."

"Why are you nervous?"

"Because I want to kiss you, and I don't know if you want to kiss me back." She swallowed hard and rushed on. "But I've learned that sometimes you have to take matters in your own hands." She leaned up on her toes and cupped her hand around the back of his neck. "I'm taking matters into my own hands."

"I like a woman who knows what she wants."

As she closed the distance between their lips, his arms wrapped around her, pulling her body flush against his, the evidence of his desire nudging her belly.

And she kissed him, her mouth covering his, her tongue tracing the seam of his lips until he opened to let her in. He tasted of garlic and wine, a heady and delicious combination.

For a long time, Megan stood, locked in Daniel's embrace, wishing she could stay there forever.

A rasping sound broke through the cocoon of passion. She jerked back and glanced around. "Did you hear that?"

"I did," Daniel said.

"It sounded like someone skidding in gravel." Megan called out, "Hello?"

The only sound in response was the thump of her pulse against her eardrums.

Daniel stepped away, his arms falling to his sides. "We should head back."

Kicking herself for being so jumpy, Megan fell in step beside him on the way back through the garden, keeping a lookout for movement. The hair on the back of her neck prickled and stood. She could swear someone was watching her. But every time she shot a glance over her shoulder, all she saw were the lights from the garden and the shadowy images of ornamental trees, bushes and flowers.

As they walked, she convinced herself her guilt was making her paranoid. She'd rather leave the next day than continue to live the lie in front of her parents, afraid she'd reveal something that would expose her and Daniel. Then all the effort they'd gone to for their marriage of convenience would be for nothing. Her father would retract his offer of giving her the horses, and her mother's disappointment at not getting the grandbabies she so desperately wanted would make Megan feel like a complete and utter heel.

"Yes, we should head out tomorrow," she said as they stepped onto the pebbled concrete patio surrounding the pool.

"How was the garden?" her mother asked, smiling at Megan and Daniel as they closed the distance.

"Lovely as ever," Megan responded. "Mother, Father, would you two be terribly disappointed if we left tomorrow?"

Her mother sat forward. "What? So soon?" She turned to her husband. "Did your father say something to make you angry?"

Megan laughed. "No, of course not. It's just that we have a commitment for a symposium in Reno in four days, and we haven't even told Daniel's family of our marriage."

Daniel picked it up from there. "We'd like to go back to Oklahoma and break the happy news. Trust me, they will be excited to welcome Megan into the Colton family. They already love her. And then we will have time to get ready for the symposium."

Her mother wilted. "Oh, well, then, I suppose you

should. But I'd hoped you'd stay longer. The last time you were here, we spent so much of our visit in the hospital with your father."

"Which you didn't have to do," her father grumbled. "But I was glad to see you."

"I promise to bring her back soon, and it's easy enough in our ranch airplane."

"Oh, dear." Her mother's hand fluttered to her chest. "I'd forgotten that you'd come in such a small plane. Are you sure you'll be okay flying back? Shouldn't you book flights on a commercial airliner?"

"Mother, I'm more likely to die in a car crash, as I almost did, than in an airplane crash. Daniel is an excellent pilot."

"Well, then." Mrs. Talbot sighed. "At least have breakfast with the family in the morning before you leave."

"Please do. We'd like to visit one more time," Christine entreated her. "We're rarely in the same place at the same time."

Megan looked to Daniel. "Do we have to leave early?"

"No, as long as we leave by noon. I'd like to clear the mountains in daylight."

"Okay, then. We'll leave after breakfast." Megan pretended to yawn. "If you don't mind, though, I'm tired from all the excitement, and I'm sure Father needs his beauty rest."

"Hey, don't count me off as old and decrepit. I was just temporarily incapacitated."

Megan leaned over and kissed her father's cheek. "I'm glad you're feeling better." She crossed to her mother and kissed her, too. "Good night."

Once she and Daniel left the patio, her heartbeat kicked up a notch. By the time they reached her room, her imagination had her clothes off and Daniel's, too, and she could almost feel his naked skin against hers.

"You can have the first shower," he told her.

She almost asked if he'd like to join her. She might have been forward enough to initiate the kiss in the garden, but hadn't he kissed her back? Though she'd been the instigator for a kiss, she didn't quite have the nerve to initiate making love in the shower. And since he offered to let her go first, she could only hope he'd join her. She left the door to the bathroom open slightly, giving him the option.

After fifteen minutes languishing under the hot water, she got out, dried off and realized he wasn't that into her.

When she left the bathroom, Daniel wasn't anywhere to be seen.

Wearing her T-shirt and jogging shorts, she crawled into her bed and pulled the sheet up over her. Half an hour later, she gave up trying to stay awake and let her eyes drift closed. He wasn't coming to bed with her.

If they stayed married for six months like this, it would be the longest six months of her life.

Chapter 13

Daniel walked around the grounds until well past midnight, afraid to go back to the room until Megan was soundly asleep. After seeing all she had at the Triple Diamond, he was certain that when she got tired of paying her own way, she'd want to go back to the life of luxury any woman would be happy to live in.

And he couldn't give her that life. Yes, his father would deed him a parcel of land to build a house on. He might even help him pay for a house, but Daniel refused to take any more than what he considered compensation for the work he did on the ranch. Living in the two-bedroom guest cottage was part of what he considered his compensation, and it kept him close to the breeding barn where he concentrated his efforts.

When he finally went back to the bedroom he was sharing with Megan, she was asleep, as he'd hoped. He lay on a chaise longue, his legs and feet dangling off the end. Sleep didn't come to him until somewhere around two-thirty in the morning. He'd have gotten no sleep whatsoever if he'd attempted to lie in the same bed with his new wife. Not after that kiss. His body was wound tighter than a rattlesnake with a new button. Sleep was out of the question.

By the time Megan woke at seven, Daniel was already up, showered, shaved and ready to go.

Megan sat up in the sheets. "Did you even come to bed last night? I wouldn't have bit you if you shared the bed with me."

"I managed on the longue."

Megan's mouth pressed into a thin line as she threw aside the sheets and rose. "I'll only be a few minutes." Her long legs seemed even longer when she wore such short shorts and the baggy T-shirt that did little to hide her sexy form. With her strawberry blond hair rumpled and her face soft from sleep, she was so adorable. More than ever, Daniel wanted to kiss her, take her back to bed and make love to her.

Grabbing her clothes, Megan disappeared into the bathroom and closed the door with a firm click. As promised, she emerged a few minutes later, her face clean and fresh, her hair pulled back into a ponytail. She wore a flowing peach-colored dress that barely came down to the middle of her thighs.

The only thought Daniel could muster in his sleep-deprived brain was how good it would feel to have those long, slender legs wrapped around his waist as he drove into her.

"Ready?" Megan stood in front of him, her brows cocked, a slight smile on her lips.

Daniel sucked in a deep breath and let it out slowly, forcing back his body's natural urge to take her into his arms. He had to remind himself over and over again that this was a marriage of convenience, not a real marriage. Megan was in a class far above his, and he didn't belong in her world. Though the argument had seemed valid only yesterday, it was fading by the minute. "Ready."

She slipped her bare feet into a pair of high-heeled sandals and straightened. "Breakfast and we're out of here."

Daniel nodded and opened the door for her to step into the hallway.

Christine stood in front of the door, her hand raised to knock. "Oh, good. I was just about to tell you breakfast is served."

Daniel followed Megan, carrying their cases down the stairs. He set them in the hallway by the front door and then entered the formal dining room, where the table had been set with fine porcelain plates, large covered platters and crystal glasses filled with orange juice.

Mr. and Mrs. Talbot stood by their seats and waited for the three of them to join them. As she had the night before, Mrs. Talbot directed Megan and Daniel to the seats they'd been assigned the night before.

"Josh sent his apologies," Christine said. "He ate a quick breakfast a few minutes ago and left for an appointment with a title company in Santa Rosa. He would have loved to have been here to see you off. However, he has a business to run."

"He made his apologies to me in person," Mrs. Talbot said. "I was sure he had an ample breakfast to see him through the day."

As they took their seats, a maid stepped forward,

lifted the covers off the platters and helped serve fluffy scrambled eggs, pancakes and toast. Breakfast proceeded in relative silence.

As they finished, Mr. Talbot offered, "I will arrange for the horses to be delivered to the Lucky C Ranch within a couple weeks."

"Thank you, Father." Megan drank the last of her orange juice and pushed back from the table. "Daniel and I have so much to do back at the Lucky C in preparation for our important meeting with Kennedy Farms."

Her father's brows rose. "I know Marshall Kennedy. I could make a discreet call to him if you'd like."

Megan smiled. "Would you, Father?"

"I'll make that call this afternoon."

Daniel held out his hand. "We appreciate your help. Thank you and Mrs. Talbot for your hospitality. Perhaps next time we come to visit, we can stay longer."

"Good. This was such a short visit, I didn't really get to know you." Mrs. Talbot bypassed his extended hand and hugged him. "Although I should be angry at you for keeping Megan in Oklahoma, welcome to the family. Please take good care of our baby. We love her so very much."

"As soon as we get settled, we'll invite you out for a visit," Daniel said.

Megan gave him an almost imperceptible frown and then smiled up at him. "We should be going. I don't know how you feel, but I don't like flying in the dark."

Mr. Talbot chuckled. "Our Megan can be a bit demanding when she wants to be, but she has a heart of gold."

"I've noticed." Daniel slipped his arm around her waist and pulled Megan to him. "If you want to make it over the mountains before dark, we have to hurry to turn in the rental car and arrange for fuel."

"Mother, Father, I love you. Please take care of each other. I'll see you soon." Megan hugged her parents.

Her mother's eyes glazed. "Don't stay away so long, dear."

Mr. Talbot pulled Megan into a big bear hug. "I'm sorry I had to threaten you to get you to come home. Had we known you were engaged, we wouldn't have been so insistent."

Her mother hugged her again. "I worry about you so much. But now—" she waved a hand "—now you have a husband to protect you and love you. I suppose I'll get used to it. But it will be hard."

"You don't have to worry," Daniel said. "I'll make sure she's okay."

"And just so you know," Megan said, "Daniel isn't replacing you two."

"We understand. He's an addition to our little family." Her mother reached out to squeeze Daniel's hand. "We have someone else to love. And if Megan loves him, we will love him, as well."

Daniel's stomach knotted around the scrambled eggs. He had been prepared to dislike the Talbots based on Mr. Talbot's threat to sell Megan's horses. The man had never intended to sell them so soon. He'd just wanted Megan back home. Understanding why Mrs. Talbot smothered Megan brought their actions into perspective.

Mr. Talbot crossed his arms. "Megan wouldn't marry someone she didn't love completely." Though he was talking about his daughter, his stare pinned Daniel.

"I'm honored by her love and will do my best to make her happy." Daniel dropped a kiss on Megan's forehead, lingering for a moment, inhaling the scent of her hair and loving the warmth of her skin. He could get used to the feel of her against him.

Megan rested her hand against his chest, her fingers curling into his shirt. "I know you'll make me happy," she said, her gaze rising to lock with his.

Christine hugged Megan and shook hands with Daniel. "It was nice to meet you. I wish you both the best."

Mr. Talbot held out his hand, and Daniel grabbed it. "We look forward to coming out to Oklahoma to visit. Once you get past the honeymoon, let us know."

"I will," Daniel promised, the lie sticking like a sock in his craw.

As he left the house, one of the Talbots' servants appeared behind the wheel of the rental car they'd picked up at the airport in Santa Rosa.

Once Daniel and Megan were driving through the gates of the Triple Diamond Ranch, he let go of the breath he'd been holding.

"Just so you know, I like your parents. And I didn't like lying to them."

Megan stared out the window, her hands twisting the hem of her dress. "I never knew my mother had trouble with her pregnancies. Had she told me, I might have better understood why she was so clingy and why she didn't want me to do anything dangerous."

"You're her only child. Her baby forever."

Megan's lips twisted. "I'm with you. I hated lying to my parents. If I'd known my father was bluffing about selling the horses, none of this charade would have been necessary."

"You heard him, though. He's downsizing his herd."

"I bet if I'd just talked to him about the horses, he'd

have come around." Megan cast an apologetic look Daniel's way. "I'm sorry I got you into this."

"You still need the money from your grandmother's estate to support the horses, so this marriage was not a total waste of time." If he was honest with himself, he liked having her as his bride, and he wished it would last longer than it took for the paperwork on her grandmother's estate to be finalized. But when Megan got tired of working for a living, surely she'd want to go back to California and live in comfort.

"Again, we don't have to stay married for the full six months. I can keep the horses a long time on the initial installment of my grandmother's money. I'll figure out how to support them when that money dries up."

"I don't mind committing to the six months. It's not like I've been dating anyone else, and I'd hate to lose my assistant because she had to find a better paying job to support her horses." He winked at her.

She smiled at him, her face solemn but happier than he'd seen it in days. "Thank you for all you've done for me."

Daniel didn't feel like he'd done all that much. In fact, the trip would prove to be more beneficial to him if Mr. Talbot actually made that call and the association with Megan Talbot set him up for a successful business deal with Kennedy Farms.

Once he and Megan had what they wanted, they could annul their wedding or get a quickie divorce and go their separate ways.

The thought of walking away from Megan and their marriage of convenience left a weighted, sour feeling in his gut.

* * *

Soon Megan was settled in the plane beside Daniel, and they took off from the Santa Rosa airport into cloudy skies, headed back to Oklahoma. Though the takeoff was smooth, the weightlessness of flying in a small aircraft unsettled her stomach more this time than when they'd left Vegas and Oklahoma.

She leaned back, adjusting the headset over her ears. "Let me know if I can help you out with anything. Otherwise, I'm going to sleep."

"Sleep," Daniel said, the electronic voice crackling in her ear reassuringly. "It's a long flight in a small plane. You might as well get as comfortable as you can."

Megan closed her eyes and leaned her head against the window, suddenly tired and achy. Hoping she'd feel better after a little rest, she willed herself to sleep.

"Megan, wake up. Megan!" Static rattled in Megan's ears, and she jerked awake.

"Daniel?" she said, her voice hoarse, something warm dripping from her nose. She raised her hand, embarrassed, and brushed away thick liquid. When she stared down at her finger, it had a long streak of blood.

"Sweetheart, are you okay? You were moaning in your sleep." Daniel glanced over at her, his eyes widening. "You have a nosebleed." His brows sank into a V. "There's a tissue in the box behind my seat."

Megan leaned forward and coughed, her breathing a little labored. She figured it was the altitude. "How far are we from home?" she asked, pressing her fingers to her pounding temples.

"An hour. You've been asleep for a while I didn't want to wake you, but you were moaning as if in pain."

He shot another glance her way, a worried frown settling on his forehead. "Are you okay? Your face is pale."

"I don't feel so great," she admitted, fumbling for the tissue box, her arms weak and her fingers numb. When she finally managed to grab a tissue, lifting it to her bleeding nose seemed to take all her energy. "I don't usually get nosebleeds from flying."

"I'm going to make an emergency landing." Daniel glanced at the GPS device on the instrument panel. "We should get you to a doctor."

"How far are we from Tulsa?" she asked, leaning her head back to stop the flow of blood. The movement made her head spin and her vision blur.

"Not too far."

"I can make it," she said. "Please. Don't stop until we get home." Her stomach roiled and her belly cramped. She drew her feet up in the seat and hugged her arms around her knees, willing the cramps to go away.

"Babe, you're not well. I can divert to Oklahoma City."

"No," she moaned. "Just get us to Tulsa. Please." She coughed, the muscles in her belly clenched and she nearly passed out from the pain. Damn it, she didn't want to stop until they got all the way back to Tulsa.

"Are you sure?"

"I think I'll be okay once we land. I just want to go home," she said, her voice fading out, the effort to talk almost too much. She wished she could click her heels and get home in the blink of an eye.

Daniel pushed the little Mooney as fast as its single engine would take it, but no amount of wishing would make the trip pass any quicker.

Thankfully the flight over the mountains had passed without a storm or any major downdrafts. At first the silence had been welcome, giving him time to think through everything that had happened. Megan slept soundly beside him.

Then Megan became ill, and the last hour in the flight was the longest. Several times her face creased in pain, and she bunched into a tight ball, groaning.

Twice he almost set down. If there had been a decent airport with access to a hospital, he would have. When he came close enough to tune in to the air traffic controller at the Tulsa International Airport, he called for an emergency landing for medical reasons. He asked that an ambulance be waiting on the tarmac.

Fifteen minutes away from the airport, Megan sagged in her seat, her face slack. Her arms around her legs loosened, and her feet fell to the floor of the aircraft.

"Megan!" Daniel called out.

She didn't respond.

He stared at her chest, watching for the rise and fall of steady breathing. For a moment, his heart stopped. Daniel reached out to touch her cheek. It was cool and clammy, and her nose continued to bleed. When her chest rose and fell on a long breath, he nearly cried in relief. "Hang in there, sweetheart. We're almost there."

The air traffic controller gave him clearance. Daniel hit the switch for the landing gear. Nothing happened. His pulse kicked up a notch, but he focused on the training he'd received on this particular plane. He reached for the backup landing gear lever and pulled. The cord should have engaged and let the landing gear down. Instead, the handle and the cord came up in his hand. He pulled the cord again, hoping to engage. The end flew up in his face. It had been severed cleanly.

Daniel had no way of lowering the landing gear. "Mayday, Mayday, Mayday," he said into the radio. He reported the problem and was instructed to perform an emergency landing.

Daniel circled around and came in low and slow. If he tilted even at the slightest angle, he risked touching the tarmac with a wing. If that happened, the plane would cartwheel out of control and disintegrate, killing Megan and him.

Steeling himself for the landing, he gripped the yoke and steadied the wings. The tarmac seemed to rush up at him even as he slowed.

The belly of the craft touched the tarmac, metal scraping concrete in a piercing screech.

Once the plane hit the ground, there was nothing Daniel could do but pray they would come to a smooth halt before the plane shook apart.

Sliding down the runway, the plane eventually slowed to a halt.

Sirens screamed around him. A fire engine pulled up beside them, and an ambulance stopped close by.

Daniel peeled his fingers off the yoke, unclipped his safety straps and bent over Megan to unclip hers.

She moaned and stirred but didn't wake.

Daniel was thankful they'd burned up most of the fuel in flight but didn't trust that the plane wouldn't burst into flame after the crash landing. He opened the door to the plane, gathered Megan in his arms and handed her out to the waiting emergency crew.

They loaded her onto a waiting stretcher and hurried away from the craft. Daniel insisted on going with them.

Since he wasn't injured, he was forced to remain behind to answer questions from airport officials.

"Daniel," a voice called out in the confusion.

He turned to face his half brother Ryan wearing his Tulsa PD uniform. "Oh, thank God you're here. Help me get out of here and find Megan."

"I heard over the scanner your plane had crashed and one passenger was taken to the hospital." Ryan asked, "Was Megan injured?"

"Not in the landing. She got sick on the flight over from California. She said she could make it to Tulsa." Daniel shook his head. "I should have insisted on stopping. By the time we were in range of the airport, she'd passed out."

"From what?"

"I don't know." The longer he was away from her, the more worried he became. "I need to go to the hospital."

"Come on. I'll get you through."

Ryan found the airport security guard in charge and cleared Daniel to leave. He led him toward the exit, where his patrol car waited at the curb.

"Sorry, but you'll have to sit in the back. With all the computer equipment we have now, there's no room for a passenger."

"I don't care as long as we get to Megan."

Ryan opened the door for Daniel and closed it once he got in. Then he slid behind the steering wheel and switched on the siren and lights. He radioed to dispatch to find the hospital where Megan was taken. With the correct location, he sped across town.

In minutes they were pulling into the emergency entrance of the hospital.

Ryan had to open the door for Daniel. Once he did,

Daniel erupted from the backseat of the vehicle and raced inside, Ryan on his heels.

"Where did they take Megan?" he demanded of the receptionist.

"Megan who?" She stared down at the computer screen in front of her, her fingers poised over the keyboard.

"Megan Talbot," Ryan responded.

"Are you a relation to the patient?" the young woman asked.

"No, she works for our family," Ryan responded.

Daniel touched his brother's arm. "She's more than that," he said. "Megan's my wife. We were married three days ago in Vegas."

Chapter 14

Daniel paced in the emergency room lobby, waiting for a doctor, anyone, to come out and tell him what was going on with Megan. So far, even after telling them that he was her husband, they wouldn't let him into the room with her.

Ryan stood by, shaking his head. "Married? Why didn't you tell any of us that you were headed to Vegas to get married?"

Daniel shrugged and passed Ryan on another lap across the lobby. "We didn't want a lot of fanfare. We had a simple wedding, just the two of us." *And Elvis.*

Ryan grinned as he keyed a text message into his smartphone. "Wait until the others hear about this. Prepare yourself for some heavy ribbing from the family."

Daniel stopped in front of Ryan, his hands clenched in tight fists. "I don't care what the family does as long as Megan is okay."

Finally a nurse emerged from a door marked Authorized Personnel Only. "Officer Colton," she called out.

Daniel hurried toward her. "How's Megan? Is she going to be all right? May I see her?"

"I'm sorry." She looked around Daniel to Ryan. "I need to talk to Officer Colton."

Anger erupted like a volcano. "I'm her husband. I have the right to see her." He pulled his wallet from his pocket and yanked the marriage certificate from it, whipping it open. "See? She's my wife. We're married. Let me see her."

"The doctor will be out shortly." The nurse snagged Ryan's arm and led him through the doorway. The door shut behind him.

"What the hell is going on?" Daniel asked the empty air.

"Sir, please, take a seat," the receptionist pleaded. "You're scaring the others."

Daniel didn't give a damn about the other people waiting in the lobby. He wanted to see Megan. Then a thought hit him and his heart seized. The only reason he could think of for them to refuse to let him see her yet was that she hadn't made it. A solid block of lead settled in the pit of his stomach, and, for a moment, his heart quit beating.

He took two steps toward the door to the restricted area and raised his fist to bang and demand to see Megan.

Before his knuckles hit the door, it swung open and Ryan stepped out, his face grim. "Daniel, come with me." He grabbed Daniel's arm and turned him toward the exit.

Daniel shook off his hand and spun away. "I'm not going anywhere until I know how Megan is doing."

"They are treating her now and expect her to come through okay."

"Then why won't they let me in to see her?"

"If you'll come with me outside, I'll explain."

"I'm not going anywhere."

Ryan's jaw tightened. "Very well, I'll spell it out here in front of everyone."

"Shoot."

He glanced at the faces of the people waiting to see the on-call doctors. "Preliminary blood tests indicate that Megan had arsenic in her system."

His chest squeezed so tight he could barely breathe. "Oh, God. How?"

"They don't know. There will be questions, like what you had to eat for the last couple of days and where. They might want to do a blood test on you to see if you've been poisoned, as well."

Daniel shoved a hand through his hair. "Anything. Just let me see her."

"The doctor is monitoring her progress with the antidote. They'll let you see her in a few minutes."

"Daniel Colton," a doctor in a white smock called out.

Daniel pushed past Ryan. "I'm Daniel."

"I'm Dr. Baxter." He held out his hand and smiled. "Your wife has been asking for you."

Daniel reached for the man's hand and gripped it. "Where is she?" He looked over the doctor's shoulder as if he could see through the door to where they were keeping Megan. "When can I see her?"

The doctor's smile faded. "She's been moved to a room in the hospital for the night."

"How is she?"

"She's going to be okay," the doctor said, pulling his hand free. "She'll need a few days of rest and plenty of clear liquid. Fortunately, you got her here in time, and the medicine is doing its job."

"How could she have been poisoned?"

The doctor nodded toward Ryan. "The police will have to conduct an investigation. The amount of arsenic in her system was enough to raise red flags."

"I can't imagine where she'd have gotten it. I've been with her for the past two days and eaten what she's eaten. Wouldn't I be sick, as well?"

"Normally, if the poisoning was accidental or the food was tainted. The amount of arsenic in her system was more than what we consider accidental."

"Holy hell." Daniel frowned. "Who would possibly want to poison her?"

The doctor shrugged. "That's for the police to determine. You'll need to list all the places you ate, the people you were with and what you ate to help trace back to the source."

"Sure. But may I see my wife now?"

"Of course." The doctor waved toward a nurse standing nearby. "The nurse will take you back for a blood test and then let you know Megan's room number and floor."

Daniel shook the doctor's hand. "Thank you for helping Megan."

"I understand you two were recently married." The doctor chuckled. "It's not the ideal way to spend your honeymoon. She'll need some extra tender loving care."

"She'll get it. I'll make sure." Daniel went with the nurse into a side room, where she drew a blood sample.

She gave Daniel Megan's room number and pointed to the elevator.

Ryan stepped in with him. "Who would want to hurt Megan?"

"I don't know."

"When you were talking to the airport personnel, you said you'd flown in from California, but you were married in Vegas."

"We got married in Vegas and went to California to inform Megan's parents. We stayed one night at her folks' ranch."

"How is her relationship with her parents?"

"From what I saw, her parents love her. They'd never hurt her."

"I've seen instances where parents loved their children so much, they'd hurt them to keep them dependent on them."

Daniel shook his head. "Megan is their only child. They tried really hard to have that one child. I can't imagine them poisoning her to keep her close. If we had not gotten her to the hospital when we did, she might have died. They wouldn't risk it."

The elevator door opened, and the two Coltons stepped out.

Daniel found the room and knocked gently.

A weak voice answered, "Come in."

His heart hammering against his ribs, Daniel pushed the door open and stepped into a dimly lit room. The curtain was open to the outside, but the sun had slipped below the horizon, casting the room in a dull, dusky light.

Megan lay against crisp white sheets, her face almost as pale as the sheets. "Hey," she said, a smile curling the corners of her lips. "You can turn on a light. It's one of the buttons on this." She handed him the remote control for the bed.

Her hand felt cold to his touch as he took the remote, found a button with a lightbulb on it and clicked it.

The reading light over the bed snapped on, casting a glow over her bright strawberry blond hair.

She raised her hand to her head. "I must be a mess."

He laid the remote on the bed beside her and took her hand in his.

Her freckles stood out against her pale skin, but her green eyes shone, and her bright hair fanned out against the pillow.

"You're beautiful."

She chuckled. "Liar."

"Ryan's here."

She tipped her head to look around Daniel. "Oh, hey. I'm sorry to cause so much trouble."

"Don't be sorry. You didn't cause it," Ryan said.

Megan frowned. "The doctor said I got a hold of arsenic." Her pretty brow furrowed. "How could that be?"

"We don't know. But we need to find out."

She pinched the bridge of her nose. "Did I eat something I shouldn't have?"

Daniel shook his head. "The doctor seemed to think it was more than just tainted food."

Her frown deepened. "He thinks I was poisoned?"

Ryan came to stand beside Daniel. "That's what it looks like."

Her eyes widened and she stared up at Daniel, her hand tightening around his. "Are you okay?"

His chest swelled. It was just like Megan to be more worried about others when she was the one who'd nearly died. "I'm fine. But you have to take it easy for the next couple of days."

A knock sounded on the door.

As Daniel turned, the door opened and Jack's shaggy, dark head stuck around the side, his green eyes shadowed with concern. "Is our best ranch assistant up for visitors?"

Ryan touched Daniel's arm. "I let the family know about your plane wreck and Megan being taken to the hospital."

"Anything else?" Daniel asked.

His half brother's lips twisted. "I might have mentioned that you two got hitched."

Daniel had forgotten to worry over what the Colton clan would think of his marriage to Megan. Well, he was about to find out.

"So, may we come in?" Jack asked again.

Daniel glanced back at Megan, and she gave a weak smile. "Sure."

"Not for long," Daniel said. "Megan needs rest."

"We won't stay long." Jack entered with his wife, Tracy. He crossed to Daniel and enveloped him in a bear hug. "I don't know whether to congratulate you or give my condolences, brother. Married, plane wrecked and a sick wife. What a combination."

Tracy smiled softly as she pecked Daniel on the cheek and then Megan. "I'm so happy for you both, and I hope you get well soon. However, I have to warn you to be prepared for a Colton gathering. There are more of us waiting outside the door."

Daniel held Megan's hand and stood by her side, bracing himself for the Colton inquisition.

Brett appeared in the doorway after Jack and Tracy

moved aside. "Hannah would have come, but her ankles were swollen from being on her feet all day. She sends her love and congrats to the newlyweds." He made his way to Daniel, wrapped his arms around him and pounded him on the back. "You dog! When did you two make the decision to elope? None of us saw it coming."

Daniel was spared from responding when his half brother Eric Colton's broad shoulders filled the doorway. "Daniel, Megan. Sorry, I'm late. I was in surgery and just got the word you were here." He pulled a surgical cap from his head, his buzzed hair shining from perspiration.

"It's okay. Megan is doing much better," Daniel said.

"Good." He shone a penlight into Megan's eyes, then touched his stethoscope to her chest, listened and finally nodded. "You have a good doctor. He was quick to pick up on the symptoms even before the blood test results came back."

"Thank God," Tracy said. "We need more women in the Colton family."

"That's right." Eric stared from Daniel to Megan. "So, you two skipped off to Vegas without letting us all in on the plan?"

"I didn't know I had to get everyone's approval," Daniel countered.

"No, you don't," Ryan said.

"No," Brett said. "But you have to give us a chance to throw you one helluva bachelor party. Don't think that just because you jumped the gun and eloped, you're cheating us out of a chance to roast you."

"Too late. We're already married. No fanfare required." Daniel held up Megan's hand, displaying the ring. "It's done."

Tracy pushed past the men to ogle the ring. "Oh, Megan, how pretty."

Megan's cheeks reddened. "Thank you. It belonged to Daniel's grandmother."

"Then it's extra special." Tracy patted Daniel's arm. "Daniel did good."

"Yes, he did." Megan smiled up at Daniel, the dark smudges beneath her eyes making his heart hurt. The plane crash and the poison had almost killed her. He could have lost her twice in one day. "We need to let Megan sleep. She's been through a lot today."

"From what the news reported, it's probably a good thing I passed out during the landing." Megan frowned up at Daniel. "Why didn't you tell me?"

"I only now got them to let me in to see you."

Ryan chuckled. "Yeah, and he was ready to break down the doors if they didn't let him in. I'm glad you're doing better, Megan."

"Thanks, Ryan." She coughed and closed her eyes.

"That's it. Everyone out," Daniel ordered.

A disturbance at the door heralded the arrival of yet another Colton.

Daniel's father, Big J Colton, his shock of thick white hair standing on end, filled their doorway. "Daniel, what's this I hear about a crash and your assistant taking ill?"

Ryan gave their father the digest version, sparing Daniel the trouble. He ended by saying, "And before all that, the two of them managed to get married in Vegas."

"What?" Big J thundered. "Why wasn't I informed?"

Daniel touched his father's shoulder. "I'm sorry, but we made the decision and moved on it."

"Well, then, I guess there's only one thing I can do," Big J blustered, his frown fierce.

Daniel had seen his father furious, but never for something like one of his sons marrying without his permission. He braced himself, hating to disappoint the man who'd taken him in when his mother had passed.

"What's that, Dad?" Jack asked.

His father's frown disappeared, to be replaced by a big grin. "The only thing a father can do when his son gets married. That's to kiss the bride." He leaned over Megan and kissed her with a loud smack on the cheek. "Welcome to the family, Megan." He turned to Daniel. "Glad you found a good woman. May your lives be filled with love and children."

Daniel's gut clenched. His family had gathered around to wish him well on his marriage, and it was nothing but a big fat lie. What would his father think when they dissolved their vows? He'd be disappointed that Daniel hadn't tried hard enough to keep it together. Daniel couldn't tell his family that it was a farce. Megan's grandmother's trust fund depended on the marriage being legal and valid. And he needed it to make his own deal with the Kennedys.

"As a doctor," Eric spoke up, "I'd say Megan needs rest to recover from her ordeal."

"That's right. We need to get out of here and give the newlyweds a little space." Brett bumped Daniel's shoulder. "You're still on the hook for a bachelor party."

"Really, it's not necessary," Daniel assured him.

"The hell it isn't," Jack stated. "We'll skip the strippers, but there will be beer and football."

Daniel smiled halfheartedly. "Fine. Beer and football.

After Megan's well and we've had a chance to figure out what's going on."

"What do you mean?" Big J's smile disappeared.

Daniel regretted opening his mouth. Now he had to explain to the family about Megan's poisoning.

"That's awful!" Tracy pressed a hand to her breast. "Who would want to hurt Megan? She's one of the nicest people I know."

"Exactly."

Big J's frown deepened. "If someone is targeting her, she's obviously not safe right now." He faced Daniel. "You two will move to the main house until we figure this out."

"No, really, it's not necessary," Megan said.

"It most certainly is." Big J waved aside her protest. "You're going to be resting for a couple days as it is. Knowing Daniel, he'll be out feeding horses at least twice a day. What will you do while he's out puttering in the barn?"

"I can take care of myself." She tried to sit up, but Daniel laid a hand on her shoulder.

"They're right," Daniel said. "I wouldn't feel comfortable leaving you alone in the guesthouse. There's safety in the number of people at the main house. Someone will be around at all times."

"It's not up for discussion." Big J spoke with finality. "You two are moving into the main house for the time being." He bent to peck Megan on the cheek. "We'll see you tomorrow. In the meantime, I hope you feel better."

"Thank you," she said weakly, staring up at Daniel.

Although he really had no desire to move into the main house with the chance of running into his stepmother, Daniel couldn't argue with his father's reasoning.

A nurse entered the room, hitting Brett with the door. Her eyes rounded. "What the heck is going on in here?" Her forehead creased in a deep frown. "Out. All of you, get out. Mrs. Colton needs rest, not a convention."

"We were going," Jack muttered, clutching Tracy's hand as he led her out of the room. He turned at the doorway. "We'll see you guys tomorrow. Congratulations."

The others filed out, leaving Daniel and Ryan as the last men in the room. The nurse checked Megan's vitals and her IV and adjusted her bed down. Then she pointed at Ryan. "You, too. Only her husband can stay the night."

Ryan held up his hands. "I'm going."

The nurse frowned at him again, then left the room.

With a quick peck on Megan's cheek, Ryan said, "Welcome to the family." He turned to Daniel. "Take care of our new sister-in-law. The men still outnumber the women. We could use more good ones like Megan." As he headed toward the door, he tossed over his shoulder, "I'll check on the investigation. As soon as you write down all the particulars of your trip, we'll follow up."

"Thanks, Ryan." Daniel's gaze followed Ryan through the door. When he was gone, the room fell into silence.

"Was that as awkward for you as it was for me?" Megan asked.

Daniel glanced down at her, realizing he still held her hand in his. "I hate to disappoint my family."

"I know." She sighed. "They don't deserve the lies we're feeding them. I'm sorry I got you into this."

"You didn't. I was the one to suggest it in the first place."

"But you wouldn't have if I hadn't handed you my resignation."

"The main thing right now is not to worry about all this. Sleep and let your body recover."

"Yes, sir." She smiled and closed her eyes. "What happened with the plane?"

He'd been wondering that himself. "The landing gear didn't deploy." The manual emergency backup cord had been severed. He didn't mention that.

Her eyes opened, and her brow furrowed. "How did you land without landing gear?"

His lips curled. "Very carefully. On the belly of the plane."

"Oh, Daniel. The plane is ruined?"

He shrugged. "Don't worry about it. That's why we have insurance. We survived the landing and got you to the hospital on time. That's all that matters."

When she opened her mouth to speak again, he held up his hand. "You can ask all the questions you want in the morning. For now, you need to sleep and recover. I have a call to make to Marshall Kennedy to cancel our meeting."

"No." Megan pushed to a sitting position. "I'm feeling better already. You can't cancel the trip to Reno."

"We don't have a plane. It's not worth it to me to go now."

"We're going," she insisted, her voice sounding stronger. "I can arrange for flights to Reno. Or we can rent a plane for the trip. We can't cancel now. We've come too far to give up over a little hiccup in our plans."

Daniel shook his head. "You almost died twice today and you call it a hiccup?" He took her hand in his and lifted it, staring at the ring. "You're an amazing woman, and your father would kill me if he knew what you'd gone through today."

"And that's why you're not going to tell him." She lay back against the pillow and closed her eyes. "Now you can leave and let me sleep. I plan on getting up in the morning and walking out of this hospital."

Daniel chuckled. "Unless you want me to leave, I'm staying. You might have been poisoned once. They might try again. If you want me to leave, I'll sit outside your door. Your choice."

She opened her eyes and gave him a weak smile. "I really am sorry this is turning out to be more trouble than you bargained for."

"Don't you worry about me. I can take care of myself."

"Good, because I'm too tired to get up." She yawned and rolled onto her side. "See you in the morning." Megan tucked her hand beneath her chin, her hair falling over her face.

Daniel stood for a long time, staring down at her, his heart torn between anger and something else. This woman had left the easy life of the privileged behind, fighting for the freedom to make her own decisions, and ended up poisoned and the target of attacks in Vegas. And yet she was more concerned about being a bother to him. He could easily fall in love with her, and that would never do. Two people couldn't be farther apart in their social realms.

Daniel stepped out of the room and stood in the hallway to make a phone call. Ryan had said he'd check on the status of the airplane and the reason the landing gear had not deployed. Hopefully, the FAA inspector had already taken a cursory look.

Before he could dial his brother's number, his smartphone vibrated in his hand. It was Ryan.

"How's Megan?" he asked without a greeting.

"Better," Daniel replied. "What have you found out?"

"I got word from the FAA inspector. When they moved the plane, they had a chance to look at the landing gear." Ryan paused. "Daniel, it was all chewed up with something that looked like acid, and there was a broken vial strapped to the electrical wires. They think that when you raised the landing gear in Santa Rosa, the vial was crushed and the acid leaked on the wires, causing them to malfunction."

"And someone cut the emergency cord."

"Good thing you two will be staying at the big house. Sounds like someone has it in for Megan, and you could be collateral damage."

Chapter 15

Megan woke the next morning feeling pretty much back to normal, until she got out of the hospital bed and tried to stand on her own two feet. She'd waited until Daniel slipped out for a cup of coffee before she tried to make a run for the bathroom to comb her hair and make herself more presentable to her new husband.

She nearly fell flat on her face, her knees so weak she could barely stand. With concentrated effort, she was determined to make a round trip to the bathroom before Daniel returned.

Dr. Baxter arrived in her room as she settled back on the edge of the bed.

He grinned. "How's my patient?"

Megan straightened, forcing a chipper look. "I feel well enough to leave."

"I'm sure you do." He shook his head. "As good as

the food and service are here, no one ever wants to stay." He winked.

After checking her vital signs and flashing a light in her eyes, he declared, "You can go home as long as you have someone with you for the first couple of days." He held up his hand. "Not that I think anything will happen, but just to make sure you don't have a reaction to the medicine or the residual effects of the poison."

"We'll make sure she has someone with her," Daniel said, stepping into the room, a paper cup of steaming hot coffee in his hand. "She'll be surrounded by family."

"Good, good. I'll have the nurse bring in your discharge papers with instructions. Your stomach might feel a little off for a couple of days, but you should be able to return to work."

Megan glanced at Daniel as she asked the doctor, "We're supposed to go to Reno in two days."

Dr. Baxter folded his stethoscope into his pocket. "There's no reason you shouldn't." He backed toward the door. "Congratulations on your marriage. Hopefully we won't see you again until you come to deliver your first child."

Megan's cheeks flamed and her heart ached. She could imagine a little boy with dark brown hair and bright brown-black eyes like Daniel's.

Once the door closed behind the doctor, she pushed her fantasy to the back of her mind and tilted her chin upward, ready for the battle. "You heard the doctor. We're going to Reno." She eased off the bed and swayed.

Daniel was there to steady her with his empty hand.

She was happy for his warmth and strength, but quickly let go to prove she was capable of standing on her own. "If you will leave me for a few minutes, I'll dress and we can get out of here."

An hour later, they pulled up in front of the main house at the Lucky C Ranch. Megan had been in the house only on a couple of rare occasions, when she'd been invited for a barbecue on the Fourth of July and a birthday party for Big J.

Daniel lifted her out of the truck and carried her up the steps.

"I could have walked," she muttered, trying not to love the way his arms felt so warm and secure around her. When he set her on her feet, he kept an arm around her middle while he opened the door.

"There she is." Hannah, Brett's wife, hurried toward them in the grand foyer, a smile on her face, her cheeks rosy and her baby bump preceding her.

"I'll be right back with your suitcase." Daniel left her with Hannah and returned to his truck.

"We were so worried about you." Hannah hooked Megan's arm. "Do you need help getting settled in Daniel's old room?"

"If it's all the same to you, I'd rather relax in the living room. I don't feel like I'm sick. Just a little wobbly."

"Well, then, come on in the main living room. There are plenty of seats available to choose from." Hannah led the way to the living room, but she glanced back at Daniel as he entered the house with Megan's case. "And, Daniel, don't worry about the horses. Brett's been out all morning taking care of them."

"If it's all the same to you, Megan, I'd like to go check on Halo."

"Please do. In fact, I'll come with you," Megan said. "I've been concerned about her since we left."

Daniel shook his head. "I'd feel better knowing you were safe in the house, recovering."

"I'm feeling better already." Anxious to get back to normal, doing the job she loved, she spun toward him and swayed.

Daniel's jaw firmed, and he gripped her arms. "If you want to come to Reno with me in two days, rest now." Then he bent to seal her mouth with his in a brief, fierce kiss. "Please," he said when he lifted his head.

Shaken more by the kiss than she cared to admit, Megan nodded. "Okay. But promise you'll tell me how she is when you get back."

"I will. I won't be gone but a few minutes." He brushed his lips across her forehead and glanced over her shoulder at Hannah. "You'll be with her all the time?"

She smiled. "You bet. The way my ankles have been swelling, I'll be somewhere inside with my feet up."

Daniel left them in the living room.

Megan listened for the sound of the back door closing before she could rest.

"Come have a seat," Hannah urged. "Big J is out with Brett. We have the house to ourselves."

"What I'd really like is a shower." Flying from California, feeling so sick she wanted to die and spending a night in the disinfectant-rich hospital made her yearn for a bar of soap and a hot shower.

"There's one on this floor, if you'll follow me." Hannah led the way to a guest bedroom and bathroom, where Megan dug through her case for her last clean outfit. She'd have to get someone to take her to her apartment soon.

After she took a hot shower, put on clean clothes and

brushed the tangles out of her long, wet hair, she felt almost human again.

Megan stepped out of the bathroom and ran into a solid wall of muscle. Her hands rested on Daniel's chest. His curled around her waist and held her tight against him.

"You got back awfully quickly." She smiled up at him and then frowned. "Is Halo all right?"

He nodded. "You smell like honeysuckle."

Megan's heart warmed. The man paid enough attention to know the scent of honeysuckle on her.

"My shampoo."

"You know they're going to expect us to stay in my bedroom upstairs."

"I just made use of this shower for now. I'm sure we can figure out the sleeping arrangements. I can sleep on the floor. It doesn't really matter to me."

Daniel's brows furrowed, his hands tightening around her middle. "You're not sleeping on the floor."

She bit her bottom lip. "I hadn't thought past telling my parents. I kind of assumed that when we got back here, we'd go on living the same as before. You in the cabin. Me in my apartment."

Already shaking his head, Daniel said, "Not possible. Now that the Colton clan knows, we have to keep up the appearance of a newlywed couple."

She sighed and cupped his face. "I guess I really didn't think this through. I'm sorry."

"I'm not." He bent, laid his cheek against her temple and sniffed. "After all that's happened, I feel better having you close enough to keep an eye on. Besides, you smell good."

Megan leaned into him, loving the solidity of his body

against hers. She'd have no trouble playing the part of the loving wife in their new role. The problem would be turning off the real feelings.

"Daniel!" A shout jerked her out of the warm haze of loving a man who didn't love her.

Daniel inhaled, his chest moving against her before he set her away from him. "The problem with living in the main house is that you don't have much privacy."

"Daniel!"

"That would be Ryan. We'd better go see if he's got any news for us."

Megan almost opened her mouth to beg him to hold her a little longer. Instead she nodded her head. "Let's go."

With his hand resting at the small of her back, he led her through the guest bedroom and down the hallway to the living room.

Brett, Hannah and Big J stood with Ryan in the living room, their faces drawn. Ryan still wore his uniform from the Tulsa PD.

"No way," Brett was saying. "He would never have done it."

Daniel stepped into the room with Megan. "What's going on?"

Ryan faced Daniel. "Actually, I shouldn't be here, but as your brother, I felt I owed it to you."

Megan's gut knotted, and she braced herself for what she was sure wouldn't be good news.

"Owed me what?" Daniel asked.

"A heads-up." Ryan drew in a long breath. "When they discovered just who Megan Talbot is, and that you'd married her in a quickie Vegas wedding, they put two and two together. Their number one person of interest in Megan's poisoning is the one man who stands to gain the most if Megan dies."

Megan shook her head. "You don't think Daniel poisoned me, do you?" She laughed out loud.

Ryan didn't crack a smile. "I don't think he did, but he has plenty of motive to make him a prime suspect."

Daniel's face hardened, and a muscle ticked in his jaw. "I didn't poison her. I'd never do anything to hurt her."

"I trust Daniel with my life. He wasn't the one who poisoned me. He's the kindest, gentlest man I know." Her eyes widened. "Besides, he wouldn't inherit anything from my death. When my parents pass, and if I pass on as well with no heirs, everything I stand to inherit will go to the next blood relative. My cousin, Christine."

Ryan pulled his smartphone out of his back pocket. "What's her full name?"

Megan reluctantly gave the details about her cousin. "But she wouldn't hurt anyone. She and I grew up together. She's the closest thing I have to a sister."

"Still, if she stands to inherit the Talbot fortune, she's another suspect on the list." Ryan keyed in the data and hit Send to text the information to the Tulsa PD. Then he glanced up. "We have to chase all leads."

A shiver slipped down Megan's spine. She'd spent her young life in the shadow of her father's notoriety, had her own bodyguard at the age of six and thought she'd escaped that life when she'd run away to Oklahoma. No one here should have known about the connection between Megan Talbot and Frank Talbot, the highly successful international businessman from California.

"Why target me?" Megan asked. "My father is still alive. I haven't inherited anything. For all I know, he could have all his money going to one of his favorite charities—the children's hospital, an equine research center, anything."

"According to news accounts, your father's health is already precarious. Am I right?" Ryan asked.

Megan's chest tightened. "Yes, but he's getting better."

"The loss of their only daughter could send your parents into a tailspin. I've seen families fall apart upon the death of their child."

"You think if I died, my father would pass away? That would leave my mother alone." Megan's hand found Daniel's, and she held on through the pain radiating in her heart. Knowing now how her parents had tried to have children before her, she understood her death could be the fatal blow to her father. And her mother might prefer to join him. "Who would want me and my family dead?" She shook her head, sadness sapping her strength.

"We don't know." Ryan's face softened, and he reached out to touch her arm. "We'll do our best to find out. In the meantime, stick with one of us Coltons. We'll take care of you."

Brett stepped forward. "That's right. We Coltons take care of our own."

"Damn right, we do," Big J said. "You're part of the family now that you're married to Daniel."

Daniel's hand squeezed hers gently. "That's right. You're a Colton now."

"Yes you are. You're one of us, Megan." Brett slid an arm around his pregnant wife.

Feeling only slightly mollified by the show of Colton support, Megan couldn't shake the feeling of impending doom. Someone was after her. But would that someone come all the way to Oklahoma to attack her?

"Come on. You look like you could use some rest." Daniel scooped her off her feet.

"I can walk, thank you very much," she said, her cheeks heating, embarrassed at his masculine manhandling in front of his family.

Brett grinned. "Yeah, we're pretty sure she can walk, Daniel."

Hannah swatted at her husband's arm. "Leave Daniel alone. It's much more romantic to be swept off your feet." She winked at Megan. "Enjoy it now. When you're seven months pregnant, it's a little harder to manage."

"What do you mean?" Brett bent and swept Hannah up in his arms. Then he groaned loudly. "Yeah, you're right. It is a little harder. Packed on a few pounds, sweetheart?"

Hannah glared at him. "Darn right I have."

"And still as beautiful as the day I met you." Brett kissed her soundly and set her on the couch.

Megan watched how Brett and Hannah teased each other, kissed and touched. The love shining from their gazes only made Megan's heart squeeze harder. Safe in Daniel's arms, she couldn't help but wish they were as in love as Brett and Hannah.

Instead of depositing her on the couch in the living room, Daniel carried her up the stairs as if climbing with a full grown woman in his arms was nothing. He pushed open the door to one of the bedrooms and closed it behind him with his foot. They were alone at last. She glanced away from his face, afraid she'd see indifference when what she wanted to see was a love to equal the feelings she had for him.

Daniel set her on her feet, his hand lingering at the small of her back.

A little shy at being alone with him, Megan scanned the clean, crisp lines of the room, from the khaki-colored paint on the walls to the gold, tan and antique-blue comforter on the bed. It didn't say much about the boy he'd been. "No trophies? Pictures from high school? Old guitars?"

"I didn't play guitar. I was outside with the horses most of the time."

She chuckled. "Big surprise."

"My stepmother had this room redecorated as soon as I moved to the cabin. She was glad see me leave her home."

"How sad."

Daniel shrugged. "You can't blame Abra for hating me. My father had an affair with his housekeeper and then brought me to live under his roof. What woman would happily take in a child who wasn't hers?"

"Like a painful reminder of your father's indiscretion." Megan nodded. "I guess I could see her side, but at the same time, it wasn't your fault Big J had an affair."

"No. But Abra couldn't let it go and accept me in her home."

"It must have been uncomfortable for you." Megan frowned. "We don't have to stay here if it's too painful."

"Since Abra was attacked by an intruder back in June, and even while she was in a coma, there have been some other minor accidents on the ranch. Because of this, she's been a little less antagonistic toward me, more vulnerable. I actually think she'd be happy to have more people in the house. She hasn't felt completely safe since that time."

"The Lucky C hasn't been so lucky lately. You'd think by now the police would have all the incidents tied together."

"We thought the hit man after Tracy was the one who attacked Abra, but Ryan assures us the evidence proves otherwise. And that man was caught before the fire." Daniel's brow furrowed. "Perhaps we should hire a bodyguard and get you far away from the Lucky C."

"No." Megan rested a hand on Daniel's chest, liking how solid it was and how safe she felt when she was with him. "I'd rather be closer to you…and the horses."

"Good. Because I'd rather you were close, as well. And don't worry. There are plenty of people around. Hannah's now here with Brett. Big J isn't out and about as often. He's letting my brothers and me run most of the day-to-day operations of the ranch, though he still has a say in the way he likes things."

"Still, I've already put you out so much. I'd feel better if we were at the cabin." She also would have felt more relaxed if it were just the two of them. Keeping up the lie would be more difficult the more people she was around.

He cupped her cheeks in his hands and gazed down into her eyes. "The cabin is too isolated. I can't leave you alone and risk someone making another attempt to take your life." When she opened her mouth to protest, he pressed his finger to her lips. "And don't say it. I know you can take care of yourself, but just this once, let us take care of you."

She nodded, finding herself falling into his incredibly dark, bottomless gaze. She shook her head, bringing herself back to the ground. "Do you suppose the intruder in Vegas was the same person to sabotage the plane and poison me?"

Daniel nodded. "It all makes sense now. When we were in Vegas, the attack seemed like a random event."

"Now it doesn't." She shivered.

Daniel's gaze raked over her. "You should get some rest. You've gone through a lot."

"I am a little tired." She glanced at the big bed. "I'd feel better in my own apartment."

He dragged a finger along her cheek. "Sorry, sweetheart. We're married now. It just won't do to have us sleeping across town from each other."

"I suppose not." She hugged her arms around her middle. "I'm just not comfortable being here."

"Would it help if I stayed until you went to sleep?"

Her lips quirked. "I wouldn't ask you to."

"You're not asking. I'm offering." Once again, he swept her up in his arms and carried her across to the bed.

Megan draped her arm around his neck and sighed. "You're making a habit of carrying me around."

He grinned. "I know. I find that I like it." He laid her in the middle of the bed and pulled her shoes off her feet, dropping them to the floor. His hands lingered on her ankles, and his nostrils flared.

A spark of desire lit a flame at her core, and Megan held her breath, praying he'd take her in his arms and make love to her.

Instead, he toed off his boots and lay on the bed beside her. Pulling her back to his front, he spooned her with his big body. "Sleep," he said, his voice sounding strained.

How in the hell was she going to sleep when all she wanted to do was turn in his arms, strip him naked and force him to see her as a desirable woman? Not just his assistant and the woman he'd entered into a bargain with for a marriage of convenience.

As she lay cocooned in Daniel's arms, Megan couldn't help but think this marriage of convenience was anything but convenient. She wanted so much more. If he couldn't love her, she'd do well to let him go sooner rather than later. The longer she was with him as husband and wife, the harder it would be to let go. To get over him, she'd have to give up her job on the Lucky C and move far away.

Her hand curled around his where it rested against her belly. God, she didn't want to let go.

Chapter 16

"Ready?" Daniel glanced up at the porch where Megan stood wearing a royal blue dress that hugged her curves to perfection. Sleeveless and cinched in the middle with a thick belt, the dress accentuated her narrow waist. The hem came halfway down her long, slender thighs, displaying a healthy amount of her legs while maintaining a conservative appeal.

The black high heels made her seem even taller than she was, and her beautiful burnished gold hair had been artfully piled on top of her head, exposing her long, graceful neck.

Daniel's heart pounded against his ribs as he stared up at the woman he found himself falling deeper and deeper in love with. After he'd brought her home to the main house at the Lucky C Ranch, he'd made it his mission to be there as much as possible and yet to maintain his hands-off approach. He'd given in to his desire to sleep in the same bed with her, but the effort it cost him not to make love to her had nearly been his undoing.

She had been through enough and was still on the road to recovering from being poisoned. The least he could do was let her sleep.

Big J appeared behind her with Abra, who was looking better than she had in a long time, her neatly dyed brown hair cupping her chin in a stylish bob. She gave Daniel a hint of a smile and patted Megan's shoulder in a minimalist hug. "Please do be careful, Megan. I've enjoyed having you in the house for the past couple of days. I'd hate it if anything happened to you."

"Thank you, Mrs. Colton."

"Oh, please. Call me Abra." She stepped back and waited at the top of the stairs.

Big J offered Megan his arm, descended the steps and he held out a hand to Daniel. "I hope you get the contract you want, son."

Daniel shook his father's hand. "You and me both. It will make all the difference in our horse-breeding operation."

"Son, when you get back, we need to talk about that. I realize the program is a success because of you. Hell, you could be making a lot more money for yourself if you didn't have the Lucky C holding you down."

"I love this ranch and the people on it. It's home."

Big J pulled him into a bear hug. "And we love you, too. When you were a bachelor, that cabin worked out just fine. But now that you're a married man, you need to think of your growing family." Big J draped an arm over Daniel's shoulder and grinned at Megan. "I expect half a dozen grandchildren running around this place."

Megan's face reddened, and her gaze dipped to her feet.

Daniel's gut clenched. He could imagine two or three little girls with strawberry blond hair wearing blue jeans and miniature cowboy boots, whooping and hollering as they ran around the barn. Megan's babies would be adorable. He found himself wanting to be their father and wishing he could give Megan the lifestyle she'd been born into. Even if he took his horse-breeding program out on his own, he'd make good money, but not anywhere near what Frank Talbot brought in.

"You'd better get going. Your plane will be waiting at the airport." Big J clapped a hand on Daniel's shoulder. "Good luck."

Daniel handed Megan into his truck and climbed in the driver's seat.

"We're not flying commercial?" Megan asked.

"No, Big J arranged for a charter airplane."

"Isn't that expensive?"

Daniel nodded. "I tried to talk him out of it, but he insisted. He has the money for it, and he wanted you to be comfortable after your last experience."

"I would have been fine flying commercial," she said, staring straight ahead.

"I still feel as if we should have called off this meeting. With someone trying to hurt you, it's too dangerous to take you out in public."

Megan's lips tightened. "I went along with resting for the past couple of days, but if I'd had to stay inside any longer, I'd have gone completely nutty. Now I know what it feels like to be under house arrest. I left my parents' home because they wouldn't let me breathe."

Daniel nodded. "Fair enough. But please keep close to

me. There should be a lot of people in Reno for the symposium. Promise me you'll stay where I can keep an eye on you. If not for you, then do it for my peace of mind."

"Okay. I get it. I'll stick to you like a fly on fly paper." She winked across at him, making his pulse pound and his desire flame.

At the general aviation hangars, Daniel located the charter company and performed the preflight with the contracted pilot, carefully checking the landing gear and the emergency landing gear cord.

Someone had sabotaged his plane before. He'd be damned if the same someone got away with it again. After a thorough once-over, he helped Megan up the steps into the airplane and settled in a seat across from her.

As the plane taxied down the runway, Daniel's gaze slid to the closed door to the cockpit, his fingers digging into the armrest.

"Not used to someone else doing the flying?" Megan asked softly.

Daniel forced himself to relax. "Not really. I've been flying since before I was old enough to drive a car. I prefer to be at the yoke in small planes."

"Flying in big planes doesn't bother you as much?"

"Not as much."

"Think about something else, like what you're going to say to Marshall Kennedy at dinner tonight."

For the rest of the trip, they went over the program Daniel had in place, the pedigrees and lineage. He'd worked so hard to create a firm basis on which to build one of the finest horse-breeding operations in the country.

By the time they landed, he wasn't even thinking

much about his sabotaged plane. They touched down without incident in Reno what seemed like only minutes after they'd left Tulsa but had actually been a few hours.

Megan smiled across at him. "You'll have a lot to talk about with Marshall at dinner tonight."

Daniel reached out to take Megan's hand. "What would I do without you? If you hadn't come along when you did, I'd still be digging my way through my filing system."

"You were doing fine without me. But I am glad I could help. Makes me think my degree in biology wasn't a waste."

"Hardly. You're amazing." He stood and pulled her to her feet. "You're not only smart but also look great."

"Let's go seal this deal." She started toward the door. Before she could take a step, he pulled her back into his arms.

"Just so you know, I appreciate everything you and your family have done for me."

She laughed up at him. "Are you kidding? You've saved my life not once, but three times." She stood on her tiptoes and pressed her lips to his in a brief kiss. "I guess that makes you my hero."

The husky tone of her voice sent Daniel all the way over the edge. He crushed her body against his. "I can't decide whether I like you better in that dress or in jeans and boots."

"I'm the same person inside."

"That's why I can't decide. You're amazing no matter what you wear—" his voice dropped to a whisper "—or don't wear." Then his lips met hers, and he forgot everything but kissing her.

Megan sank into him, her mouth opening on a sigh.

He swept in, caressing her tongue in a long, slow glide, his hands skimming along the curve of her waist and downward to the swell of her hips and buttocks.

She made him want so much more of what he couldn't have. Even if she wasn't his employee, and if they didn't have to go back to the way things were before their sham of a marriage, she far outclassed him in every way.

A soft cough sounded over Megan's shoulder. "Sorry, I didn't mean to interrupt."

Daniel stepped back and glanced at the pilot standing by the hatch. His face was red. "I was just going to lower the stairs."

"Please do," Daniel directed him.

"I'll be here when you're ready to return to Oklahoma. You have my number." The pilot spoke as he lowered the stairs into place. Then he stood back. "Take your time disembarking. I'll deliver your luggage to the hotel where we're staying."

Megan's cheeks glowed a pretty pink, and her green eyes danced. "Let's get this show on the road."

She went down the steps first. Daniel followed, wishing they were going straight to their hotel to finish the kiss they'd started, instead of meeting Marshall Kennedy for dinner.

Alas, pleasure would have to wait. He was there on business. He hoped all would go well and they could be on their way back home.

Megan settled in the backseat of the limousine that whisked them from the airport to the convention center, where the symposium would have a meet and greet for the attendees. They were to find Marshall Kennedy there and leave the convention center to have a private dinner with him and whomever he'd brought with him.

"My father said Kennedy was open to dialogue and spoke well of you."

"Remind me to thank your father for placing the call."

"He did say that Mr. Kennedy liked to make up his own mind. But hopefully a little bug in his ear will help smooth the path." Megan reached for Daniel's hand. "Just tell him the truth. You've done your homework, and you excel at choosing quality horses. This is your passion, and that will shine through."

Daniel lifted her hand to his lips and pressed a kiss against the backs of her knuckles. "Best pep talk ever. Thank you."

The rest of the ride was made in silence, Megan's heart nearly bursting with Daniel's praise. He didn't let go of her hand until they got out of the vehicle in front of the convention center.

He alighted first and reached in to take her hand.

She let him help her out and onto her feet. Then, hand in hand, they walked toward the convention center.

Megan was so proud to be with the most handsome man there. He stood a head taller than most men, and he looked so sexy in a crisp white shirt, black jeans and black cowboy boots. He had on his best black cowboy hat and a plain black tie that he tugged at several times. Obviously uncomfortable in the semiformal attire, he squared his shoulders and marched through the door.

"Just so you know," she said, "I think you look pretty darned sexy."

He stopped short, a frown creasing his brow. "You think I should have worn blue jeans instead?"

Megan laughed. "No, I think that if Mrs. Kennedy comes, you'll have someone else batting for you."

"I'm more afraid I won't make it across the room with you at my side. The prettiest woman in the building is bound to cause a riot."

"In this old thing?" She winked. "Let's go make some waves."

Megan strode into the convention hall feeling like a million bucks. She refused to look past the deadline of her marriage. For the moment, she had the man she loved at her side, he thought she was beautiful and that was all that mattered.

The majority of symposium attendees were men in jeans and cowboy boots, nice button-up shirts and cowboy hats. Wives, if they brought them, were dressed in a mix of nice dresses, pantsuits or jeans and cowboy boots. Megan would have preferred her jeans and cowboy boots. But with so much riding on this meeting, she felt more prepared in the blue dress she knew looked good on her.

They made their way around the large room, introducing themselves. Daniel had brought up several pictures of Marshall Kennedy online the night before so they wouldn't miss him. Megan had seen him on only one occasion when he'd visited the Triple Diamond, and that had been when she was more concerned about riding horses than breeding them.

In the crowd, she caught a glimpse of a woman with shiny blond hair and for a moment thought it was Christine. After all that had happened, she had to admit to a case of mild paranoia, the feeling she was being watched. Even at the Coltons' main house. Yet every time she turned around, no one was there. Now was no different.

The shiny blond-haired woman she thought was Christine turned out to be a woman with bleach-blond hair in her midfifties.

Megan laughed at herself, her smile growing when she spotted a man fitting the images they'd seen on the internet of Marshall Kennedy.

Kennedy was reportedly tall, like this man, with a head full of strikingly white hair. Dressed in a black button-up shirt, black jeans and a silver bolo tie, he was handsome and commanding, with a crowd of people around him.

Megan leaned toward Daniel and smiled. "In the corner by the bar."

"I see him." Daniel smiled down at her instead of staring hard at his target. "And if I'm not mistaken, he sees you." He lifted his head and nodded. "He's headed this way."

"Daniel Colton?" The white-haired gentleman, surrounded by his entourage, made his way across the room, his hand held out in front of him. "You are Daniel Colton?"

"Yes, sir." Daniel took the hand and shook it.

Megan adopted all her mother's grace and charm from years of sponsoring charitable events. She shone her best smile on the man who could make all the difference to the breeding program Daniel had worked so hard to perfect.

"And you must be his new bride, Megan." He leaned forward and bussed her cheek. "Your father gave me permission to kiss the bride. What a beautiful bride you are. The spitting image of your mother when she was your age." The older man turned to Daniel. "You're a very lucky man. If I'd had a lick of sense thirty years ago, I'd have married Megan's mother instead of chasing horses around the world." Marshall held up both hands. "Don't get me wrong. I married a beautiful, successful woman, and we've been together for the past twenty-five years."

"I'm sure my father is happy to hear that." Megan smiled.

"Colton, you had the good sense to put a ring on Josephine's daughter's finger before you got too caught up in the business. A good woman can help keep you grounded."

Daniel slipped an arm around Megan's waist and smiled down at her. "I am a very lucky man that she chose me. She's not only beautiful but also smart. She has been a huge help to my program already. We work well together."

The heat rose in Megan's cheeks. "He's being too kind. Daniel had the program going strong before I ever showed up at the Lucky C Ranch."

Daniel kissed her temple. "You helped me position it for the next level." He shifted his direct gaze to Kennedy.

The older man nodded, his lips quirking at the corners. "What I've learned from Frank, the internet and the grapevine is that you've done pretty well for yourself, and at a young age."

Daniel tipped his head up. "Thank you, sir. I'm proud of my horse-breeding strategy, and I hope to take it a step further with Kennedy Farm's Striker's Royal Advantage stud services."

Kennedy nodded. "Precisely. We can talk details at dinner." He introduced Daniel and Megan to his ranch manager, Tom Miller, and the head of his breeding program, Gary Callan.

The five of them loaded into Kennedy's waiting Hummer limousine, and they were taken to one of the nicest steak houses in Reno in one of the most prestigious casinos.

"Daniel, are you a gambler?" Mr. Kennedy asked as he took his seat at the table.

Daniel settled in next to Megan and reached for her hand beneath the table. "Only in the sense of weather and crops. However, I like to take what I call educated risks."

Kennedy's eyes narrowed, and he leaned forward. "How's that?"

"I do my homework to find the best solutions to problems. I consult my expert biologist—" Daniel tilted his head toward Megan "—and make the environment as stable as I can when ranching and working with animals before I commit."

The older man sat back, giving Daniel an assessing glance. "Sounds pretty calculated."

"I didn't build my program based on the seat of my pants."

"Have you ever taken an uncalculated risk?"

Daniel squeezed Megan's hand beneath the table. "As a matter of fact, I did. That risk was asking Megan to marry me."

Kennedy chuckled. "How do you figure that as uncalculated?"

"We were in the barn. I'm sure I smelled of horse manure and hay when I asked her."

Megan smiled up at him. "He'd saved me from a runaway horse a few days earlier, I smelled about the same and it was the most romantic proposal I could have imagined. I wouldn't have had it any other way."

Daniel grinned at Mr. Kennedy. "See what I mean? She's perfect."

"Common interests and goals are the keys to a successful merger." Kennedy nodded. "You two will do well together."

"I hadn't met a woman as interested in horses as I am." Daniel gazed at Megan. "Until a pretty redheaded female answered my ad for an assistant. I have to admit, I was hesitant to hire a woman to work with horses. But she convinced me to give her a try. I was pleasantly surprised that she was more than just a pretty face."

Megan's mouth twisted in a wry grin. "You're sounding pretty chauvinistic, sweetheart." She shifted her glance to Mr. Kennedy. "I told him I'd been working around horses all my life. My father bred both quarter horses and Thoroughbreds. I knew the nose from the tail and how to manage the records of a much larger operation."

Daniel's gaze fixed on Megan, giving her a warm feeling. "She talked the talk."

"How did she convince you?" Kennedy asked.

"I challenged her to ride with me." Daniel crossed his arms, a grin spreading across his face. "Bareback."

Butterflies fluttered in Megan's belly at the way Daniel's dark eyes danced. He loved telling this story, and it made her feel special and proud to have passed his test. Her parents would have been appalled that he'd asked her to ride bareback. But bareback was how she'd learned and felt most natural.

Mr. Kennedy laughed out loud.

Daniel's chuckle made Megan's chest swell. "I figured if she was afraid of horses, she'd refuse to ride bareback, and she'd know immediately she didn't have the job. I couldn't have an assistant afraid of horses."

Megan's chin tilted upward. "I'm not afraid of horses. But I have a healthy respect for them."

Kennedy leaned forward. "Did you ride the horse bareback?"

A grin spread across her face. "Damn right I did." Her mother would have washed her mouth out with soap had she heard her daughter curse in front of anyone. Megan felt she'd earned the right to be adamant. She was good with horses, and when her parents refused to give her permission to work with the Triple Diamond breeding stock, she'd been even more determined to prove them wrong.

Daniel's chest puffed out. "Not only did she ride that horse, but she also cleaned her hooves, checked her teeth and gave me advice on what feed was best and how often. She asked questions only someone with an intimate knowledge of horses would ask."

"Now he doesn't know how to live without me," Megan said with a bright smile. She wished her words were true. When the time came for their marriage to end, she knew she wouldn't be able to stay. Daniel already meant so much to her that she couldn't work at his side as just his assistant. What if he fell in love with another woman?

Her heart ached at the thought.

No, she couldn't work alongside him if he had another woman in his life. She'd have to leave the Lucky C Ranch in order to get over him. Seeing him with someone else would tear her apart.

Tom Miller and Gary Callan asked questions.

Megan gave Daniel the lead. It was his program. When she was gone, he'd still be there, raising the finest horses.

Daniel didn't let her sit by, nodding and smiling. He pulled her into the conversation. Soon the five of them were leaning over the table in a lively discussion about studs or mares from other breeders that Kennedy Farms and the Lucky C could benefit from.

Marshall Kennedy finally glanced at his watch. "Good Lord. Is it really eleven o'clock?"

Megan looked around the restaurant. The waitstaff was hovering around their table, ready to clean up and get out of there. "We shouldn't have kept you so long." She started to stand, but Daniel put a hand on her knee beneath the table.

She waited until he stood and held her chair. Though she hated all the formality of living the lifestyle of the rich and famous, it was nice to be treated like a lady, with respect and care. When it was convenient, Daniel opened doors for her on the Lucky C. There were times that, as an assistant, she opened them for him.

"Tomorrow I would like to show you the stud you were interested in. The symposium arranged for breeders to show their horses at the arena. Will you be available to view him?" Mr. Kennedy asked. "I'll have several of our broodmares, as well."

Daniel slipped an arm around Megan's waist. "We'd be honored."

Outside the restaurant, Kennedy, Miller and Callan shook hands with Daniel and Megan.

"We're staying at this hotel," Kennedy said. "But the limousine is at your disposal. It will drop you off at yours." The older man held out his hand to Daniel. "So that you're not left hanging, I want you to know that I like what I've seen in the way you run your program, the horses you've bred and, of course, your choice of a lifelong assistant." Mr. Kennedy dropped Daniel's hand and lifted Megan's to cup it in both of his. "And you're absolutely right. She is beautiful and intelligent. Your father must be proud."

Megan now knew her father was proud of her, and hearing Kennedy say that he must be made it all the more real. "Thank you for your time, Mr. Kennedy."

"Call me Marshall. I like to be on a first-name basis with the people I do business with." He winked at Daniel. "Once you've had a chance to see Striker's Royal Advantage, if you're still interested, we'll draw up the papers."

Daniel nodded, his face serious. "Thank you, Mr. Kennedy. I appreciate your confidence in me."

Kennedy clapped a hand on Daniel's shoulder. "You've earned it, son."

Kennedy and his two men returned to the hotel while Daniel handed Megan into the limousine.

Once he was seated, a huge grin split Daniel's face, and he grabbed Megan in a bear hug. "Sweetheart, I could not have done it without you. You were absolutely amazing. I could kiss you."

She stared up into his shining eyes and asked, "What's stopping you?"

Daniel cupped her cheek and tilted her face up, bringing his mouth so close to hers, his warm breath tickling her lips.

"I could so easily fall in love with you," he whispered.

"Again, what's stopping you?"

He brushed her mouth with his, dragging her close against him.

The limousine pulled away from the hotel and was halfway down the road before Daniel broke away to breathe. But only for a minute. Then he kissed and nibbled a trail along her cheek and chin, down the side of her neck to where the pulse beat hard at the base of her throat.

Her body was on fire with need. She couldn't wait to reach the hotel and have this man. Nothing would stop her or get in the way of them making love. Until they broke it off, Megan and Daniel were married. Making love was part of the gig. There was no shame in it and no reason to hold back.

A quick glance at the divider between the driver and the back of the limousine reassured her of their privacy. Megan pushed Daniel to arm's length, grabbed for the buckle cinching the belt around her waist and pulled it free. Then she winked. "Are you afraid to go for a ride, cowboy?"

Chapter 17

Daniel's eyes flared, and his pulse pounded so hard against his eardrums he could barely hear. "Hang on." He fumbled with the buttons on the side of the door and said, "Driver, could you circle Reno for twenty minutes? My wife hasn't seen all the city has to offer."

After the driver responded, Daniel hit the Mute button.

Daniel barely had his finger off the button when Megan reached for the hem of her dress, pulled it up over her head and tossed it to the side.

Daniel froze, and his breath caught in his throat. He reached out to touch the soft skin of her cheeks and then dragged the backs of his knuckles down her neck. He memorized the curves and edges as he crossed her collarbone, smoothed across the muscles of her shoulders and moved downward to the swell of her breasts.

The lace of her bra had an erotic coarseness that set

his world on fire. Daniel tweaked the distended nipples through the lace, his mouth watering for a taste of her luscious fruit.

Megan moaned and leaned into his palms.

There would be no stopping him this time. All the best intentions of staying away from her and keeping his hands off this woman were null and void. He had to have her. He wanted her so much he'd make love to her in the backseat of the limousine.

His need for her was like a physical pain in his heart.

Megan reached behind her back and flicked the catches on her bra, freeing herself for him. Then she wove her fingers through his hair and guided his mouth to her nipple. Daniel tugged the straps down her arms and tossed the undergarment away. He palmed a breast in one hand while he tongued the other, angling Megan downward onto the leather seat.

The vehicle slowed for a stop. Daniel wasn't even vaguely aware of the world around him.

Megan reached between them and unbuckled his belt and the top button of his jeans. "I want you. Now." She gripped the zipper and tugged it downward.

"Shh, sweetheart. We have the limousine long enough to do this right."

"I don't want right. I want now." Her fingers slid into his jeans and wrapped around the steely hardness of him.

"At the rate we're going, I won't last long."

"Anyone ever tell you that you talk too much?" She leaned up on her elbow and wrapped her hand around his neck, pulling him down on top of her. Her mouth found his, and she kissed him long and hard.

Daniel hooked his thumb in the elastic of her panties, dragged them down her long legs and tossed them to the side. Then he parted her legs and moved between them, nudging her entrance with his erection.

She pushed his jeans over his buttocks and sank her fingernails into his skin. She gasped, "What about protection?"

"Back pocket," he gritted out, afraid he wouldn't be able to control himself much longer. "In my wallet."

While he balanced over her on his arms, she reached for his wallet, extracted the little foil packet, ripped it open and rolled it down over him. "Now!"

Megan wrapped her legs around his waist and dug her heels into his buttocks.

Daniel drove into her, hard and fast, burying himself deep inside. Her slick channel contracted around him, drawing him deeper.

Holy hell, how was he supposed to make this last when she felt so damned good? He thrust in and out, unable to slow to pleasure her first. The need to have her drove his actions.

Megan let her heels drop against the seat. She pushed off to meet him thrust for thrust, the friction creating an overpowering heat he was sure would light the leather cushion on fire.

Her moans turned into soft mewling cries that sent him rocketing over the edge of reason. He thrust one last time and held steady, deep inside her.

Megan's legs clamped around him, holding him there until his member stopped throbbing and he could redirect the blood flow back to his brain.

He pulled free and handed Megan her clothes, helping her by hooking the bra in the back. Dressing her was almost as sensual as undressing her, and he wished they had more time in the limousine. But they had a room they would share in one of the swanky hotels. "Hey, the sooner we get back to the hotel, the sooner we can resume our negotiations." He tugged the dress over her head and down her torso.

Then he zipped, buttoned and buckled, ready to get on with the night. Alone in their room.

Megan was smoothing her hair and adjusting her hem when the driver slammed on the brakes and the limousine's tires screeched. Without their seat belts on, Megan and Daniel slid off the backseat and dropped to the floor. Then there was a loud crashing of metal on metal. The limousine was tossed to the side, and they were flung with it.

When all movement stilled, Daniel leaned over Megan. "Are you all right?"

"I think I am," she said, touching her hand to her temple. She'd hit something. A long trail of blood oozed down the side of her face.

"You're hurt." Daniel reached for the door and tried to open it. It had been shoved into the interior three or four inches. The other door was worse.

"Are you two all right back there?" The driver lowered the dividing wall between the front and the back seats.

"Mrs. Colton was injured."

"I'm all right. But can you get us out of here?"

"Both doors have been damaged. You have two choices. Climb through the window between the front and the back or out through the sunroof, if I can get it to open. The electronics aren't working exactly right." A motor whined. The sunroof opened halfway and stopped. After several attempts by the driver, the roof opened.

"I'll go first, then help you out." Daniel pulled himself through the sunroof and reached in to help Megan. The blood on her face made him so angry he could have put his fist through a brick wall.

Once he had her on the roof, he dropped to the ground and held out his hands to help her, sliding her down his body. Then he hugged her tight. "We're going to get you to the hospital."

"No. I'm fine." She turned to the driver. "Are you okay?"

"I'm fine. My seat belt held me, and the air bags deployed. I was more worried about you two."

"What happened?" Daniel demanded.

"It was a hit-and-run. I started through a green light, and a vehicle ran the red and broadsided the limousine, smashing us against a light pole." The driver ran a hand through his gray hair. "Before I could get a license plate number, he was gone."

Several police cars and an ambulance converged on them, blocking traffic on the busy road.

The police took their statements while the emergency medical technicians did their work. They gave Megan and Daniel a once-over, cleaned up Megan's wound and advised her to take a ride in the ambulance to see the ER doctor.

Megan refused. "I really didn't hit that hard, and I'd like to get to bed sometime tonight."

"I think you should let me take you to the hospital," Daniel said.

"No," she said firmly. "Take me to the hotel. I just want a hot shower and a bed."

Short of throwing her over his shoulder and forcing her to go the hospital, Daniel had to concede to her wishes. "Okay, but for the record, I don't like it."

"So noted." Megan leaned against him. "It's been a long day. Let's go."

What had started as a great evening ended on a disturbing note. Daniel called Ryan to let him know what had happened. Ryan would fill the Reno police in on the information the Tulsa PD had collected on the attempts on Megan's life.

When they finally got to bed, Daniel crawled in beside Megan and spooned her body with his. No sexual overtones, just holding her, feeling her body against his.

"Do you think whoever is trying to hurt me crashed into us tonight?" Megan asked, her fingers resting on his arm dug into his skin, her body trembling.

"I don't know." He tightened his arms around her. "Just to be safe, stay close to me tomorrow."

Megan draped her arms over his. For a long moment, silence filled the room.

"Daniel?" she whispered, her voice quivering.

"Yes."

"If someone is after me, you could be collateral damage. I don't want you to be hurt."

"Sweetheart, it's a chance I'm willing to take to keep you safe."

If the person after Megan was in Reno, tomorrow could be more of a challenge than he or Megan originally thought.

Perhaps he should check on security services in Reno. It was time to get some help.

Daniel prayed they'd make it through the following day and return home intact.

When Megan woke the next morning, she stretched out her arm, searching for Daniel's solid form, only to find an empty bed. On the pillow beside hers, Daniel had left a note explaining he would be back in less than ten minutes with breakfast and coffee.

She sat up and pressed a hand to her head, hoping to get a handle on a mild headache plus alternating feelings of euphoria and impending doom before Daniel returned. If all went well that day, they'd have a deal with Kennedy Farms, and the marriage of convenience would have fully served its purpose.

Once they sealed the deal with Kennedy Farms, she and Daniel had no reason to stay married. Oh, maybe for a couple of weeks to give the appearance of having at least tried to make it work.

She'd come up with some excuse, maybe throwing a fit over something stupid as a debutante would do. That way Daniel would save face, and Marshall Kennedy wouldn't hold their subsequent divorce against Daniel.

The issue of someone being after her had her equally concerned. Megan didn't want Daniel to be hurt. Perhaps she should hop on a plane, head back to the Triple Diamond and let her father assign a bodyguard to her. Then she wouldn't be putting Daniel in harm's way, and she could start getting over him.

Megan suspected getting over Daniel would take a very long time.

Pushing aside all the thoughts that had whirled through her mind and kept her awake most of the night, she dressed for the day in pressed blue jeans, riding boots and a white blouse. She added a filmy turquoise scarf for a splash of color to cheer her up. As she finished running a brush through her hair, the door to the hotel room opened and Daniel entered, balancing two cups of coffee and a pastry bag.

"You like cream and sugar, right?"

She smiled, happy that he'd remembered. "I do."

"I grabbed a couple of muffins. We meet Marshall in thirty minutes at the arena."

"I don't have to have coffee or a muffin. We can leave now," she said.

"No need."

They ate at the room's tiny table with a view of Reno and sipped their coffee, rehashing the discussion with Kennedy the night before.

When they finished, they brushed their teeth in the bathroom like an old married couple. Megan's headache had disappeared, but a new ache settled in her chest.

She stood at the door to their room without reaching for the knob.

Daniel's hands descended on her shoulders, and he pulled her back against him. "What's wrong?"

"You realize that once we seal the deal with Kennedy, we don't have to continue being married."

Daniel turned her toward him, a frown settling deep on his brow. "We have to stay married for at least six months to fulfill your grandmother's stipulation or you won't get the rest of your trust fund until you're thirty."

She shrugged. "I don't need that money. I only needed the funds we were able to secure to take care of the horses my father is giving me."

He shook his head. "I disagree. You need to have that money for emergencies. You have a couple years before you turn thirty." Daniel smiled. "Tell you what. We can discuss it when we get back to the Lucky C. We'll come up with a timeline if we need to. For today, we're Mr. and Mrs. Colton." He brushed a light kiss over her lips, then bent to seal her mouth with his.

Megan sank into him, loving the way his tongue tasted fresh from the toothpaste.

When he finally raised his head, he stared down at her. "What say you and me skip this meeting? I can think of a dozen other things we could do as newlyweds that don't involve leaving this room."

Megan laughed up at his teasing grin. "I'm in."

He took her hand and tugged her back toward the bedroom.

She started to follow him, but reason kicked in and she dug in her heels. "We can't miss this meeting."

"I don't need this deal. I can find another breeder." Daniel pulled her into his arms. "Stay with me today. Forget the crash last night. Forget the meeting with Kennedy."

Megan cupped his cheek and leaned up on her toes. "We've worked too hard to let this fall through the cracks. If you want to spend the day here with me, let's take care of business first. Then we can come back to our room and attempt all those dozen things we can do without leaving."

Daniel sighed. "You are too smart for my own good." He gripped her hand in his and opened the door to the room. "Come on, let's go make a deal. The sooner we do, the sooner we can start celebrating."

The first real day of the symposium was packed, especially at the arena, where breeders from all over the country had brought horses they had up for stud or for sale.

Daniel and Megan wove through the crowd, searching for the Kennedy Farms stalls with the stud Daniel was most interested in using for his breeding stock.

Daniel nodded toward a group of men gathered

around a pen with a black stallion pawing at the sawdust. "There's Marshall."

Megan glanced in the direction Daniel gazed. "He appears to be looking for you. Go on. I'll catch up in just a moment. I need to visit the ladies' room."

"I'll go with you."

"Don't be silly." She batted at him playfully. "You can't go into the ladies' room."

Daniel frowned. "After what happened last night, I'm not leaving you."

"I'll only be a moment. Go on before you lose him in the crowd."

Daniel's gaze switched from Megan to Marshall and back. "No. I can find him again."

"Daniel." Marshall Kennedy waved at Daniel, ending the argument.

"I'll be right back." Megan slipped through the crowd toward the last sign she'd seen indicating bathrooms.

A flash of blond hair made her stop short in the hallway and she stared at the back of a woman wearing jeans and a soft pink blouse, her blond hair hanging loose down to the middle of her back. Something about the way she carried herself struck a chord of familiarity in Megan. When she turned to glance out at the arena, Megan got a clear view of her profile and gasped. "Christine?"

Her cousin ground to a halt and turned toward her. "Megan!" She flung her arms around her and hugged her. "It's so good to see a familiar face in the crowd."

"What are you doing here?"

"When Josh and I get married, we want to start a horse ranch and breed horses. He thought the symposium was a good idea to give us a chance to see what it's all about and how much is involved." Christine's brows rose. "All those years we played at the Triple Diamond, sneaking out to ride, I never knew how much went into the actual operations of a horse-breeding facility."

"There is a lot to it," Megan conceded. "I thought Josh was into real estate."

"He is. But he comes across deals on ranches. He thinks it would be a great investment." Christine glanced over her shoulder. "Are you here with Daniel? Shouldn't you two be on your honeymoon or back in Oklahoma?"

"We'd planned on coming to the symposium before we decided to get married. So, here we are." Megan nodded toward the bathroom. "If you'll excuse me, I had too much coffee this morning. Maybe we can meet up and talk later."

"Sounds good. I can't wait to let Josh know you two are here." Christine waved and stood on her toes, searching the crowd.

Megan left her and entered the ladies' room. No one else was in the facility. She took care of business and washed her hands. When she turned to the exit, a speck of dust landed in her eye and she blinked. The particle felt like sand, scraping across her cornea.

Megan didn't want to keep Daniel waiting and wondering where she was—already, her presence had caused him so many delays and problems. But she couldn't open her eye without tearing. She leaned toward the mirror and lifted her eyelid with her finger. She couldn't see the speck so she blinked several times until the irritation cleared.

With one bloodshot eye, Megan walked out of the restroom, and ran into Josh, Christine's fiancé. "Josh, I was surprised to see you and Christine here."

He gripped her wrist. "No time to talk. Christine told me I could find you here. Daniel's been injured by Kennedy's stud. I was sent to get you and take you to the hospital where they're transporting him."

Megan's heart plummeted to the pit of her belly. "Daniel's hurt? What happened? Where is he?" She pushed past him and would have run out into the arena, but Josh's hand held tight.

"He was kicked in the head. They had an ambulance on standby, and they loaded him up."

"So quickly?" Megan tugged her arm, trying to shake loose of Josh's grip. "I have to go with him."

"That's what I'm telling you. I know which hospital they're taking him to. Come with me."

Her pulse raced through her, her heart thumping against her ribs. Megan nodded. "Okay. Take me there. I have to get to him."

"They went out the back way." Josh held tight to her wrist and half led, half dragged her deeper into the back rooms surrounding the arena.

Megan's breath lodged in her throat. After all that had happened in Oklahoma and Vegas, had someone finally succeeded? Her stomach clenched and she hurried alongside Josh. Daniel was injured. *God, please don't let him die.*

Chapter 18

Daniel stood beside Marshall Kennedy at one of the stock panel pens constructed for Kennedy Farms. Inside, Marshall's Striker's Royal Advantage, the black quarter horse stud Daniel had kept his eye on for the past four months, pawed at the sawdust as if impatient to get back to familiar surroundings.

Daniel had wanted this deal so much, he'd married his assistant to make it happen. In the process, he'd come to realize he'd fallen head over heels in love with the beautiful woman, and his priorities had shifted.

If this deal didn't go though…so what? There would be another. But there would not be another Megan.

Kennedy laid a hand on Daniel's shoulder. "My driver told me what happened last night. Are you and Megan all right?"

Daniel turned in the direction Megan had gone, his

gaze searching the crowd, hoping she'd emerge. "She got a bump on her head but was too stubborn to rest."

Kennedy chuckled. "She's Frank's daughter, all right." He tilted his head toward the stallion. "So, what do you think?"

Daniel cast a quick glance at the stallion and returned his gaze to the direction Megan should have come from by now. "Mr. Kennedy—"

"Call me Marshall." The man stuck his hand out. "So do we have a deal?"

"He's exactly what our program needs…" Daniel looked over his shoulder again. "Excuse me, Marshall. I'm worried about my wife. I need to find her. I hope we can finish this discussion later."

"Certainly. A pretty lady like Megan needs a man to watch out for her." The old man waved Daniel away. "Go. We'll be here all of today and tomorrow."

"Thank you," Daniel called out as he trotted back the way he'd come, searching for the bathrooms.

"Daniel!" a female voice called out. "There you are."

Daniel turned toward the sound and found Megan's cousin Christine hurrying toward him. "I ran into Megan a few minutes ago and told her we should get together for dinner. Josh has so many questions about horse ranching, and I know you two are the experts."

Daniel stared at her, trying to wrap his head around the fact Christine was in Reno. "Why are you here?"

"Like I told Megan, Josh has considered purchasing a horse ranch. He wants to start a breeding program like you and Megan have." Christine smiled broadly. "Wouldn't that be wonderful? Megan and I grew up riding together. It gave us lots in common besides being cousins."

Something clicked in Daniel's head. "Christine, where were you the day before we saw you in California?"

"I was staying at the Triple Diamond." She tilted her head. "Why do you ask?"

"Where did you say Josh was the day before we arrived at the Triple Diamond?"

"He was out of town on some real estate training trip."

Daniel gripped her arms. "Where?"

"I don't know." Her pretty brows descended. "He goes on so many."

A lead weight settled in Daniel's gut as he recalled Megan correcting Ryan about who stood to inherit the Talbot fortune should Megan pass away. Not her husband but the next living Talbot descendant. Christine.

And Josh was poised to marry the beautiful Christine.

Daniel demanded, "Where is Josh now?"

"I don't know." Christine stared down at Daniel's hands on her arms. "I ran into him a minute ago and told him I'd seen Megan. You're hurting me."

Daniel let go of Christine. "Did you tell him where you'd seen her?"

"Of course. I saw her right here." Christine pointed toward a sign leading to the ladies' room. "She was going into the bathroom."

Daniel ran for the bathroom and burst through the door. A woman stood at the sink, washing her hands. Her eyes widened and she smiled. "I think you have the wrong bathroom. The men's room is next door."

Daniel slammed through the stalls, finding each one empty. When he came out, he stopped by the woman washing her hands. "Did you see a woman with strawberry blond hair leave this room?"

The woman dried her hands on a paper towel, her

brow furrowing. "There was a woman headed down the hallway with a man when I entered the bathroom. She looked upset. And yes, she had strawberry blond hair."

"Which way were they going?"

The woman stepped out of the bathroom and pointed. "That way."

Christine stood in the hallway. "Megan wasn't in there?"

"No." Daniel grabbed her arms again. "If you know where Josh might be, tell me now."

Christine's eyes widened. "I don't know. I thought he'd find you." She squirmed under the intensity of Daniel's stare. "You're hurting me."

"Are you the one who has tried more than once to kill Megan?" Daniel shook her. "Are you?"

Christine's eyes widened. She shook her head. "Of course not. I love Megan like a sister. I would never hurt her." She flung her hand in the air. "I didn't even know she was being targeted. Does her father know?"

"Four times already. Someone broke into our room on our honeymoon in Vegas. Then she was poisoned before we left California, and someone sabotaged our plane."

Christine started to cry. "Josh wouldn't do that… would he?"

"Who else other than you stands to gain from Megan's death? You inherit her father's wealth. If Josh is married to you, he benefits."

"I don't believe you."

"Believe what you want, but help me find Megan or your fiancé. I have a feeling he's behind the attempts." Daniel set her to the side and raced down the hallway, ducking into every unlocked room along the way and banging on the ones that were locked. "Megan!" he yelled. Dear God, where was she? If Josh was the one responsible for all of the attempts on Megan's life, he had her and could possibly succeed this time.

Daniel couldn't let that happen.

The deeper Josh led her into the maintenance corridors of the arena, the more terrified Megan became. Finally she pulled to a stop. "If we're going to the hospital, we should be working our way out of the arena, not deeper into it."

"This is a shortcut," he insisted.

"I don't think so." Megan yanked her hand loose. "I'm going back out the front and catching a taxi to the hospital."

"Sorry, that can't happen. I've spent too much time and money chasing after you." He grabbed her arm and yanked her so close his cologne nearly overpowered her. A scent that sparked a dark memory.

"What do you mean you've been chasing me?" The scent memory of that cologne hit her, and an image of being in the hotel in Vegas with an intruder washed over her. "You!" This was the man who'd attacked her in Vegas.

Despite Josh's boy-next-door good looks with his sandy-blond hair, tailored jeans and white cotton shirt, the glare in his eyes turned Megan's blood to ice.

"Yeah, what about me?" Josh jerked her around and clamped her to him with his arms, dragging her deeper into the darkened corridors.

Megan fought him, twisting and turning, but he had her arms pinned and her body pressed tightly to his. She didn't have room to lever herself free. "You were the one who attacked me in Vegas," she said.

"Says who?"

"I recognize the cologne."

"And you think the scent of cologne will stand up in court?" He dragged her into a room and shut the door behind him. "Look, you've already been enough trouble. We end this now."

"Damn right we do." She stomped on his instep and dug her elbow into his gut.

He loosened his hold long enough for her to break loose and dart past him to the door.

She was twisting the knob when Josh cursed. His low voice cut across the room. "Open the door and I'll shoot you."

Megan glanced over her shoulder.

The man held a small but deadly-looking pistol pointed at her.

"What have I done to make you want to kill me?" she asked, refusing to remove her hand from the knob.

"Call it an accident of birth."

She snorted. "If it's my parents' wealth you want, I never wanted it in the first place. But you'll have to take it up with them."

"I will, once you're out of the picture."

A chill slithered down the back of Megan's neck. The man was insane. To think he could get away with one murder was bad enough. "What makes you think you won't be caught?"

"You're a wealthy man's daughter. Anyone could take a potshot at you."

"The Tulsa and Las Vegas police departments are already searching for the person responsible for the attacks on me. It's only a matter of time."

"I left no trail."

"Are you certain?" She raised her brows, twisting the knob on the door so slowly, she hoped he didn't notice. "They're already looking at Christine as a possible suspect because she stands to inherit my father's wealth if I die." Megan shook her head. "Did you ever really care about her?"

"She's a means to an end."

"The end being that you want my father's fortune." Megan had the knob twisted around. All she had to do was jerk the door open and dive out into the corridor. "How do you know my father hasn't already changed his will? I told him I didn't want his property and that he could leave it all to the charity of his choice."

"He hasn't changed his will. I've seen it."

Anger shot through her. "My parents trusted you in their home."

"Yeah, and your cousin is gullible enough to marry me. Seems the entire family is too trusting." He shrugged. "Makes it easier."

"You might have gotten away with poisoning me or sabotaging the airplane. But you won't get away with shooting me."

"No? Are you willing to bet your life on that?" His eyes narrowed, and he leveled the gun on her.

If he was going to shoot her, she'd be dead, anyway. Megan threw open the door, dove into the corridor and rolled to the side and onto her feet.

Josh lunged for her, snagging her long hair. He jerked her back and locked an arm around her throat.

Megan bent double, trying to throw him over her. The man was bigger and stronger than she was and had her in his grasp, tightening his hold.

Her vision blurring, Megan knew she couldn't give

up. Her parents would be next and then Christine. She wouldn't let this greedy bastard win. But she couldn't quite shake him loose, and her own strength was waning.

A shout down the hall made Josh twist around, still holding her throat.

"Let her go, Josh. You won't get away with it." Daniel stood several feet away, holding his hands up in surrender. "Everyone knows you're behind the attempts on Megan's life."

"If by 'everyone' you mean you, that's hardly a threat." He whipped his gun out and pointed it at Daniel, tightening his arm on Megan's throat.

Her voice cut off with the air to her lungs. Megan could do nothing to help Daniel.

"Oh, Josh." Christine stepped up beside Daniel, tears flowing down her cheeks. "You didn't need my uncle's money. You were doing so well on your own."

"What do you know?" Josh said. "You see what you want to see."

She swiped at her tears. "You're right. I saw a man I thought loved me and wanted to marry me because of me, not my uncle's fortune." She walked toward him. "You were going to kill me, weren't you?"

"Christine, don't." Daniel grabbed her and flung her behind him.

Josh shifted his aim from Christine back to Daniel. "You all deserve to die. You certainly don't deserve to inherit Talbot's millions."

Yeah, and neither do you. Megan did the only thing she could and let her knees buckle so suddenly, Josh didn't suspect it. Her weight tipped him forward along with the aim of his weapon.

Daniel dove at him, knocking the gun from his hand.

It hit the floor and slid out of reach. Before Josh could recover, Daniel swung a fist at the man's face, hitting him so hard he fell backward, taking Megan with him. She landed on top of his chest.

His hold loosened. Megan rolled to the side and away from him, the dizziness fading as she filled her lungs with gulps of air.

Daniel yanked Josh up by the collar and slammed his fist into his face again. Josh fought back, but Daniel was bigger, faster and stronger.

Megan crawled across the floor, reaching for the gun.

Christine grabbed it first and pointed it at the two men fighting. "Stop it!" she screamed. "Stop it or I'll shoot." Tears ran down her face.

Daniel rammed his fist into Josh's gut one last time and stood back.

Josh, a hand pressed to his belly, his face a bloody mess, looked across at Christine. "Give me the gun."

"Don't, Christine," Megan said. "He doesn't love you. He only wants your money."

She shook her head. "I trusted you."

He looked up at her, the charming man Megan had first met, a desperate battered face now. "I did it for us." He took a step forward.

Christine pointed the gun at his chest. "You tried to kill the only family I have left." She held the gun out, her finger on the trigger.

Megan's breath caught and held. "Christine, don't shoot the bastard. He's not worth it. It's over. Let the police take him."

"He lied to me."

"He lied to all of us." Megan stood and inched her

way toward Christine, sliding an arm around her waist. "What's important is that you still have your family."

"He would have killed you." Christine looked to Megan. "You're the sister I never had."

"I'm okay, sweetie. Let me have the gun."

Her hands shaking, Christine gave Megan the gun and buried her face in Megan's shoulder.

Josh made a fast move toward Christine and Megan.

Daniel grabbed his arm and yanked it up behind his back, between his shoulder blades. "Give it up. This is over."

Within minutes they had the Reno police collect Josh and take him away. Megan called her parents, and her father agreed to fly out to bring Christine back to the Triple Diamond. When the dust cleared and the police assured Megan and Daniel that they were free to leave the arena, Daniel pulled Megan into his arms and held her for a long time.

"I didn't think I'd find you in time."

She laughed, the sound choking on a sob. "I didn't think you would, either."

He set her at arm's length and pushed a strand of her long hair back behind her ear, his touch so gentle it made Megan want to cry. "The attempts on your life made me realize something."

She looked up into his deep brown eyes and gasped at his expression.

"I love you, Megan Talbot Colton." He cupped her cheek and brushed his lips across hers. "I can't give you what your parents can, but I can love you more than I love to breathe."

"How many times do I have to tell people that I don't want what my parents have?" She wrapped her arms around his waist and hugged him. "I have everything I want, as long as I have you."

"Well, it's a good thing, because that's all I can promise. You can have me, and all of my wealth, which isn't much, and my whole heart."

"Then I'd have all I'd need, and I'd still be the richest woman in the world."

His lips descended on hers, and he held her wrapped in his warmth and strength.

A discreet cough brought them back to the arena, and Megan lifted her head.

Marshall Kennedy stood with his arms crossed and a big smile spreading across his face. "I heard what happened, and I'm glad to see you both aren't too worse for the excitement." He stuck out his hand. "I can offer you two a ride back to your hotel or to the hospital."

Daniel tucked Megan in the curve of his arm and shook Mr. Kennedy's hand. "Thank you, sir."

"I also want you to know," Marshall said, "I'm ready to sign whatever deal you want to make. You're the kind of people I want to work with. You're smart and tough and believe in taking care of your family."

"That's right." Daniel grinned down at Megan. "And I want Megan to be part of my family for a very long time."

She stared up at him, butterflies beating in her stomach. "You mean that, don't you?"

He nodded. "Like I promised in front of God and Elvis, I do."

Chapter 19

Daniel sat in the chair of honor, the most comfortable easy chair in Jack's living room, with his feet kicked back and a bowl of popcorn in his lap, happier than he'd been in…well…forever.

"You didn't think you'd get by without letting us throw you a bachelor party, did you?" Brett tossed a piece of popcorn into the air and caught it in his mouth.

"You guys didn't have to go to all this trouble." Daniel glanced around the room at his brothers, gathered in front of the large television screen at the halftime of the football game.

"Now that we're getting so many females in the Colton family, it's nice to have an excuse for a guys' night out," Jack said.

Daniel knew Jack was perfectly content to spend all his evenings with his beautiful wife, Tracy, and his son, Seth.

"It also gives us a chance to impart our wisdom on you without getting slugged," Brett said. "Like, if your wife asks you if the outfit she's wearing makes her look fat, you tell her what you know she wants to hear, or go to bed in the guest room."

"Never go to bed mad," Jack said. "Makeup sex is so much better than a cold shoulder."

Eric dropped onto the end of the couch nearest Daniel's seat. "If you want to make your marriage last, just remember to tell her you love her. A woman never gets tired of hearing that."

Daniel nodded. "I appreciate all the advice. Megan and I are so new to this marriage thing. I don't want to screw it up right out the chute."

"What about you, Ryan?" Brett nudged Ryan with his foot where he lay sprawled on the floor in front of the television. "Got any advice for Dan?"

Ryan shrugged. "Since I'm the lone stag at the stag party, don't go with any advice I've got to say. Apparently my methods aren't working."

"That's right," Jack said. "You're the last single man standing. Tracy and I are hitched, which is a good thing considering she's pregnant."

"No kidding?" Brett grinned. "Hannah will be happy to hear there will be another little one to play with."

Daniel leaned forward and clapped a hand on his older brother's shoulder. "Congratulations." He couldn't wait to start a brood of his own. A couple of strawberry blond-haired girls and strapping boys were what he had in mind. More family to love.

"Well, Ryan, that puts the pressure on you to find a woman to love and marry." Daniel sat back in his chair. "My advice to you is to elope. It's much easier than all the planning and trouble Greta's going through in pulling her wedding together."

"I'd love to skip all the hoopla," Jack admitted. "But I told Tracy that whatever she wanted was fine with me."

"Speaking of Greta." Ryan sat up. "I swear I saw her the other day. Is she back in town and no one bothered to let me know?"

All heads shook.

"Not that I know of," Daniel said. "I'll be glad when her wedding's over. I never would have thought Greta would go for a big wedding. She struck me as a tomboy."

"Well, I guess we can't all go as classy as our man Daniel and get Elvis to officiate." Ryan laughed.

Daniel threw a piece of popcorn at him. "As far as I'm concerned, I wouldn't change a thing. I'm married to a helluva woman, I love her and she loves me."

Jack sat back, staring at the television commercials. "Can't ask for more than that."

Daniel couldn't agree more. He loved Megan so much, he wanted to be with her every waking moment. The party couldn't end soon enough. He pushed to his feet. "Boys, thank you for the party. But I have a beautiful wife waiting for me back at the cabin and…well, she's a lot better looking than the lot of you."

He hurried out the door, climbed into his truck and drove the short distance to the cabin.

Before he could climb out of the vehicle, the door to the cabin opened and Megan stepped out on the porch, her brows knit. "What's wrong? The game's not over yet. I've been watching it."

Daniel strode toward her. "I couldn't concentrate on the game when I knew you were here. Alone. I thought maybe we could make good use of our day off and get a little naked." He swept her up in his arms and carried her across the threshold.

"Sweetheart, you know how to sweep a woman off her feet."

"I'm full of interesting talents," he said, nuzzling the curve of her neck. "Wait until you see what I can do when I get your clothes off."

Megan's laughter was low and sultry, her fingers already working at the buttons on his shirt. "I didn't know I'd be marrying an insatiable man."

With a full heart, he laid her on their bed and kissed her, finally coming home to the start of his very own family. "Darlin', you bring out the beast in me."

* * * * *

Read on for a sneak preview of FATAL AFFAIR,
the first book in the FATAL *series by*
New York Times *bestselling author*
Marie Force

ONE

T<small>HE SMELL HIT</small> him first.

"Ugh, what the hell is that?" Nick Cappuano dropped his keys into his coat pocket and stepped into the spacious, well-appointed Watergate apartment that his boss, Senator John O'Connor, had inherited from his father.

"Senator!" Nick tried to identify the foul metallic odor.

Making his way through the living room, he noticed parts and pieces of the suit John wore yesterday strewn over sofas and chairs, laying a path to the bedroom. He had called the night before to check in with Nick after a dinner meeting with Virginia's Democratic Party leadership, and said he was on his way home. Nick had reminded his thirty-six-year-old boss to set his alarm.

"Senator?" John hated when Nick called him that when they were alone, but Nick insisted the people in John's life afford him the respect of his title.

The odd stench permeating the apartment caused a tingle of anxiety to register on the back of Nick's neck. "John?"

He stepped into the bedroom and gasped. Drenched in blood, John sat up in bed, his eyes open but vacant. A knife spiked through his neck held him in place against the headboard. His hands rested in a pool of blood in his lap.

Gagging, the last thing Nick noticed before he bolted

to the bathroom to vomit was that something was hanging out of John's mouth.

Once the violent retching finally stopped, Nick stood up on shaky legs, wiped his mouth with the back of his hand, and rested against the vanity, waiting to see if there would be more. His cell phone rang. When he didn't take the call, his pager vibrated. Nick couldn't find the wherewithal to answer, to say the words that would change everything. *The senator is dead. John's been murdered.* He wanted to go back to when he was still in his car, fuming and under the assumption that his biggest problem that day would be what to do about the man-child he worked for who had once again slept through his alarm.

Thoughts of John, dating back to their first meeting in a history class at Harvard freshman year, flashed through Nick's mind, hundreds of snippets spanning a nearly twenty-year friendship. As if to convince himself that his eyes had not deceived him, he leaned forward to glance into the bedroom, wincing at the sight of his best friend—the brother of his heart—stabbed through the neck and covered with blood.

Nick's eyes burned with tears, but he refused to give in to them. Not now. Later maybe, but not now. His phone rang again. This time he reached for it and saw it was Christina, his deputy chief of staff, but didn't take the call. Instead, he dialed 911.

Taking a deep breath to calm his racing heart and making a supreme effort to keep the hysteria out of his voice, he said, "I need to report a murder." He gave the address and stumbled into the living room to wait for the police, all the while trying to get his head around the image of his dead friend, a visual he already knew would haunt him forever.

Twenty long minutes later, two officers arrived, took a quick look in the bedroom and radioed for backup. Nick was certain neither of them recognized the victim.

He felt as if he was being sucked into a riptide, pulled further and further from the safety of shore, until drawing a breath became a laborious effort. He told the cops exactly what happened—his boss failed to show up for work, he came looking for him and found him dead.

"Your boss's name?"

"United States Senator John O'Connor." Nick watched the two young officers go pale in the instant before they made a second more urgent call for backup.

"Another scandal at the Watergate," Nick heard one of them mutter.

His cell phone rang yet again. This time he reached for it.

"Yeah," he said softly.

"Nick!" Christina cried. "Where the *hell* are you guys? Trevor's having a heart attack!" She referred to their communications director, who had back-to-back interviews scheduled for the senator that morning.

"He's dead, Chris."

"Who's dead? What're you talking about?"

"John."

Her soft cry broke his heart. *"No."* That she was desperately in love with John was no secret to Nick. That she was also a consummate professional who would never act on those feelings was one of the many reasons Nick respected her.

"I'm sorry to just blurt it out like that."

"How?" she asked in a small voice.

"Stabbed in his bed."

Her ravaged moan echoed through the phone. "But who... I mean, *why*?"

"The cops are here, but I don't know anything yet. I need you to request a postponement on the vote."

"I can't," she said, adding in a whisper, "I can't think about that right now."

"You have to, Chris. That bill is his legacy. We can't let all his hard work be for nothing. Can you do it? For him?"

"Yes...okay."

"You have to pull yourself together for the staff, but don't tell them yet. Not until his parents are notified."

"Oh, God, his poor parents. You should go, Nick. It'd be better coming from you than cops they don't know."

"I don't know if I can. How do I tell people I love that their son's been murdered?"

"He'd want it to come from you."

"I suppose you're right. I'll see if the cops will let me."

"What're we going to do without him, Nick?" She posed a question he'd been grappling with himself. "I just can't imagine this world, this *life*, without him."

"I can't either," Nick said, knowing it would be a much different life without John O'Connor at the center of it.

"He's really dead?" she asked as if to convince herself it wasn't a cruel joke. "Someone killed him?"

"Yes."

OUTSIDE THE CHIEF'S office suite, Detective Sergeant Sam Holland smoothed her hands over the toffee-colored hair she corralled into a clip for work, pinched some color into cheeks that hadn't seen the light of day in weeks, and adjusted her gray suit jacket over a red scoop-neck top.

Taking a deep breath to calm her nerves and settle her chronically upset stomach, she pushed open the door and stepped inside. Chief Farnsworth's receptionist greeted her with a smile. "Go right in, Sergeant Holland. He's waiting for you."

Great, Sam thought as she left the receptionist with a weak smile. Before she could give in to the urge to turn tail and run, she erased the grimace from her face and went in.

"Sergeant." The chief, a man she'd once called Uncle Joe, stood up and came around the big desk to greet her with a firm handshake. His gray eyes skirted over her with concern and sympathy, both of which were new since "the incident." She despised being the reason for either. "You look well."

"I feel well."

"Glad to hear it." He gestured for her to have a seat. "Coffee?"

"No, thanks."

Pouring himself a cup, he glanced over his shoulder. "I've been worried about you, Sam."

"I'm sorry for causing you worry and for disgracing the department." This was the first chance she'd had to speak directly to him since she returned from a month of administrative leave, during which she'd practiced the sentence over and over. She thought she'd delivered it with convincing sincerity.

"Sam," he sighed as he sat across from her, cradling his mug between big hands. "You've done nothing to disgrace yourself or the department. Everyone makes mistakes."

"Not everyone makes mistakes that result in a dead child, Chief."

He studied her for a long, intense moment as if he was making some sort of decision. "Senator John O'Connor was found murdered in his apartment this morning."

"Jesus," she gasped. "How?"

"I don't have all the details, but from what I've been told so far, it appears he was dismembered and stabbed through the neck. Apparently, his chief of staff found him."

"Nick," she said softly.

"Excuse me?"

"Nick Cappuano is O'Connor's chief of staff."

"You know him?"

"Knew him. Years ago," she added, surprised and unsettled to discover the memory of him still had power over her, that just the sound of his name rolling off her lips could make her heart race.

"I'm assigning the case to you."

Surprised at being thrust so forcefully back into the real work she had craved since her return to duty, she couldn't help but ask, "Why me?"

"Because you need this, and so do I. We both need a win."

The press had been relentless in its criticism of him, of her, of the department, but to hear him acknowledge it made her ache. Her father had come up through the ranks with Farnsworth, which was probably the number one reason why she still had a job. "Is this a test? Find out who killed the senator and my previous sins are forgiven?"

He put down his coffee cup and leaned forward, elbows resting on knees. "The only person who needs to forgive you, Sam, is you."

Infuriated by the surge of emotion brought on by his softly spoken words, Sam cleared her throat and stood up. "Where does O'Connor live?"

"The Watergate. Two uniforms are already there. Crime scene is on its way." He handed her a slip of paper with the address. "I don't have to tell you that this needs to be handled with the utmost discretion."

He also didn't have to tell her that this was the only chance she'd get at redemption.

"Won't the Feds want in on this?"

"They might, but they don't have jurisdiction, and they know it. They'll be breathing down my neck, though, so report directly to me. I want to know everything ten minutes after you do. I'll smooth it with Stahl," he added, referring to the lieutenant she usually answered to.

Heading for the door, she said, "I won't let you down."

"You never have before."

With her hand resting on the door handle, she turned back to him. "Are you saying that as the chief of police or as my Uncle Joe?"

His face lifted into a small but sincere smile. "Both."

TWO

SITTING ON JOHN'S sofa under the watchful eyes of the two policemen, Nick's mind raced with the staggering number of things that needed to be done, details to be seen to, people to call. His cell phone rang relentlessly, but he ignored it after deciding he would talk to no one until he had seen John's parents. Almost twenty years ago they took an instant shine to the hard-luck scholarship student their son brought home from Harvard for a weekend visit and made him part of their family. Nick owed them so much, not the least of which was hearing the news of their son's death from him if possible.

He ran his hand through his hair. "How much longer?"

"Detectives are on their way."

Ten minutes later, Nick heard her before he saw her. A flurry of activity and a burst of energy preceded the detectives' entrance into the apartment. He suppressed a groan. *Wasn't it enough that his friend and boss had been murdered? He had to face* her, *too? Weren't there thousands of District cops? Was she really the only one available?*

Sam came into the apartment, oozing authority and competence. In light of her recent troubles, Nick couldn't believe she had any of either left. "Get some tape across that door," she ordered one of the officers. "Start a log with a timeline of who got here when. No one comes in or goes out without my okay, got it?"

"Yes, ma'am. The Patrol sergeant is on his way along with Deputy Chief Conklin and Detective Captain Malone."

"Let me know when they get here." Without so much as a glance in his direction, Nick watched her stalk through the apartment and disappear into the bedroom. Following her, a handsome young detective with bed head nodded to Nick.

He heard the murmur of voices from the bedroom and saw a camera flash. They emerged fifteen minutes later, both noticeably paler. For some reason, Nick was gratified to know the detectives working the case weren't so jaded as to be unaffected by what they'd just seen.

"Start a canvass of the building," Sam ordered her partner. "Where the hell is Crime Scene?"

"Hung up at another homicide," one of the other officers replied.

She finally turned to Nick, nothing in her pale blue eyes indicating that she recognized or remembered him. But the fact that she didn't introduce herself or ask for his name told him she knew exactly who he was. "We'll need your prints."

"They're on file," he mumbled. "Congressional background check."

She wrote something in the small notebook she tugged from the back pocket of gray, form-fitting pants. There were years on her gorgeous face that hadn't been there the last time he'd had the opportunity to look closely, and he couldn't tell if her hair was as long as it used to be since it was twisted into a clip. The curvy body and endless legs hadn't changed at all.

"No forced entry," she noted. "Who has a key?"

"Who *doesn't* have a key?"

"I'll need a list. You have a key, I assume."

Nick nodded. "That's how I got in."

"Was he seeing anyone?"

"No one serious, but he had no trouble attracting female companionship." Nick didn't add that John's casual approach to women and sex had been a source of tension between the two men, with Nick fearful that John's social life would one day lead to political trouble. He hadn't imagined it might also lead to murder.

"When was the last time you saw him?"

"When he left the office for a dinner meeting with the Virginia Democrats last night. Around six-thirty or so."

"Spoke to him?"

"Around ten when he said he was on his way home."

"Alone?"

"He didn't say, and I didn't ask."

"Take me through what happened this morning."

He told her about Christina trying to reach John, beginning at seven, and of coming to the apartment expecting to find the senator once again sleeping through his alarm.

"So this has happened before?"

"No, he's never been murdered before."

Her expression was anything but amused. "Do you think this is funny, Mr. Cappuano?"

"Hardly. My best friend is dead, Sergeant. A United States senator has been murdered. There's nothing funny about that."

"Which is why you need to answer the questions and save the droll humor for a more appropriate time."

Chastened, Nick said, "He slept through his alarm and ringing telephones at least once, if not twice, a month."

"Did he drink?"

"Socially, but I rarely saw him drunk."

"Prescription drugs? Sleeping pills?"

Nick shook his head. "He was just a very heavy sleeper."

"And it fell to his chief of staff to wake him up? There wasn't anyone else you could send?"

"The senator valued his privacy. There've been occasions when he wasn't alone, and neither of us felt his love life should be the business of his staff."

"But he didn't care if you knew who he was sleeping with?"

"He knew he could count on my discretion." He looked up, unprepared for the punch to the gut that occurred when his eyes met hers. Her unsettled expression made him wonder if she felt it, too. "His parents need to be notified. I'd like to be the one to tell them."

Sam studied him for a long moment. "I'll arrange it. Where are they?"

"At their farm in Leesburg. It needs to be soon. We're postponing a vote we worked for months to get to. It'll be all over the news that something's up."

"What's the vote for?"

He told her about the landmark immigration bill and John's role as the co-sponsor.

With a curt nod, she walked away.

AN HOUR LATER, Nick was a passenger in an unmarked Metropolitan Police SUV, headed west to Leesburg with Sam at the wheel. She'd left her partner with a staggering list of instructions and insisted on accompanying Nick to tell John's parents.

"Do you need something to eat?"

He shook his head. No way could he even think about eating—not with the horrific task he had ahead of him. Besides, his stomach hadn't recovered from the earlier bout of vomiting.

"You know, we could still call the Loudoun County Police or the Virginia State Police to handle this," she said for the second time.

"No."

After an awkward silence, she said, "I'm sorry this happened to your friend and that you had to see him that way."

"Thank you."

"Are you going to answer that?" she asked of his relentless cell phone.

"No."

"How about you turn it off then? I can't stand listening to a ringing phone."

Reaching for his belt, he grabbed his cell phone, his emotions still raw after watching John be taken from his apartment in a body bag. Before he shut the cell phone off, he called Christina.

"Hey," she said, her voice heavy with relief and emotion. "I've been trying to reach you."

"Sorry." Pulling his tie loose and releasing his top button, he cast a sideways glance at Sam, whose warm, feminine fragrance had overtaken the small space inside the car. "I was dealing with cops."

"Where are you now?"

"On my way to Leesburg."

"God," Christina sighed. "I don't envy you that. Are you okay?"

"Never better."

"I'm sorry. Dumb question."

"It's okay. Who knows what we're supposed to say or do in this situation. Did you postpone the vote?"

"Yes, but Martin and McDougal are having an apoplexy," she said, meaning John's co-sponsor on the bill and the Democratic majority leader. "They're demanding to know what's going on."

"Hold them off. Another hour. Maybe two. Same thing with the staff. I'll give you the green light as soon as I've told his parents."

"I will. Everyone knows something's up because the Capitol Police posted an officer outside John's office and won't let anyone in there."

"It's because the cops are waiting for a search warrant," Nick told her.

"Why do they need a warrant to search the victim's office?"

"Something about chain of custody with evidence and pacifying the Capitol Police."

"Oh, I see. I was thinking we should have Trevor draft a statement so we're ready."

"That's why I called."

"We'll get on it." She sounded relieved to have something to do.

"Are you okay with telling Trevor? Want me to do it?"

"I think I can do it, but thanks for asking."

"How're you holding up?" he asked.

"I'm in total shock…all that promise and potential just gone…" She began to weep again. "It's going to hurt like hell when the shock wears off."

"Yeah," he said softly. "No doubt."

"I'm here if you need anything."

"Me, too, but I'm going to shut the phone off for a while. It's been ringing nonstop."

"I'll email the statement to you when we have it done."

"Thanks, Christina. I'll call you later." Nick ended the call and took a look at his recent email messages, hardly surprised by the outpouring of dismay and concern over the postponement of the vote. One was from Senator Martin himself—What the fuck is going on, Cappuano?

Sighing, he turned off the cell phone and dropped it into his coat pocket.

"Was that your girlfriend?" Sam asked, startling him.

"No, my deputy."

"Oh."

Wondering what she was getting at, he added, "We work closely together. We're good friends."

"Why are you being so defensive?"

"What's your *problem*?" he asked.

"I don't have a problem. You're the one with problems."

"So all that great press you've been getting lately hasn't been a problem for you?"

"Why, Nick, I didn't realize you cared."

"I don't."

"Yes, you made that very clear."

He spun halfway around in the seat to stare at her. "*Are you for real?* You're the one who didn't return any of my calls."

She glanced over at him, her face flat with surprise. "What calls?"

After staring at her in disbelief for a long moment, he settled back in his seat and fixed his eyes on the cars sharing the Interstate with them.

A few minutes passed in uneasy silence.

"What calls, Nick?"

"I called you," he said softly. "For days after that night, I tried to reach you."

"I didn't know," she stammered. "No one told me."

"It doesn't matter now. It was a long time ago." But if his reaction to seeing her again after six years of thinking about her was any indication, it *did* matter. It mattered a lot.

Continue reading Sam and Nick's story in
FATAL AFFAIR, available in
print and ebook from Carina Press.

REQUEST YOUR FREE BOOKS!
2 FREE NOVELS PLUS 2 FREE GIFTS!

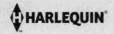

ROMANTIC suspense

Sparked by danger, fueled by passion

YES! Please send me 2 FREE Harlequin® Romantic Suspense novels and my 2 FREE gifts (gifts are worth about $10). After receiving them, if I don't wish to receive any more books, I can return the shipping statement marked "cancel." If I don't cancel, I will receive 4 brand-new novels every month and be billed just $4.74 per book in the U.S. or $5.49 per book in Canada. That's a savings of at least 12% off the cover price! It's quite a bargain! Shipping and handling is just 50¢ per book in the U.S. and 75¢ per book in Canada.* I understand that accepting the 2 free books and gifts places me under no obligation to buy anything. I can always return a shipment and cancel at any time. Even if I never buy another book, the two free books and gifts are mine to keep forever.

240/340 HDN GH3P

Name	(PLEASE PRINT)	
Address		Apt. #
City	State/Prov.	Zip/Postal Code

Signature (if under 18, a parent or guardian must sign)

Mail to the **Reader Service:**
IN U.S.A.: P.O. Box 1867, Buffalo, NY 14240-1867
IN CANADA: P.O. Box 609, Fort Erie, Ontario L2A 5X3

Want to try two free books from another line?
Call 1-800-873-8635 or visit www.ReaderService.com.

* Terms and prices subject to change without notice. Prices do not include applicable taxes. Sales tax applicable in N.Y. Canadian residents will be charged applicable taxes. Offer not valid in Quebec. This offer is limited to one order per household. Not valid for current subscribers to Harlequin Romantic Suspense books. All orders subject to credit approval. Credit or debit balances in a customer's account(s) may be offset by any other outstanding balance owed by or to the customer. Please allow 4 to 6 weeks for delivery. Offer available while quantities last.

Your Privacy—The Reader Service is committed to protecting your privacy. Our Privacy Policy is available online at www.ReaderService.com or upon request from the Reader Service.

We make a portion of our mailing list available to reputable third parties that offer products we believe may interest you. If you prefer that we not exchange your name with third parties, or if you wish to clarify or modify your communication preferences, please visit us at www.ReaderService.com/consumerschoice or write to us at Reader Service Preference Service, P.O. Box 9062, Buffalo, NY 14240-9062. Include your complete name and address.

"Why don't we get married?"

Even though she'd known it was coming, it still hit her square in the chest. The air rushed from her lungs and a tsunami of feelings washed over her. A surge of joy made her heart beat so fast she felt faint. She crested that wave and slid into the undertow of reality. "A marriage of convenience?"

"Exactly." Daniel reached for her hands.

When she hid them behind her back, he dropped his arms. "It wouldn't have to be forever. Just long enough to satisfy the stipulations of your grandmother's will and save your horses, and that would help me get past the Kennedy gauntlet. We could leave tomorrow, spend a night in Vegas, find a chapel and it would be over in less than five minutes."

With her heart smarting, Megan forced a shaky smile. "Way to sweep a girl off her feet."

He waved his hand and Halo tossed her head. "If you want, I can make an official announcement in front of my family."

Megan shook her head. "No."

"No, you won't marry me?"

"No." She pushed past him to pace down the center of the barn. "Your plan is insane."

"Do you have a better one?" he asked. "I'm all ears."

The plan was the same as the one she'd been thinking of before Daniel had woken up. Only when she'd dreamed it up, it didn't sound as cold and impersonal as Daniel's proposal. Somewhere in the back of her mind she'd hoped that marriage to Daniel would be something more than one of convenience.

After yesterday's kiss, she wasn't sure she could be around Daniel for long periods of time without wanting another. And another.

Don't miss
PROTECTING THE COLTON BRIDE
by New York Times *bestselling author Elle James,*
available September 2015

www.Harlequin.com

HRSEXP0915

Limited time offer!

$1.⁰⁰ OFF

Mixing romance and politics can be fatal in the *New York Times* bestselling *Fatal Series* by

MARIE FORCE

Fall for fast-paced political intrigue, gritty suspense and a romance that makes headlines.

Save $1.00 on any one book in The Fatal Series!

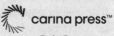

www.CarinaPress.com
www.TheFatalSeries.com

$1.⁰⁰ OFF the purchase price of any book in *The Fatal Series* by Marie Force.

Offer valid from September 1, 2015, to October 5, 2015. Redeemable at participating retail outlets. Limit one coupon per purchase. Valid in the USA and Canada only.

52612998

Canadian Retailers: Harlequin Enterprises Limited will pay the face value of this coupon plus 10.25¢ if submitted by customer for this product only. Any other use constitutes fraud. Coupon is nonassignable. Void if taxed, prohibited or restricted by law. Consumer must pay any government taxes. Void if copied. Inmar Promotional Services ("IPS") customers submit coupons and proof of sales to Harlequin Enterprises Limited, P.O. Box 3000, Saint John, NB E2L 4L3, Canada. Non-IPS retailer—for reimbursement submit coupons and proof of sales directly to Harlequin Enterprises Limited, Retail Marketing Department, 225 Duncan Mill Rd., Don Mills, Ontario M3B 3K9, Canada.

5 65373 00076 2   (8100)0 12091

U.S. Retailers: Harlequin Enterprises Limited will pay the face value of this coupon plus 8¢ if submitted by customer for this product only. Any other use constitutes fraud. Coupon is nonassignable. Void if taxed, prohibited or restricted by law. Consumer must pay any government taxes. Void if copied. For reimbursement submit coupons and proof of sales directly to Harlequin Enterprises Limited, P.O. Box 880478, El Paso, TX 88588-0478, U.S.A. Cash value 1/100 cents.

® and ™ are trademarks owned and used by the trademark owner and/or its licensee.

© 2015 Harlequin Enterprises Limited

CARMF00257COUP

THE WORLD IS BETTER WITH

Romance

Harlequin has everything from contemporary, passionate and heartwarming to suspenseful and inspirational stories.

Whatever your mood, we have a romance just for you!

Connect with us to find your next great read, special offers and more.

f /HarlequinBooks

🐦 @HarlequinBooks

www.HarlequinBlog.com

www.Harlequin.com/Newsletters

◆ HARLEQUIN®

A *Romance* FOR EVERY MOOD™

www.Harlequin.com